# Shadow of the Dolocher

By
European P. Douglas

By the same Author:

The Dolocher

Rattleyard

Join my mailing list at http://eepurl.com/bWwroj
for news of upcoming books and a free copy of the
books listed above.

# Chapter 1

The sticky tangle of bloodied hay hung from what served as a bed in the cell in the tower of 'The Black Dog' prison. The smell, sickly sweet and warm, punctured now by the harsh tang of urine as the guards searched through the hay for something that could have slit the prisoner's throat. The body lay in the hall at the top of the stairs with a sheet pulled over it. It had been stripped and probed, clothes checked separately, but nothing had been found before he had been removed from the cell. Alderman James watched in silence from the doorway. He studied the drips of blood on the stone floor that led to where the body had been found by the bars, a pool of blood around the upper half of it. There couldn't have been all that much blood left in the man.

"Nothing in there, sir," one of the guards said after they had been at the hay and rotted frame for a few minutes. The Alderman looked around the room; it was spare of any other furnishings.

"You check with your hands the whole wall here, look for cracks or holes or loose stone where something might be hidden," he said to one and then to the other, "Go downstairs and search in the space below that window, perhaps he dropped it outside when he cut himself." The guards looked at one another and then did as they were told. James could feel their unease, in fact, he shared it.

The blood led from the window, which was where James assumed the man had cut himself; searching the walls was unlikely to yield anything, the man hardly slit his throat and then hid the weapon like that. If it were anywhere, it would be outside on the ground or else in the hay, missed by the men. Soon the guard had finished searching the wall, and he turned to James for further instruction.

"Call down and see if the other guard has found anything," James said. The guard went to the window and called out,

"Arthur!"

"What?" came the reply.

"Did you find anything?"

"No, there's nothing here." He turned back into the room from the window.

"There's nothing down there," he said to James.

"Burn this bed," James said to him. The guard looked back at him in confusion. "Burn it here in this room," James said, but still the guard stood there as if not knowing what to do. "Take that lantern from the wall there and burn the bed; it's fine, there is nothing else here to catch flame, and once we stand back we'll be unharmed." The guard went to the top of the stairs and took the lantern and brought it into the room. He looked at the Alderman once more, who nodded at him in encouragement and then lit the hay.

They both stood back in the hallway and watched the hay burn and then the wood frame it lay on too. Singed hair smell flooded the air, and the blood burned black and bubbled nastily before beginning to disappear. They had to fan the smoke back into the room towards the window to stop it going into their eyes or overwhelming them. It didn't take long for there to be nothing but a smouldering mess of dust and sinews of scorched hay on the floor. The air began to feel fresher as the wind came in and the smoke dissipated. The ash was sand coloured and formed a small pile.

"Sweep that up and go through it again for a weapon, it could be something very small so be sure to sweep up little sections at a time and run the ash through a sieve before it goes into a bucket. You can get the gaoler to let me know if you find anything," James said, and he set off down the stairs.

At the bottom of the stairs he looked about for a moment, it had been a long time since he was inside this place. It hadn't changed in the slightest. Apart from the gaoler of course. The last one, Brick, had been killed by Cleaves as part of the Dolocher murders. That whole mess had originated in this very place with the suicide -in the very room, James had just been in- of the murderer Thomas Olocher, in very similar circumstances to the new death. He could only hope that word of this wouldn't get out; he knew full well the way these local people thought, they would be howling about the return of the Dolocher before the end of the day, and he didn't need that fear and tension rising in the community again. Things had been relatively calm for the last two years, and that was the way he would like it to remain.

James looked down to the doors of 'The Nunnery,'- that basement room where streetwalkers were housed in the gaol. It was dark inside, and he couldn't see anyone in there. Cabinteely; the new gaoler appeared from the back corridor and greeted the Alderman. He was a man of about five feet eleven inches, slim and stiff looking, his blonde hair and smiling eyes belied his dour career.

"Alderman, did you find anything?" he asked gaily.

"No Marcus, but I've one of your guards doing a last search."

"Well he can take his time, it's not very busy at the moment."

"Is there no one in 'The Nunnery' tonight?" Marcus Cabinteely smiled at the question.

"There's some fleet going out tomorrow, and all the women had their fines paid this morning, so they're out. Most of them belonged to that French one, what's her name?"

"I know who you are speaking of," James said dryly. "Has anybody been in asking about the dead man?"

"No, we didn't even know his name, so if they had, we wouldn't have known who they were talking about anyway."

"You didn't know his name?" Alderman was sure he had heard the name Trevor in relation to the prisoner.

"No, he was brought in by some of the parish watch lads, drunk as anything and kicking and screaming. He was put up there to sleep it off more than anything else."

"Which watchmen brought him in?"

"I'm not sure, but I heard they were almost as drunk as he was." This was nothing unusual; the watchmen were always missing from their posts or drunk or asleep at them. It was a wonder anyone paid them at all for all the good they did. As far as James could see they made little or no difference to safety at night. "I can probably find out for you," Cabinteely offered.

"Yes, that would be good if you can. I'm going home now but if your man upstairs finds anything, or if you get those watchmen's names send a boy over to my house with a letter. You know where I live?"

"I do, and if I didn't I'm sure the letter carriers would," the gaoler smiled.

The Alderman said goodbye and went to the gate where he was let out onto Back Lane. He stood looking over the area on this quiet night. The Dolocher was on his mind, and he recalled the two murders committed not fifty feet apart from where he now stood; in; both the victims were guards of this very prison, savaged to death. He still couldn't believe the strength Cleaves held in that frame of his; he wouldn't have thought even a man twice his size could have been so powerful. He shook his head and looked up at the tower; all that was in the past. Up there was what was going on now. The light was growing and the silhouette of the tower on the new morning was mesmerising, looking as though the tower was swaying slightly against the slow moving clouds of predawn.

James decided to walk home, and he asked the carriage driver to trot along beside him in case he changed his mind. The walk would do him good, he thought. He was ever restless on nights when he thought about the Dolocher case. The similarities tonight were scary, the same room and the same cause of death. The people of the Liberties would have a field day with that.

These were the people he had sought to protect. He had made them his priority a long time ago when he learned from his own youthful mistakes in this position he held. He thought of all the nights he had spent walking the streets at the time of the killings; how he had put his own life in danger on a few occasions to chase the killer. In the end, it had been the blacksmith Mullins who got all the credit, but he had simply been in the right place at the right time. James felt cheated by this, he was only streets away when it happened, and he couldn't shake the belief that if not for Mullins, he would have caught Cleaves that night.

Then the people would know what he did for them and understand. He smiled at his rising anger; this was all silly, wishful thinking.

It had been two years since then, and things had been quiet. Well, quiet in comparison; there was no shortage of people willing to do bad things. There was also plenty of talk of rebellion these days, and that kept his office and the soldiers busy. Still, the thought came back to him about catching the Dolocher. He needed to sleep, to forget about the past.

# Chapter 2

The sky was dark and threatened rain as Kate got to the market stall. Mary Sommers, her friend, and former housemate was working the stall this morning and there was a brisk trade. Kate caught her eyes, and they exchanged smiling nods while Mary finished with the few customers who milled about her.

"Well, you look busy," Kate said when they could finally talk

"It's well this morning, I think it's the dark clouds all day," Mary said looking up at the sky. "It gets people out early for fear of getting caught in a downpour."

"Same as myself," Kate laughed. As she was talking, she saw that there was a new ship coming up the river to moor at the market harbour. In her previous life, she would have known about this ship coming in and would have been here waiting for it, trying to sell herself to the men on board to make her living. How she was glad those days were over now. She hadn't thought of it as being so bad a life at the time, but now that she no longer had to live as a streetwalker, or in Madame Mel's brothel, she felt ashamed that she ever did such things.

"You've not long missed Sarah; she's gone on home to start a fire for later," Mary said interrupting the flow of her thoughts.

Kate felt the first drops of rain on her cheek as the new ship docked at the nearest point to the vegetable stall.

"Looks like the rain is finally started," she said. Mary looked up too.

"Well, you can't live in Ireland and complain about the

rain."

"I better get going all the same and get this stew on for Tim."

"You should call in some evening soon to catch up," Mary said.

"I'd like that, talk to Sarah and see what night suits you both and I'll pop back tomorrow to see you."

"I'm sure any night will do, but I'll talk to you later."

Kate said goodbye, and she walked across the square at the docks of Templebar. She was always proud of herself that she was able to come back to this place so readily after she had been attacked and nearly lost her life here. She would often look at the fish sellers and the delivery carts and thank them all silently for the mess they made that had Cleaves slip that night when he attacked her and that made possible her escape. Mary had been one of the victims too, and Kate knew she had not been able to pass by the street where her encounter had taken place. As far as Kate knew, Mary never went out after dark on her own to this day.

Kate was lost in thought as she went up the narrow cobbled lanes of Templebar and she was shook and frightened when a heavy arm landed on her shoulder and pulled her against the body of a man who reeked of drink.

"There's my favourite flower!" he said in a loud drunk voice that drew glances from people who were passing. "Where have you been? I've looked for you so many times at the..."

"I don't do that work anymore," Kate snapped before he said the word brothel. She shrugged his arm off her, and he nearly fell with his loss of support. He looked at her as though she had wounded him and she tried to place him from her past.

"You're a terrible loss to the profession," he said, and he bowed so low that almost fell forward on his head. Kate didn't know if he was trying to be sweet or if this was intended as an insult, but suddenly she recalled this man. His usual voice and then his normal, sober face from before came back to her. She remembered him, he'd much been changed by drink and night living by the looks of him. He hadn't been a handsome man, but he was not so ugly as now, but he'd a nice way about him with the girls, and he had always tipped well in the past. She couldn't for the life of her remember his name.

"Thank you, I have to go now," she said and rushed off as fast as she could through the crowds.

"A flower!" she heard him call out to her and it brought a smile to her face. She felt sorry for him now, for what he had become in the short space of time since she stopped being a street walker. This was the type of meeting she wouldn't be able to tell Tim about either; he was still very troubled by her past, and she was never to speak of it or the people she knew through it while he was in earshot.

At first, Kate had been reluctant to leave the profession on a purely financial basis. She didn't think Tim's blacksmith shop would bring in enough for the two of them, but he had proved her wrong. Now she had nothing to do most days but errands and looking after her husband. She would have liked to work at something but it was a sore spot with him, and she brought it up very infrequently.

She loved him very dearly, however, and she could put up with these things for that sake. Deep down she knew that he only wanted her to be happy. She knew that it had been hard for him to accept what she had been, and she could only imagine what must go through his head when he wondered if he knew men who had been with her. She had been coy with him and told him that it rarely went that far, that most of what went on in the brothels was mundane compared to the stories that came out of them. She knew that he had never been to a madam's house, but she doubted he believed that nothing went on there at all.

Still, they were happy in the transparent lies they told one another. She did not believe for a second that Tim ever got a black eye from mishandling equipment in the shop or some other type of accident. He was violent at times, and she knew he always would be. He had never displayed anything of this toward her, but she knew that when he went out to the whiskey cabins, it wasn't always just for a drink. People had all sorts of things inside them that needed to be let out every now and then, and Kate was happy to get along with things with this frame of mind.

She realised too late that she hadn't started home in a way whereby she could have dropped into the blacksmith's on her way, and with the rain threatening she didn't want to chance it now. She was sure to be drenched if she attempted it; that was the kind of luck she had. As she moved hurriedly away from Templebar, there were less and less people on the streets, nothing close to deserted but she could feel and hear the difference, and she raised her head a little, not so cautious about meeting eyes with an old customer here. Heavy raindrops splatted against the ground intermittently around her.

Kate heard a horse and carriage behind her a little, and she turned to look at it; it was unusual to see one down this particular narrow street. The horse was large and chestnut coloured, and its coat gleamed in the light. The carriage was black and sprung and very polished, and she wondered who might be in it and what business a person with that kind of money would have here. She stepped to the side of the road to let it pass. She felt the horse's hot breath as it sidled by slowly, grunting a little and then she noticed that its gait was slowing. The door of the coach was beside her now, and it opened a little. Kate realised that she had stopped walking and she knew then who it was in the coach.

"Do you want a lift? The rain is going to come down before you get home," Mr. Edwards said smiling down at her.

"No, I'm fine thank you," Kate replied, getting her senses back. She was about to walk away when she saw that the horse's head was tilting to the left and it leaned in a way that stopped her from going that way. She looked back the way she'd come, and it was clear, but she didn't want to go the longer way home because of him.

"How have you been Kitty?" he asked.

"I'm very good," she said looking up at him, an expression of anger on her face.

"How's the blacksmith?" She didn't like Tim being referred to by Edwards, and she looked at his eyes to convey this to him.

"My husband is fine; not that it's any of your business!" She heard the coachman chuckle a little at this and she shot a glance in his direction, but her view of him was blocked by the shell of the carriage.

"Why don't you both come over for dinner tomorrow night?" Edwards asked, pretending not to notice her tone.

"You know full well that's never going to happen!"

"I suppose so," Edwards mused, "It's only really you I want to come over anyway," he added.

In her previous life, Mr. Edwards had been one of her most generous and frequent customers. He often asked for her specifically at the brothel and made a fuss when she was not there. Since she stopped being a prostitute, he had accosted her a few times in the street like this and asked her to come to his house. She had always assumed he just wanted to sleep with her, but there was something different in his voice this time. Something she didn't recognise that made her curious as to what he was after. There must have been something in her face that gave away what she was thinking for he leaned forward then and handed her a letter.

"Read it when you are alone," he said, and then he tapped the roof with his cane, and the carriage set off down the street and around the corner out of sight.

Kate looked at the letter. It was sealed with wax, red and shiny smooth and the paper was cream coloured and felt thick and looked expensive. She was tempted to open it there and then, but she had the sense of eyes on her, so she put in her bag and continued on her way home.

## Chapter 3

Timothy Mullins's huge form took up most of the frame of the doorway to his blacksmith shop as he looked out at the street in the late morning sun. It had been a quiet morning so far, just some odd bits and pieces to mend and strengthen but he wasn't too concerned. Business had been going well the last few months, and now that he was with Kate he didn't go to the whiskey cabins anywhere near as much as he used to. As a result of this, he was able to put some money aside every few weeks, very little, it must be said, but it was something for the future. From where he stood he could see the tower of Newgate Prison, 'The Black Dog' as it was known locally and he knew that there had been another suicide there last night. There were rumours all about as to who the prisoner was, but no one seemed sure of the information they passed on.

Timothy felt an odd mood with the news of the death; it brought back to him the time of the Dolocher and the fact that the killer had been none other than his best friend, a man who Mullins had been so sure hadn't a wicked bone in his body. He had even tried to kill Mullins; resulting in the fact that he was the one who had unmasked the Dolocher in the end. Even now over two years later he still found it hard to believe. His business had taken a bit of battering at that time as he was a suspect in the murders for no reason other than his immense height and strength, and then through his association with the real killer. During this time he'd had to take on work from the gangs, something he had always been loath to do in the past, to pay the bills. He would mend their weapons but that was all, he still refused to make anything for them. As soon as he was able to, he stopped doing this work. This was just as well as soon after the gang warfare had all but ceased.

Lord Muc, the leader of the Liberty Boy's, a group that started out as weaver's but soon took on all type of men who loved violence, took the battle to such extremes that more and more men died during them that no one wanted to face him anymore. There was the odd scuffle now and then with members of the Ormonde Boys, but nothing organised or as violent as things had become before. Mullins saw Lord Muc from time to time, looking for trouble outside taverns or causing a nuisance in the streets but he'd had nothing to do with him for a long time.

Checking the time he saw that it was near lunch and he thought about going home for a while. Scally, his errand boy and helper- not yet an apprentice- sat on a tiny stool outside the shop whittling on a stick. Mullins looked to him just as the boy made some mistake in his whittling,

"Stupid fuckin' thing!" Scally exclaimed, and he threw down the piece of wood in temper. Mullins laughed, he had seen this in him before; it didn't take much to set him over the edge.

"Do you have anything to eat with you?" Mullins asked him.

"No," Scally said; this was often the case. Mullins went inside to his satchel and pulled out some sandwiches wrapped in cloth and handed them to him.

"Go home and split these with your mother," Mullins said to him.

"Thanks, Mr. Mullins!" Scally said, and he set off towards home. Mullins closed the door to the shop and walked along Cook Street towards his own home, happy to have been able to do something nice.

When he came in the door, he called Kate, but there was no answer. He looked into the bedroom and saw that it was all made up and she was nowhere to be seen. He wondered was she down at the market with the women she used to live with. He decided he would wait long enough to eat and have tea before he went back to the shop.

There was a low fire going, and he stoked it to boil water. As this was going on, he cut two thick slices of bread and buttered them thinly and put some tomatoes and lettuce on them and a sliver of a slice of meat. He sat down in front of the fire and chewed as the bubbles dotted the water and soon it began to boil. He was almost finished his sandwich by the time he poured the tea, and he went to the cupboard and took out some biscuit and ate that with it. The biscuit was almost stale, and he didn't enjoy it as much as he'd hoped to.

He'd been home half an hour by now, and he decided that it was time to go back. He couldn't afford to sit around doing nothing. It was disappointing not seeing his wife, but he would see her later in the day. She might even drop by the shop on her way home if she was indeed at the market at Templebar as he guessed. He stepped out onto Dog and Duck Yard and headed back towards Cook Street. As he walked along here, he was tempted to stop into his favourite cabin and see if there was any more news on the man who'd killed himself in the gaol, but he avoided this, staying on the side of the road he was on and going straight to the shop. Scally was there waiting for him, back on his tiny stool, the same whittling piece as earlier in his hands.

"Anyone come with business?" he asked the boy.

"No, but I'm only here about ten minutes. Do you want

me to go looking for customers?" Mullins thought about this and shook his head,

"No, we'll see how the next couple of hours treat us."

An hour later, as Mullins worked on some pieces he had lying around for his own projects, the door darkened, and Mullins turned to see Lord Muc standing there; that same cocksure grin on his scarred and battle hardened face as ever. He was the last person Mullins wanted to see. Wherever the gang leader went trouble followed close behind.

"Muc," Mullins said in greeting.

"Hello Blacksmith, long time no talk."

"It has."

"Haven't seen you brawling much of late."

"Haven't been brawling much of late."

"All down to the love of a good woman eh?" Muc laughed as he said this. Mullins stiffened at the mention of Kate.

"What can I do for you?" he asked.

"I need something made."

"You know I don't do weapons," Mullins reminded him, sure that this was what he was going to ask for.

"It's not a weapon I need, it's a replica of a weapon I want you to make."

"A replica?"

"Yes, of the boar's tusks that I used to do battle with." Mullins looked at him and saw that he was serious.

"You want me to make iron boars tusks?"

"Yes, the battle days are over, and I want something to commemorate them."

"I can't do it Muc," Mullins said turning back to what he had been doing.

"Why not?" Muc asked; there was an edge to his voice and Mullins turned to him again lest he attack from behind.

"I can't be associated with anything to do with the Dolocher; if word got out about that, no one would use my shop anymore."

"It has nothing to do with the Dolocher; that was a human, your friend as I recall, I just want tusks done in steel."

"You know that everyone around here still links all of those things, the pigs and the boar with the Dolocher, as well as Cleaves."

"You're getting very soft Blacksmith. There was a time when you didn't care what anyone thought, but now you're almost like a little housewife."

"Do you want to step outside and discuss this?" Mullins rankled, leaned into him but Lord Muc didn't flinch.

"I've no desire to hit women most of the time."

The talk of the Dolocher and this scene reminded Mullins of the time he'd been suspected; Muc had rubbed that in then too as now. Mullins stepped back and put down the tool he held and silently took in a deep breath through his nose. He was determined not to get into a fight now. Muc looked a little disappointed, and he too backed off away towards the door.

"I'll find someone who will do it. Just thought I'd offer you the business," Muc said, and he nodded goodbye and left.

Mullins came out and watched him walk away, and he saw Scally looking up at him.

"Why didn't you make it for him?" the boy asked.

"Because if I did it would be the death of someone,"

Mullins said. Scally nodded in understanding and looked after Lord Muc as he mingled in with the street crowd and slowly disappeared.

# Chapter 4

Alderman James sat with Sheriff Dunbar at breakfast in his home looking out on Henrietta Street. It had been a large breakfast, and now they drank coffee as they went through the finer points of a case involving a gentleman and a severely beaten servant man. It was clear that the man would get away with the crime, but it was how best to approach it, to keep it from court if possible that they were engrossed in. A knock came on the door, and the butler brought in a letter from Marcus Cabinteely, the Gaoler of Newgate Prison. James put the letter to one side without opening it and continued on with his coffee until Dunbar was gone.

He picked it up again when he was alone expecting it to read that there was no weapon found in either the ashes or the courtyard and perhaps a name or two of the watchmen who brought in the prisoner who had killed himself in the tower. When James opened it, however, he was stunned to see that it concerned a murder that had been committed outside the prison during the previous night. There was no more information than that and James hurriedly called for his coach and left for the scene.

As he bounced across the cobbled streets, he looked at the letter trying to garner further information from it, but there was simply nothing there. Cabinteely wasn't much of a letter writer; it didn't even say who the victim was or if there had been anyone apprehended for the crime or not. Scant was the best word to describe it, and James meant to tell him to be more specific if he ever had call to write to him again. The Alderman was going in cold to this, and he didn't like it. Normally he was told by a watchman or soldier what to expect and if there were any witnesses or any other pertinent information that he should be aware of. As it stood now, he didn't even know if the army had been notified or if he was going to be the first person of authority to arrive there.

The carriage crossed the Liffey at Essex Bridge, and James looked out at the boats down by the docks at Templebar, busy loading, and unloading, and he could see the teeming market there too, part of it anyway, and then they were climbing the road towards the prison. There was a crowd of people there but nothing like he'd feared there would be, only about twenty in all. When James got out and saw that an area by the gate was cordoned off, he felt another chill of recognition go through him as he had felt in the tower a couple of nights ago.

He made his way through the people who paid him no heed, and he saw the blood on the ground. There was a lot of it, and some was slathered onto the wall of the prison by the window to 'The Nunnery' as well. There was a guard standing by so no one came too close to the mess.

"Where is the body?" James asked.

"Inside Sir," the guard replied, his face was white, and James thought he was in a state of shock at having seen the body. He mused that it must have been in a bad way for this kind of reaction. Still, it couldn't be worse than what he had seen in the past. James made his way to the gate. He wanted to look at the faces of the people, to see what they were thinking, but he was afraid that his own face would give something away. He went inside, and the gate was closed behind him. The pressure of their eyes came off his back as though something physical had been on there.

"Alderman! Hello," Cabinteely was coming across the courtyard to him with a hand outstretched.

"Good morning," James said shaking his hand.

"You saw outside?"

"Yes, who was it?"

"Don't know that yet."

"Not one of the guards then?"

"No, our guards don't go outside the gates at night."

"Is that as big as the crowd of onlookers has been out there?"

"No, it was a little bigger earlier, but a lot of people left after we brought the body in."

"People saw the body then?"

"Yes."

"It would have been better if that had not been the case." Cabinteely didn't say anything to this.

"I'll take you to the body, but I have to warn you it's pretty gruesome."

"Murder always is."

Cabinteely led James through the archway into the building proper and down a short corridor with a large wooden door at the end of it.

"Open up Jack, it's me," Cabinteely said as he banged on the door. They could hear footsteps and a lock behind lifted, and then the door opened to another tired looking guard. This one had the same white face as the other and James wondered why he had been in a locked room with the body like this.

From the hall James could see the body on the large table, it was covered with a white sheet, but there were blood stains all over it as though it had soaked through. Every part of the body seemed to be cut. They walked in, and the air was pungent in the room. They all held their noses, and the guard who had waited for the others to do this seemed most relieved to get to do it once more as he must have been before they came in.

Cabinteely went over and took hold of the sheet and looked at James as if for permission to pull it back. James nodded, and the sheet was pulled back to reveal the body of a man, not very tall and with black hair matted with blood. His eye sockets had been stabbed, and eyeballs were missing, and his face was shredded so much to make knowing what he used to look like impossible. The rest of the body was covered in cuts and slice marks, but thankfully there was no sign of a serrated weapon being used.

"Was he naked when you found him?"

"Yes."

"So he must have been dumped there and killed someplace else," James thought out loud.

"I'd say so, surely one of the men would have heard something of this if it happened just outside the gate," Cabinteely added.

"Do you have any idea of when it was dropped off?"

"It can't have been long before six." James thought about this for a moment. There was very little to go on, nothing really. He looked at the guard, skin white and slick with nausea and he wondered if there were any guards here at all from a few years ago. Would anyone else have noticed the similarities to that case? Probably not if none of them worked here at the time. Cabinteely himself didn't arrive until months later, he hadn't even been in Ireland while all that was going on.

"Has the doctor been called?" James asked.

"He's been and gone; he said he'd send for the body when you were finished with him." James had never cared for the doctors at the barracks, there was nothing of pleasantness in them, and the way they treated the dead was abominable.

"What did he say?"

"Killed by stabbing through the heart and multiple knife wounds."

"Did he indicate if he thought the wounds were inflicted after the man died?"

"No, he wasn't here for very long, to be honest."

James walked closer and looked at the wound by the heart; it was deep and wide, and the edges jagged as though the knife had been twisted while in the body. There were scratch marks on the exposed ribs too and something else that didn't look quite right. James asked for a lantern to be brought to him, and he held it up to the body. The skin was white yellow now in this glow and looked almost like wax.

"There's something in there!" James said, and he handed the lantern back to the guard. Cabinteely looked where James was looking but didn't seem to understand.

"What do you see?"

"In the chest wound, there is something in there that doesn't belong."

"Oh, I see, you're right!" Cabinteely exclaimed, "What do you suppose that is?"

"I have no idea, but we're going to find out." James rolled up his sleeve and looked about for something to reach inside the man's body with. There was nothing he saw that would do the job, so he had to bite his lip and stick two fingers into the hole. He felt something steel and cold, and it moved a little. He pushed against the dead muscles to get his fingers in behind the things and finally got there. It was cylindrical and small and had a ridged surface. He pulled at it, but it was wedged in so he had to push it in a little more and then tip it so that he could take it out by one end.

James took it to the light but couldn't make out what it was with all the blood. There was a basin of bloody water that the doctor might have used earlier on a shelf beside the table and he dipped a rag into it and wiped away at the object. He held it to the light and looked at it, the guard and Cabinteely leaned in as well to get a better view.

It was a piece of lead coloured metal and had a loop at the top where a chain or string might have gone through to make this thing an amulet or necklace of some kind. There were some letters engraved, but they didn't make any sense. The raised parts were of another engraving, and it was clear as James turned it what this figure was supposed to be.

"That's the Devil," the Guard said, and James nodded.

"Have you seen something like this before?" Cabinteely asked looking to James.

"No, have you?" Both of the men of the prison shook their heads.

James had the amulet in his possession when he left the prison, and as he rode back home in his coach, he looked it over again. Any reference or depiction of the Devil always brought the same thing to his mind. Mr. Edwards and his godforsaken Hellfire Club. He hadn't seen Mr. Edwards much since the Dolocher case and even less so of late. If there was anyone who would know what this thing was and where it might have come from it would be him.

James didn't like the idea of approaching him at all because he knew that the prospects of murders and mayhem delighted Edwards and he would want to get involved with the investigation. It was true that he was a source of information that the Alderman would never have been able to get on his own, but his whole demeanour and the satanic side of his life, as well as the drunkenness and who knew what else struck James sourly. There was so much to Edwards that James knew he didn't see. There were the rumours about the Hellfire Club and what went on there, but James didn't put a whole lot of stock in those stories. To his mind, it was most more than likely that they all just sat around, drank and gambled the night away.

He put the amulet away and sat back in the coach. The Dolocher was on his mind again; everything seemed to be reminiscent of it today. He recalled his folly of displaying the wild boar to the town, thinking that it was the Dolocher that they all so feared. In his haste to be a hero and to gain forgiveness from these local people, he had rushed to believe against his better judgment. The boar hadn't been the Dolocher, and while James had wasted time with it, the real killer continued unabated until he was apprehended by that blacksmith Mullins. James had received none of the credit despite his hours and sleepless nights searching for the killer. Was this going to be a new chance to redeem himself? Was this the start of something? He shook his head as though to dispel the thought; the last thing he wanted was another murderer in the Liberties.

Rain began falling on the canopy of the coach, and it brought his attention to the outside world. There were some children playing at the corner, some game that he didn't recognise and some women stood near them talking, each one carrying something. They were either on the way to or from some errand. The sky grew darker, and he saw some of the women cast apprehensive looks to the sky. He envied those children and those women whose daily worries never involved murders and scenes the like of which he had been party to this morning.

# Chapter 5

Kate was shaken from her accosting by Edwards in the street, and she locked the door and looked out the window to see that she had not been further followed. There was no sign of anyone she didn't recognise, and children played football in the square as ever. She went to the back room and took out the vegetables and started to peel and cut them up for tonight's dinner. She stopped cold when she realised that something was different in the house than when she left this morning; she couldn't put her finger on it immediately, and she looked about for somethings out of place. There was a small mess on the table, breadcrumbs and some pulp from a tomato- that was it; she had left the place spotless. Tim must have been home, yes that was all; she sighed thankfully. The door had been locked when she came in, she was sure of that, and who would come in and just make a sandwich and tidy up, mostly, if not her husband? But then she was worried afresh; hadn't she sent him to work with his lunch? She had, she was sure of it; she remembered making it this morning and handing it to him as he went out.

She went to the door and checked that it was locked, and then looked out the window again. Still nothing. She wondered about Edwards, and she reasoned that it would not be his style to come into a house and do something like this. Then she remembered the letter he had given her. She went to her bags and found it down beside the cabbage head. She took it out and opened it; inside there was a single handwritten page. Kate was not great at reading, but she could make out some of it. She would have to go to Mary Sommers if she wanted to know exactly what it said, but she was sure that he was proposing that she go back to her old profession and he would see that she was well looked after! She knew words like 'protection,' and she recognised Melanie's name, the Madam of the house where she had once worked.

Edwards had asked her this before. There had been a couple of times that he had come to her in the most unexpected of places and said that she should go back to her old life and that he would ensure that she was happy. She grew angry at the thought that he could just 'buy' her. She felt like throwing the letter directly into the fire at that very moment, but something stopped her. There was more to the letter than she could understand and something in her made her curious as to its content. She reasoned that she needed to know what it said so that she could berate him about it if she should speak to him again. But she also knew that some of her anger was at her embarrassment of not being able to read and the shame of letting him know this. He clearly didn't know, or he wouldn't have written her a letter. On more than one occasion she had made up her mind that she was going to learn but she had never done anything about it, and each time her life went on as it had the day before.

She would have to hide the letter and take it to Mary at the market tomorrow. She didn't think Tim could read either, but she couldn't take any chances. If he knew that Edwards had been in contact with her and trying to get her away from him, he could do anything. Edwards was rich and powerful and not someone who Tim could match. She had no doubt that in a fight her husband would come out easily the victor, but in the long run, Edwards could make serious trouble for them if he really wanted to.

She looked for a place to hide the letter but nowhere seemed safe enough. Finally, she decided that she would have to get it out of the house. She looked in her purse and found a small coin and went to the front door. She called one of the boys playing football over and offered him the coin if he brought the letter to the vegetable stall and gave it to Mary Sommers. She made him repeat the name and said that he should get a time from her to come to the market tomorrow as a reply. The boy ran off happy with his money, and Kate felt the ease of the letter being out of Tim's way run through her body, and she went back to making the dinner.

She couldn't get Edwards out of her head and images of times she had slept with him came to mind. Sometimes he could be caring and considerate, and at others, he was cold and distant. She remembered the time she spent in his fabulous house and then how humiliated she was when he used her for sex once he'd gotten the information from her that he wanted. She had dreamed of living in a house like his, but she knew that it was never going to be. She was here on Dog and Duck yard, and the best she could hope for was another small house somewhere very close by. She wished she'd never seen the inside of Edwards' house or slept in that bed or used that bath. Those things had spoiled her for the life she had lived up to then and since. She hated Edwards for that too, for showing her what a life out of the gutter could be like. Perhaps that was what she hated him most of all for; for moments like this when she felt that her life with Tim was not all that it could be. She loved Tim; loved him dearly and she owed him for catching the Dolocher as he promised he would for her, but she knew that where they were now was probably as far in life as they ever would be. She brought an image of him purposefully to mind, seeing him make the sandwiches when he came home and tidying up after himself. She smiled at what she saw, and she felt tender towards him. She went to the table and wiped the last of his mess up. He was a good man, a very good man and she was lucky to have him.

# Chapter 6

Alderman James' carriage pulled up outside the large house on Francis Street that he knew to be one of the Hellfire Club hangouts. He'd been here a few years ago at Edward's insistence, and on that day he was presented with the body of a huge dead boar that he was so sure was the Dolocher. There were some lights on the higher floors of the building, but he saw no sign of shadows or people moving around. He went up to the door and knocked loudly three times and then took a step back to wait. He knew that it was unlikely that anyone would answer as there was an ever changing coded knock that was supposed to gain a person entry and he was sure that it was not three simple bangs. He waited for a moment and then pounded three more times again but harder. Still no one came. He walked back to the kerb and looked up at the lighted rooms, and he imagined that there were people up there who were perhaps passed out drunk and incapable of even hearing the door let alone coming down to answer it.

He went back to his coach and asked to be brought to Cork Hill. The carriage moved slowly over the cobbles and turned on the road and headed in that direction. James had tried Edwards at home and at the French woman's brothel and now at one of the clubhouses with no luck. He knew that the Hellfire members often met and drank in the Eagles Tavern and that was where he was headed now.

As soon as he got out of the carriage, he knew that they were in there. The noise of drunken revelry was something so raucous that he had never heard the like of it before. Cries of men and shrieks of women echoed out into the street and laughter came from all quarters. There were street walkers walking up and down outside and propositioning the men who came out, and children played at the side of the road while their fathers spent money that should have been for their dinner inside. James told his driver to turn the carriage around and be ready to head for home in a few minutes time, and then he went inside the tavern.

The heat was immense and hit him like a wall when he went in, and he saw that there was not a person inside that could be called even half sober. Never before had he seen so many red faces and sleepy eyes on men and women; their bodies covered in sweat and the stains of spilled drinks. The floor was littered with rubbish and food, and there was even a dog under one of the tables chewing on a gnarled loaf of bread.

Looking around the sea of faces James could see no sign of Edwards, but there were men in fine clothes who he was sure he'd seen before in the same company. Another roar of laughter went up from that quarter, and James was apprehensive of approaching them in this state to ask for Edwards or word of him. A woman appeared up in the middle of the men, and her shoulders were bared- for a moment of horror, the Alderman thought she was naked and that they were performing some kind of satanic ritual in this very public place! However, one of the men moved, and he saw that it was only the shoulders that were bare and otherwise the woman was well covered. Another man moved forward with a paintbrush and drew some symbol that James didn't recognise on the nape of her neck and all the men there cheered and ordered drinks for everyone in the house for which a mighty cheer went up. This explained why everyone here, rich and poor alike was so inebriated.

"What will you have Alderman?" a voice said next to him and James turned to see a man of military bearing standing beside him looking at the same thing he'd been. "Colonel Spencer," the man said and offered his hand.

"From the 68th Foot?" James asked; he'd heard of this man.

"Yes."

"You're a member of that lot aren't you?" James said nodding at the club members.

"I am, but I'm too far behind them to even try to get involved this evening," he smiled.

"Have you seen Mr. Edwards today?"

"Not today, no," Spencer answered after a moment's thought.

"Can you give him a message for me if he shows here tonight?"

"Of course."

"Can you just tell him that I need to speak with him urgently?"

"Not a problem. Will you have that drink then?" James nodded so as not to be rude and Spencer ordered two whiskeys for them, and they stayed standing at the bar.

"So is old Edwards in trouble at last?" Spencer asked with a grin.

"No, nothing like that."

"Pity!" Spencer laughed.

"What's going on over there anyway?" James asked referring to the drunken group of Hellfire members.

"I'm not sure really, body painting is not something we usually get up to."

"What do you usually get up to, apart from drinking?"

"Not a lot Alderman, not a lot of all," Spencer was laughing when he said this.

At that moment a call came out from one of the drunks.

"Spencer! The real painter!" and some of the men came over and grabbed him, and he was dragged away towards the woman, holding a hand up in both apology and farewell to James. A paintbrush was then shoved into his hand, and the woman's now cleaned shoulders were presented to him. Alderman James took this as his opportunity to leave. He handed his drink to a man who'd just entered who though surprised thanked him effusively and drained it in one. As he left, James cast one last look back into the corner and saw Spencer begin to outline some design on the skin of the woman with black paint and a thin brush.

Out on the street, the air was nice and cool, and James stood for a moment before getting into the carriage. The driver set the horses in motion, and James sat in the back and thought about the places he'd been this evening. Brothels and Taverns were not his normal places of leisure. He knocked on the wall of the carriage in front of him, and it stopped. The driver leaned over and looked in through the window.

"Take me to Daly's," James said, "I don't think he'll be there but you never know." The driver disappeared from view and the carriage once again set off for College Green.

Daly's was a formidable club for the true elite of the city. It was the haunt of politicians and the super-rich alike. Alderman James would be able to gain entry, but he would be out of his class if he were to try to become a member. There were big men at the door and on the street outside whose job it was to keep prostitutes and undesirables away from the entrance and also refuse admittance to those not deemed worthy of entry. From the outside, James could see the torches within burning brightly, and there were people standing and talking by the windows and doors inside, secret dealings going on everywhere. He knew that Edwards came to this place from time to time, but also that it was not one of his preferred haunts. He would only come here to show his face every now and then as he knew all respectable people in Dublin society should do, and gain some news or gossip that might be of use to him at a later date. The doormen looked James over, but no one made a move to stop him coming inside. It was also one of the places Edwards's despicable club met.

Inside James was amazed at the splendid and opulent furnishing of the rooms. White marble chimney pieces took pride of place in most rooms and gold and white chairs, and elegant sofa's dotted the floors. Expensive silks covered these, and the carpets and curtains were of the finest imported materials. The club had only moved to these new premises from Dame Street in February of this year, and the opulence was something to behold and took his breath away every time he had call to come there.

James walked through the rooms looking for Edwards, but again there was no sign anywhere. He'd heard of secret rooms in these clubs, but he never knew if they existed or if it was just fancy talk. Either way, he knew that he would not be able to gain admittance to them even if they did exist. He asked a few people that he knew if they had seen Edwards, but none had, and none of the staff he spoke to had seen him for a week or more. They suggested James try the rival club on Kildare Street where he could also sometimes be found. He did this, but they also had not seen him there for about a week either.

James looked at the amulet as he jostled about in the back of his coach on his way home. It had been a wasted evening. Perhaps he should have asked Colonel Spencer if he knew what the amulet was, but then he hadn't really had the chance. He also didn't know the Colonel personally, and he didn't know what kind of man he might be behind his reputation as a soldier. He never fully knew what Edwards was about either, but he felt that there was something in Edwards that led him towards the truth, as much as he wanted to let be known of the truth anyway. A wasted night.

# Chapter 7

The young woman's skin was blue and hard, and the blood was dried out of her gashed abdomen making the wound look like a hole burst into something solid like wood or plaster. She had been dead for a few days, and the place she was found was not the place she was killed. Her face was intact, and it could be seen that she was pretty in life and not much more than twenty. Her identity was unknown for now, but James was sure that someone would come forward to claim her; this at least would give him an avenue of investigation other than questioning people in the vicinity of the find as to if they had seen or heard anything.

It was the location of the body that most upset and disturbed the Alderman. Once more he found himself on Back Lane at the walls of 'The Black Dog' looking over a dead body. This girl was in almost the exact spot that the second guard killed by the Dolocher had been slain. This time, however, there was no blood or viscera at the scene; the walls were not flecked with bodily matter, and the ground was not sticky underfoot. As far as James could see this woman had no marks on her body apart from the gaping hole in her middle. He wondered if there was another amulet or message in there. He was in no doubt that this was the same killer as the body found at the gate a few weeks ago. He didn't want to go rummaging inside the woman while there were people around to see but he would travel to the mortuary with her and check then.

"Get her on the wagon and take her!" he said to the soldiers who stood at attention waiting for his orders. James looked at the small crowd gathered, and he scanned their faces. He didn't really know what he was looking for, but he knew he would know it if he saw it. A face not disturbed enough by what it was seeing, eyes that poured too deeply into the dead woman, a smile that showed malicious intention, it could be anything, but he would know it.

The soldiers lifted the body up and covered it with a sheet.

"I'll go with her," James said holding back a soldier who was about to get up on the wagon. The young soldier stopped and looked at the Alderman with surprise, but hr didn't dare question him. "Go ask people what they saw," James said. The soldier nodded and went to the people gathered as the horse and cart was driven away from the scene.

It was still dull and early, and the streets were quiet. When James thought they were far away enough from the prison he looked about and seeing that the street was empty and the driver was looking dead ahead sleepily, he lifted the sheet and looked in at the body to locate the wound. Once he found it, he put his hand inside and rummaged as gently as he could. It was very hard in there and had he not known he would never have guessed by the feel that his hand was in the stomach cavity of a person. The whole thing felt odd, and as such he couldn't be sure that he had not felt something that was out of place. He was going to have to go into the mortuary with the body and use a lantern to look inside. He hoped that he could do this before the doctor arrived so that he wouldn't have to explain what he was doing. The fewer people who knew about this, the better.

But still he was resigned to the fact that it was going to

come out, things like this always did. People were going to be frightened, and they would jump to all sorts of conclusions. There was no doubt that the Dolocher was going to be recalled and rumours of his being back in the real world killing again were unavoidable It would be just like when everyone believed that Thomas Olocher was committing the Dolocher murders from beyond the grave. It seemed to be so easy to rattle these people; they were willing to believe in almost anything.

The cart clattered over the cobbles at the rear gate to the mortuary at the barracks. It was very quiet here, and the sun was rising and casting a strange glow over the square courtyard. Doctor Adam's was standing at the back door smoking a pipe, and he looked on the cart with interest as it pulled up. Two large dogs were stationed on either side of him like a royal bodyguard. The doctor whistled lowly, and the two dogs scurried off across the courtyard to a small construct that must have housed them.

"What have we got here Alderman," he said with a raised eyebrow on seeing who it was with the body. It was clear he was surprised to see him.

"A girl murdered and left on the street," James replied.

"Do you know who she is?" James knew he meant personally, but he answered as though he was this was all about policing.

"Not yet, but I think we will in a matter of days." The doctor came over and lifted up the sheet to look at the body.

"She's been dead a few days," he said in mild surprise; he looked questioningly at James.

"I thought so too. She was dumped at the walls of Newgate."

"Another one at Newgate? Dolocher country eh?" Adam's chuckled. James frowned, gripped with annoyance by the uttering of that name. Already someone was making casual comparisons.

The body was brought inside, stripped and laid out on a well-lit table in a small room where the doctor and the Alderman looked it over.

"There appears to be nothing but the main wound," the doctor said in a professional way having looked over the entire body.

"I noticed that too," James said. Adam's leaned over and peered into the wound, placing a scalpel inside and pushing things around a little so he could see better. He had a skilful hand, and James could see his years of battlefield hospital experience had not dulled his sensitivity with the dead.

"Look at this," he said, and James came over and leaned in for a better view. "Do you see all the serrations; here and here, and the same on the other side there?" Adams pointed.

"Yes," James nodded.

"Those are all the results of different stab wounds. It looks like this woman was repeatedly stabbed in the abdomen and then this whole section of her body was removed so as to make it look like one giant gaping hole."

"Like a massive bite?" James said nodding in the realisation that this is what it resembled.

"Exactly."

James knew what this meant for the rumour mill, and he was surprised that he hadn't seen the similarity to a bite earlier. He didn't want to dwell on this, and he looked back inside the wound.

"Is there anything else?"

"Like what?" Adam's asked in surprise, he must have thought this was enough already. James wondered was it obvious he was looking for something specific.

"Is there anything in the cavity that shouldn't be there?" James asked. Adam's looked at him askance and then he looked into the wound and poked around a little more.

"There doesn't seem to be anything," he said looking back to James. "Were you expecting anything in particular?"

"No, nothing specific." James looked over the young woman again, and he hoped sincerely that she had died quickly, though he doubted she had. He could feel the amulet in his pocket, and he ran his fingers over the grooved design on it. What did it mean?

"Did the man who was killed in the tower come here or was he just buried?" James asked. There had been no leads as to who this man was, and the men who had brought him in had been so blind drunk that they had no clue either, they only knew that they picked him up somewhere near the prison.

"He was here briefly, but there was no mystery there," Adams said

"Was there anything unusual found in his case?"

"On the body?"

"Yes."

"No. I must say these are odd questions Alderman."

"I know," James said, and he left, thanking the doctor on his way out the door.

# Chapter 8

Thin April clouds framed the door as James looked out to the street, taking in some of the chill air he'd felt through his window. He liked to stand on the steps of the house sometimes in the mornings before the street was really alive. It was quiet and peaceful here most of the time, and it was nice to be in near silent outdoor setting in the middle of a city sometimes. He breathed in and enjoyed the cold going into his cheeks and lungs. He leaned against the railing and closed his eyes and listened. In the distance, he could hear the hooves of a horse and the rattle of the wheels of a coach going somewhere. Closer to home some birds chirped from atop the houses.

As he was about to go back in he wiped his feet on the mat and as he looked down, he noticed something protruding from underneath it. He leaned down and lifted the corner revealing an envelope there. He looked around and seeing no one picked it up and examined it. It was a fine envelope, but it bore no distinctive markings. There was nothing on it save his own name as the addressee. It was not sealed, and he pulled the single sheet from within and let it fall out to full length from its folding. It read as follows:

*Dear Alderman, by now you will have realised that I am back. I have killed as before to set myself back in your mind, but now I'll have to deviate from the past so as not to make this too easy for you. I will kill again soon. It could be any person in any part of the city. I will kill at my old haunts from time to time, but I can't let you know when those will be. I have sketched an image from our shared past on the reverse of this page. I hope you like it.*

*Yours,*

*The Dolocher.*

James was stunned, and he looked about the street once more, hoping against hope to see some mildly mocking eyes or some colleague enjoying this joke, but there was nothing. He flipped the paper over and was shocked to see a rendering of the body of Thomas Olocher, as he had seen it that morning being feasted upon by the feral pigs of the city. It was detailed and gruesome and instantly brought James back to that time and place. He folded the letter back up and went back inside to his study, closing all doors behind him as he went.

He went to his desk, took out the letter once more, and placed it flat on the surface. Then he opened a drawer and took out a folder filled with letters. He ran through them quickly, letting the ones he was finished with fall to the floor as he searched for a match in the writing or even the paper, and looked out for small sketches that sometimes people put in their letters to him. He moved as though time were against him and when he got to the final letter the floor and desktop were a mess of papers and envelopes. He'd not seen a hand like it nor paper exactly the same.

He flipped the paper over and looked at the image once more. It was clear that this person had been there, had seen the body as it was that morning. It was far too accurate to have been by chance or imagination. His mind began to run through who would have been there that day.

There were plenty of names that crossed his mind, but the body was there overnight before the soldiers arrived. Countless numbers of people could have seen it, and no one could ever know.

James picked up the envelope and looked at it once more. He squeezed it to be fully sure that there was nothing inside and then he separated the folds and looked inside, and he saw something. There was another sketch inside the envelope, on the paper itself. He couldn't quite make it out, so he brought it close to the lamplight and spied inside. He couldn't be sure, but it really looked like a drawing of the amulet he'd found inside the body of the murder victim of a few days ago. He tore the paper carefully and continued to look inside to see that he was not ripping other important evidence until finally, he had the sketch on its own separated from the rest. It was a picture of the amulet, there was no mistaking it.

He sat back and let his body go limp in his chair. His worst fears had been realised. This was all related to the Dolocher, and he could see the panic and fear from two years ago already beginning to rise in front of him. Someone was acting in the name of the terror that had stalked the streets; not Cleaves, but the idea that he had managed to evoke in the public mind. James could feel the pressure rising in his head, and he put the sketch down and closed his eyes to it. It was only a matter of time now before the next murder, and then the rumours would begin once more to take hold, and God only knew where it would go from there.

Now he knew he would have to find Edwards. He needed him to find out what this amulet business was all about. His first search had been fruitless, but now he was more desperate, and he resolved that he would not sleep until he found him. He started by writing a letter that he would leave at Edwards' home if he could not find him there. In it, he would say that there was a new case like the Dolocher one and that there was a strange devilish amulet involved that he might know something about. James thought this would be enough to bring Edwards out of the woodwork and pique his curiosity.

When he wrote that letter, he called for some coffee to the be brought to his study, and he made up a list of the soldiers and people who would have been involved in the Thomas Olocher find. He didn't know the names of the soldiers off hand, but there would be a record of it at the barracks, and he would be able to ask the doctors there if they had remembered anyone there who shouldn't have been. He knew that the chances of yielding anything this way were low, but he had to give it a go. He knew from experience that you also never knew when blind luck was going to see you through something. He couldn't get the soldiers to ask questions about the find to people where the body was found as this would lead to questions being asked and wild assumptions and rumours spreading throughout the Liberties again.

The coffee was bitter, and he drank little of it. There was a sick feeling in him that he'd not felt since Cleaves was put to the gallows. How could someone be so sick and twisted as to want to emulate the madness and barbarity that went on back then? It was true that there had been murders committed since and some as violent and evil, but to wage a campaign, to be proud of it to the point of making a game of it? What kind of person could do this?

Again names and faces of the Dolocher times came back to him, the old gaoler Brick; the blacksmith Mullins; the gang leader Lord Muc- actually Alderman James hadn't heard much about Lord Muc in recent times this was unusual in itself. The gang warfare had all but ceased, and nothing else he had been involved in had ever passed James' desk. He might be worth looking into; there was something in him that sang out violence and blood lust, and James was sure that he couldn't have just turned a corner and left all that behind him.

The thoughts of patrolling dark streets once more, unsettled James and he shivered at the thought of it. At least it was nearly summer and the nights wouldn't be as they were during the other killings. He wondered again about Edwards, and he called down for his coach to be readied to leave in half an hour. He recalled that he once had his suspicions of Edwards himself in relation to the murders. He would have to find him now and use his help once more, but the blasphemies and diabolic talk that emitted from always left James with a dirty feeling. Better the Devil you know crossed his mind as he went down to his carriage.

# Chapter 9

The Liberties and the surrounding environs were swept up in the kind of hysteria not seen since the early days of the Dolocher murders. The stories were out, and the connections were being made. Enough people in the area had seen and heard about one or other of the three deaths located around 'The Black Dog, ' and now all were common knowledge. There was no mistaking the similarity to the killings of 1788. A man had died in the tower, just like Thomas Olocher, another was killed at the gate, like the first guard a few years ago and a third was killed at the walls, the same place as the second guard back then. It was almost a perfect copy. Some people heard that the murders were carried out in different places and the bodies then transported to the prison, but this was more fearful in their eyes as the imagined beast stalking the night carrying bodies about could be anywhere.

Even though all had heard about Cleaves, and how he had been the Dolocher there was still enough doubt and superstition in these people that the notion of a beast was able to gain traction again. This was especially the case when the last victim had a massive bite taken from her abdomen. Once again people tread the streets at night fearful of meeting this creature. They started to take the longer, busier routes to get to where they needed to be. Only the bravest, drunkest or most foolhardy travelled the thin alleys alone after dark.

Everyone knew that the next murder was imminent and tensions rose in line with this. Strangers to the neighbourhood were looked on with suspicion and children were kept close to home during the day. The places where it was known Dolocher murders had been committed before were vacant and quiet, and in the taverns and coffee houses, revellers argued about the order of the last murders and where the next one was likely to occur. There were those who being sensible opined that of course, this was the work of another man, a mere mortal just as Cleaves had been, but they were shouted down or ignored. It was easier for the uneducated masses to assume that something sinister prowled around at night rather than to think one of those who walked amongst them during the day was the vicious killer by night.

# Chapter 10

Mary Sommers rearranged the stock on her cart, separating the vegetables that had been dropped or moved into the wrong areas, and making the whole mess look more appealing to her customers. It was near the end of the day, and the light was fading. She would give it fifteen more minutes and then start to pack up for the day, she decided. She went back behind the cart to the seller's position just as a tall man approached from the lanes of Templebar. He was straight-shouldered, and she could tell he was a soldier, probably an officer and certainly a gentleman in civilian clothes with a tall hat and walking stick.

He stood at the cart and looked over the food and then looked up at Mary. She looked down, both afraid of making eye contact with gentlemen and also because of her shame at her scars; the reminders for all to see what the Dolocher had done to her.

"Can I help sir?" she asked timidly.

"Not with vegetables, but perhaps in another way," he said. He was definitely an officer; his voice had that commanding tone to it that she had heard as orders were barked in the streets at soldiers sometimes. The difference here was the way he was using his voice, he was almost jolly in tone.

"How do you mean?"

"I'll come straight out with girly," he said with authority. "My name is Spencer, and I am a painter. I would like to use you as a subject for a painting."

"Me!" was the only thing comprehensible thing that came out of Mary's mouth amongst a torrent of half words and sounds.

"You have a unique face, one that I am very interested in as a painter." Mary blushed at this, embarrassed by her scars being highlighted. "I know you went through a terrible thing, but from what I can see you came through it very well and have managed to get on with your life. There is a great strength in you, and I can see it in your face. I wish I had some men like you under my command!" he laughed here at his own joke and Mary smiled shyly.

"I don't think anyone would be interested in a painting of me."

"Nonsense, I'm interested, and I know plenty of others who would be too." Mary didn't say anything for a few moments. "I'll pay you very well, and I'll keep the sessions short, say about forty-five minutes a time?" She looked at him. It was true that she could always do with more money, who couldn't? It had been hard since Kate moved out, and Sarah and she had struggled a little since and hadn't found a suitable sharer. Kate still gave them a little money when she could, and she thought Tim wouldn't notice, but things were still tough. She wondered how much this man might be offering, but she was very much afraid to ask in case he should be offended. "If you are frightened of being alone with a man let me assure you that my servants will be on hand and soldiers come to me throughout the day with messages about all kinds of rubbish?" he offered.

"I don't know," she said, she was afraid of being alone with him but that hadn't crossed her mind until he brought it up. She wondered where he lived. Would she have to walk home in the dark after these sessions? "I have to work here during the day."

"Every day?" he asked.

"Mostly."

"Even if I paid you a week's wages that you get here every time you sit for me?"

"Really?" she was astounded by this offer. A week's wages for less than an hour of letting him paint her. She was embarrassed by how impressed she'd sounded, but he just smiled at her reaction.

"And, I'm sure it would take at least five or six sessions to get the basics down on canvas," he said. She couldn't turn this down, it was far too much money for so little effort, and it would really help Sarah and her out.

"What would I need to do?" she asked. She hadn't known anyone who had been painted before, and she had no clue what might be involved.

"Come to my house, and we'll get a pose that is comfortable for you and that suits my idea for the painting, and then I paint, and you sit."

"That's all?"

"Yes, it's quite simple, I can give you something to eat and drink while you are there as well." A thought suddenly struck her, and she remembered some of the men some nights looking at copies of paintings in the tavern where she used to work. Once or twice she'd caught sight of what they were looking at, and she could see that the women had little clothes on and sometimes there were parts showing. Her face must have changed for Spencer was now looking at her in a confused way

"Is everything alright?" he asked.

"Yes, I just want to know..." how could she put this?

"Yes?"

"What would I have to wear?" she felt ridiculous asking, and she was mortified afresh. Spencer laughed, and he seemed to understand her concerns.

"What you have on now is fine, anything you like. It's your face, your strength that I want to capture." Mary was relieved, and she smiled too at his answer and his beaming face which she really looked at for the first time now. He was actually quite handsome. In his forties probably but he looked fit and able. His face bore the marks of alcohol, and there was a small scar, faint against the light above his left eye, running down into the eyebrow itself, making it look as though it were two different eyebrows.

"Good," she said.

"So you'll consider it?"

"Yes, why not."

"Great, great!" he said.

"When do you want to start?"

"How about Sunday?"

"Sunday is fine."

"Good, I'll send my carriage for you at three o'clock. Where do you live?"

"He can pick me up here if that's allowed?"

"That is allowed," he smiled. "At three on Sunday so. Goodbye."

"Goodbye."

She watched him as he walked away the way he'd come. What a stroke of luck, her face had never been anything other than something to be hidden behind dropped hair or by her head turned to one side as she spoke to people. Now it was going to be making her money, as much as the vegetable stall did in a week! How odd this world was. She tidied up the stall a little earlier that she intended, the rush of knowing that there was going to be money coming in allowing her to do so without guilt. She stored the stock in the shed a lot of the market people used and then walked jollily home along to Skippers Lane and up to her room on the second floor where she waited for Sarah to come home so that she could tell her the good news.

## Chapter 11

The road started to rise a long way off from the hunting lodge at the top of Montpelier Hill. It was growing dark quickly, but Alderman James had come to the end of his wits in his search for Edwards, and he had been told with some authority this afternoon that Edwards was at the Hellfire Club lodge in the mountains, and had been there for a few days now. The house itself could be seen for a long time before he got to it. It was lit up and stood out like it was on fire on the dark mountainside making the name seem very apt. James grew uneasy the closer he got to it. There was a lot of talk of the things that went on up here, so far from the city and away from prying eyes. It was said that there were orgies and black masses and that the Devil himself would preside over gatherings here. James didn't believe in any of this, but it was hard not to be a little fearful in this wild setting. These people glorified the Devil after all, and this was reason enough to worry about them.

As he came up the road to the house, he was met by a hooded figure on a black horse who seemed to grow forth from the overhanging leaves of the trees on either side of the road.

"Who goes there?" the figure asked.

"Alderman James."

"What business have you here?"

"I've come to see Mr. Edwards."

"There is no one here by that name." James wondered was there some club name that Edwards had to be referred to as, or if there was some secret password he was supposed to say to this sentry to get by.

"I am an officer of the law, and I will go to the house and look for myself," James asserted in a bold tone.

"You are an officer of the law in Dublin city but not out here," the sentry said.

"Who are you? Why do you not show your face?" James demanded.

"You should turn and go back home, Alderman." The sentry's voice was stoic and calm, but there was something very unnerving about talking to a man all in black with a hooded face out here in the dark of night in an unfamiliar place.

"Can you get a message to him for me?"

"I don't know who you speak of." James was aware suddenly of another dark horseman watching from a small distance closer to the house. Though he tried to fight it, there was fear creeping into the Alderman's heart, and he was afraid to say anything more lest they suspect it in his voice. He nodded gravely to the sentry who had addressed him, turned the horse around and began slowly down the road the way he'd come. As he moved away, he could hear the hooves of the second horse come to join the first one, and he wondered were they going to follow him. He was afraid, and he wanted to look behind, but he did not want to give them the satisfaction, of letting them know he was afraid. He whet his lips and tested a faint whistle, and when this worked, he loudly rang out a tune until he thought he might be out of their earshot.

It was pitch black now between the trees, but he could see the road ahead with the moonlight. It was almost white against the perceived black of everywhere else up here. He looked back along the road and confident that there was no one following him, he got off the horse and led it into the trees where he tied it up and put an oat bag over its nose. He looked about once more for anyone who might have followed him down the road and satisfied he set off on foot back up towards the house.

When he thought he was close enough, he tried to make out some landmarks that he could use for his bearings, and he started to walk slowly and as quietly as he could cross country. He didn't want to go too deep into the woods, but he had to go in so far that he would not cast an easy to see silhouette. If didn't take him long to come to a point whereby he could see the sentries at the gate. He could hear the murmur of conversation between them but could make out nothing they were saying. He looked up at the house, and he saw that in two dozen or so yards he could be at the circular courtyard wall. He stayed still for a time and looked all about; there was still the chance that there were more sentries on duty. So far he had not seen any.

The house was blazing with light, and he could hear the voices of men shouting obscenities when he finally got to the wall. It was like he had passed some sound threshold, an area where all things could be heard. He peeked over and saw one man stumble to a window on the first floor of the house and vomit down into the courtyard. A roar of laughter went up from within, and someone else came up behind him and slapped the man heartily on the back and led him back inside. James got over the wall at a low point and walked to the steps that led into the house on the first floor. The sentries could still be seen at their post on the road, and they were not looking at the house.

James crept up and inside the unguarded and open door. Hr was in a small alcove, and the voices came clear and loud to him now. It was like he was at the same table with them all. They were swearing vile oaths one at a time, and James shuddered at the profanity and vileness of them. So far he hadn't recognised the voice of Edwards, so he still wasn't sure if he was here or not. He looked around the alcove and saw ten men around a large table, well lit by candles and covered with food and wine. There was a large bowl of something in the centre of the table with a ladle hanging over the side. He saw someone take from it and fill their glass and drink some. He noticed that the head of the table was left clear and he knew that it was set aside for the Devil as was the rumour. Fear came to him once more, and he told himself that he did not believe all this, but still it did not lift.

As he stood in that doorway, he suddenly felt very vulnerable and alone. He could not go in and challenge these men with no one else to back him up. They were drunk and on their own territory, and God only knew what they might do to him knowing full well that they would probably get away with it. Who would hear his calls for help out here? He regretted coming now, and he cursed the amulet in his pocket and the intrigue it had caused in him. Why did I come here? He closed his eyes and began to say a prayer, but his mind wandered to images of the carved statue of the Devil under the archway near Christchurch Cathedral; the place called Hell, and he could see it come up the steps here, go inside and take its place at the head of the table. He shook his head to try to dispel such fanciful images, but they would not lift.

At that moment hot stale-breathed air flushed his face, and he opened his eyes to the vision of a massive shimmering black beast right up at his face. Cold eyes peered at him, and huge buck teeth bared at him each tooth as long as his own hand. James called out in fright, seeing that same Devil as before taking hold of him to whisk him away. There was more noise; voices yelling and he felt a blow to his head as the beast moved away from him and back out the door. There was another blow to his head, and he felt black descend over him.

## Chapter 12

His body was warm and clammy, and his head ached. He knew he was somewhere he didn't know, even before he opened his eyes. Alderman James moved to sit up, and pain shocked his head; he knew he had come to some injury. He opened his eyes, and he could see a crackling, well-built fire that he hadn't heard up to know. He was on a couch, and there was something wet against his head where he was in pain. He lifted his hand to it and took a wet towel and saw there was blood on it. What had happened to him, he wondered. And where was he now? He could recall nothing, and he felt tired and weakened.

"You should put that back against your head," someone said, and James knew the voice. He looked around in the dim room, and he saw, by the window, Edwards sitting at a table with a brandy glass in front of him. The fire was the only light in the room, and it gleamed off the curve of the glass leaving Edwards mostly in shadow. James recalled the sentry's at the Hellfire Club, and he got images of being there and the beast that had come at him from the doorway.

"What happened?" he asked.

"You had a fall," Edwards said slyly. James got the impression that Edwards was testing his memory to see if he remembered what had really happened.

"I did not fall. I was attacked."

"If you know what happened, why ask?"

"There was some creature at the door," James said, and he looked around the room. Was this the same place?

"We are away from the lodge now Alderman, down the mountain a bit, in a house where you are safe."

"What was it at the door?" James could feel its hot breath on him, and he saw the black shape as it was nearly on him. It moved slowly, and he felt a chill at the image as his mind raced as to what it could be.

"It was a horse who stuck his head up through the doorway; he must have followed you up from the courtyard," Edwards was almost laughing.

"And who hit me?" James asked.

"Hard to tell; there was quite a melee when the alarm went up that there was an intruder on private property." James knew better than to pursue this. If there was anything Edwards was good at it was keeping secrets, he was sure of that; there was no way he was going to tell him who had struck the blow. "I would advise that you don't go sneaking around up there in the future," Edwards added after a pause.

"What was going on up there anyway?"

"Nothing really; a bunch of men having a good time."

"Good time?" Edwards nodded. There was no point going on with questions. "I've been looking for you for a while."

"Yes? What can I do for you?"

"I wanted you to look at something for me." James rooted deep in his pocket and took out the amulet and held it up.

"What is it?" Edwards asked, not getting up from the table.

"Some kind of amulet I think. It has a carving of the Devil on it. I thought you might know where it came from." Edwards walked over and took the amulet and went to the fire where he could see it better. James watched his face as he studied it but it gave nothing away, he couldn't tell if Edwards had ever seen something like it before.

"Where did you get this?"

"Do you know what it is?"

"Perhaps. Where did you get it?"

"It was at a murder site." Edwards nodded.

"I should have known really, why else would you come to me with it."

"Do you recognise it?"

"I've never seen one, but it looks like an amulet described to me before that used to be worn by members of the club in London back in the fifties."

"Hellfire Club members?"

"Yes. We've never gone in for this type of thing over here," he said. "Still, it is nice work don't you think?"

"The craft maybe but not the content," James said. Edwards laughed.

"I forgot how pious you like to be." James didn't say anything to this. "So how many murders this time?" Edwards asked.

"What?"

"How many murders have there been?" Edwards looked at him with raised eyebrows. "You haven't been searching high and low for me just to show me this. You want me to help with your investigation."

"No, I just wanted to know what this was. It pertains to one murder."

"You've always been a terrible lair Alderman."

"Can you tell me anything else about the amulet?" James ignored this.

"No, I'm not even sure it is what I think it is."

"Would any of the rest of your cabal know?"

"Possibly."

"Can you ask?"

"So you do want my help?"

"In this small matter only."

"Of course I'll help you, Alderman. I hear this body was found outside the gaol not long after the one in the tower." James didn't know how Edwards always knew these things. It was infuriating the way that he dropped things into conversation like that.

"There's been another since." At least James had that one over him.

"Yes, also at the walls of the prison. Do you think it is the return of 'our mutual friend?' This was the name Edwards had given the Dolocher when they were investigating that case.

"Of course not, don't be so ridiculous!" James snapped, as angry at his infuriating information as for his blasé attitude to people's deaths. Edwards laughed out loud again. James' head hurt, and he put the wet towel back to it to cool it.

"But you are afraid that this is what the locals will think when they find out?"

"Yes," James admitted.

"Did you find anything else on the other bodies?"

"No."

"And how were they killed?"

"The first had his throat cut; the second was stabbed many times and slashed all over, his eyes removed and the latest was stabbed multiple times, and then the area removed so that it resembled a huge bite mark."

"Bite mark?" James nodded. "And you don't think this is related to the Dolocher?"

"Someone is killing and trying to evoke that same fear and confusion, but not in the same way as before. These murders are different."

"How so?"

"Well, the last two have been killed at some unknown location and dumped at the scene near the prison."

"Any idea where the actual murders have been committed?"

"Not yet."

"The identities of the people killed?"

"No yet, but hopeful on the latest one."

"Why is that?"

"She is young and would be recognisable, her face is unharmed."

"There's something else? Something you're holding back on for some reason?" Edwards looked at him, and again James wondered about how well this man could read him so often. He hadn't mentioned the letter or the sketch, but at that moment he knew that Edwards was going to be involved, so it was as well that he knew everything. Everything within reason.

"I've received a letter from the killer." Edwards lit up at this.

"I knew you were holding out on me," he exclaimed, "What did he say?"

"He said that he will kill again soon."

"And?"

"He claims that he is the Dolocher."

"That connection was easy enough to make without his writing a letter."

"He is not the Dolocher. Cleaves is dead and buried."

"I know that, but this person wants us to think of him as

the Dolocher, and I see no reason why we should deny him this."

"There was a sketch with the letter."

"Of what?"

"Thomas Olocher's body as it was found on the morning half eaten by pigs."

"That was a gruesome sight."

"Indeed. It was a perfect rendition as though from my own memory."

"So it was done by someone who was at the scene?"

"Certainly."

"Do you have the sketch or letter on you now?"

"No, they are at home. They are on either side of the one sheet."

"Was it delivered to your house or office?"

"It was under my doormat at home."

"So he knows where you live."

"Well, that's no great secret."

"I suppose, but you should be careful; what is security like at your home. Is there any at all?"

"Not really, but I'm not too concerned about that."

"Still looking to be punished for doing your duty eh?" James didn't respond to the mocking tone Edwards had addressed this to him.

"What time is it?" James asked.

"Late, we'll stay here tonight and go first thing. Your horse is in the stable here."

"There was one more thing about the letter."

"Yes?"

"There was a sketch of that amulet on the inside of the envelope." Edwards held the amulet up and looked at it once more.

"What is this little Devil up to, eh?" he said admiringly.

# Chapter 13

Mullins was on Cook Street in the whiskey cabin, leaning against the bar with a small jug and wondering if he was going to get another, and if so should he take a seat at one of the tables. It had been a long hard day in the shop; unexpected jobs coming in and really putting him under pressure, but he knew the money coming in would make it all worth it. He was very tired but wired too from work, and he didn't want to go home and sit still as of yet. As much as the thought of being with Kate was appealing, his body wasn't ready for bed or the armchair by the fire. He ordered another one and looked again at the seats and then saw a table free up in the corner at the back. He called the barman to tell him that he was going to sit down and the barman nodded and said he would drop the jug over in a minute or two.

Mullins sat with his back to the wall, and he faced the door off to his left a little. He knew all the faces of the people here, and he had said his hellos on the way in and made small talk with a few but had managed to disengage himself and be alone after that. This was what he had wanted. He recalled how all of the people here, and many more besides, had bought him so many drinks for a while after he captured the Dolocher. Even the barman had been generous, often telling the tale of the night Mullins left this very place in a woman's cloak that led to his being mistaken for a woman and attacked that night. This was before the suspicions set in, and the mistrust in people came back to the fore.

This was the place he used to most often meet Cleaves; a good friend of his for many years before being uncovered as a murderer. Some people couldn't believe that Mullins had never gotten so much a hint that his friend might have been so twisted, and some even went so far as to suggest that Mullins might have known all along. No one had ever said this to him directly, but he knew it from overheard snippets. The drinks began to dry up then very fast, and this was when the drop off in business came too.

Just at the jug was placed in front of him, Mullins saw past the barman that Lord Muc coming in. They made eye contact, and Muc nodded and went to the bar. Mullins didn't look at him, didn't want to encourage him to come over, but just as he feared the man was in front of him with a large jug a few moments later. He pulled out the chair opposite Mullins and sat down without asking or being invited. Mullins looked at him but said nothing. Muc took a swig straight from the jug and planted it on the table roughly. He seemed to be already on the way to drunk, had probably been somewhere else before this cabin.

"We'll be in trouble again soon," Muc said without preamble.

"How do you mean?"

"Haven't you heard?"

"Heard what?"

"The Dolocher is back!" Muc said loudly; everyone in the place looked at them for a moment and then went back about their business. Muc smiled mischievously.

"That's not possible," Mullins said. He had heard about the killings, and he knew that they resembled the Dolocher murders, but he also knew that Cleaves was dead, He was as sure of this as anything else; he had been there at both his hanging and his burial; had seen the whole thing. He had to see it with his own eyes to the believe it; to be sure that Cleaves was guilty and that he was really being punished for it. To actually believe that it had all happened and that it was all finally over.

"Possible or not it's happened," Muc sneered.

"And how does that affect us?" Mullins hated saying anything collective about the two of them.

"We will be looked at again. Fingers will be pointed at us once more."

"Why would they?"

"Because of who we are."

"And who are we?"

"Men of violence," Muc said, self-satisfied. Mullins didn't say anything; he knew well how Muc thought they were alike, that they were men who needed violence in life and how potent and powerful a force it could be. Muc was smiling at him waiting for him to say something.

"Neither of us is too involved in anything violent these days," Mullins said taking another sip of his whiskey.

"Not by choice," Muc sighed looking like a bored child.

"It is for me."

"No, you have a woman now, and you think you shouldn't do the things you once did, but I know that every time you are in a place like this you have it in your heart that you hope someone will insult you and give you cause to unleash what is inside you."

"That is plainly not true."

"Look at us blacksmith, there are very few men in this city who would want to tangle with us. No one here, in this place or even the whole of the Liberties because they know what we can do."

"Most people don't want to fight in the first place, against anyone."

"I've seen you fight blacksmith both one to one and when you fought for my gang that one time. You've seen me fight. I don't know how many times you've seen me, but I know you have." Muc paused, and Mullins was not sure where he was going with this. "We could stand up now and fight all twenty men here and come out of it with barley a scratch," Muc went on. Mullins looked involuntarily about the crowd in the cabin, and he had to admit that Muc was probably right.

"So?"

"That's not what would be interesting though would it?"

"And what would?" Mullins knew now what he was getting at.

"You are the one person in the whole of Dublin who I think could give me a good fight," Muc eyes him up with a grin.

"It's not going to happen Muc."

"I know it would be hard; you are very stubborn, and even if I were to hit you right now I don't know if you would fight or not."

"I wouldn't."

"I would lean that way myself," Muc agreed and drank from the jug again. "We should work together," he then said unexpectedly.

"Work on what?"

"You know we will be questioned soon and why not be on the same side if we really are? I didn't kill those people, and I know for certain that you didn't. You don't have that inside you."

"If I get questioned, I will tell the truth, and that will be the end of it."

"Like the night you told the truth, and they shoved you

in the tower of 'The Black Dog?'"

"That was remedied only a few hours later."

"Still, if it happened again there is no guarantee that the outcome would be the same for you."

"If we are both innocent, we don't have anything to worry about." Muc nodded as though in agreement with this logic.

"This city is changing blacksmith," Muc said wistfully. "There's not much room for people like us left."

"I fit in perfectly well here," Mullins said. Muc didn't answer, he lifted his jug and drank some more.

"Do you fancy going for a stroll?" he asked after a while. Mullins was drinking form his own glass as Muc spoke.

"I'm not going to fight you tonight Muc." He was sure that this was what he was getting at.

"Not even if I tell you that I was a customer of you wife on many occasions?"

Mullins stopped dead, and he stared at Muc with ferocious intensity. He had always feared someone might say something like this, or insinuate as much to him, but thus far it had been avoided. Was Muc telling the truth? It didn't matter if he was or not.

Mullins stood and pushed forward with all his strength. The table pushed against Muc's midriff as he had tried to stand at the same time. He stumbled back, and his jug fell to the floor and shattered, Mullins own jug and glass shifted on the table but somehow stayed upright on it. His fist fell square and hard on the end of Muc's nose, and Muc fell back further into a pile of men. There was uproar in the cabin, and the barman shouted at Mullins to take it outside. The men pushed Muc back up off them and into a standing position, and it was now that Mullins saw how drunk he was. The punch had stunned him, but it was mostly drink that had him swaying like a tree in a stiff breeze. He went forward and grabbed Muc by the clothes at his chest and pulled him out into the street. Muc couldn't see as a result of the whack on his nose, but he flailed a few times and landed a crack on Mullins's temple; it glanced off but hurt a little. Mullins let go of him, and Muc stumbled back a little raising his hands in defence. He was getting his sight back.

There were shouts all around, and Mullins knew that the cabin had emptied and that everyone was watching what was going on. They had waited a long time to see this spectacle. Mullins looked around and then dropped his aggressive stance and looked at Muc.

"It's not over just like that!" Muc shouted, furious.

"It is over just like that," Mullins said back to him. Mullins was humiliated now for making such a scene; people would ask what it was about and someone was bound to come to the right conclusion or to have heard what Muc had said. Muc sprang forward as Mullins was lost in this train of thought and he felt the hard forehead smash into his mouth and nose, and Mullins was sent sprawling to the ground.

"I'm too drunk for this now blacksmith, but we'll go again," Muc said. Mullins felt the blood run from his mouth and nose and he tasted the iron of it and spat. Muc was stumbling away in the direction of his home and Mullins just looked after him. The pain was terrible in his face, and it was a cold damp ground underneath him. All in all, it could not have been a much worse end to what started out as a pleasant evening.

# Chapter 14

Kate went to Skipper's Lane the evening following Edwards giving her the letter. The boy she'd sent with the letter to Mary had told her to come tonight to the second floor room where Kate once lived with Mary and Sarah. Kate walked along the dirty street and looked about for signs of anyone watching her, or for places Edwards or one of his agents might spring from to further surprise or interrogate her. She got to the door safely and unhindered, and she went in and up the stairs to the room and knocked on the door.

"Come in!" Sarah said seeing who it was. She went in and saw Mary was standing by the fire stirring something in a pot that smelled very good. Mary smiled and said hello and Kate returned the greeting.

"Will you eat?" Mary asked when Kate sat down. She wanted to, but she knew she was going to eat at home and she didn't want to take food from them. Especially knowing that they were tight for money and needed all they had and all they could get. Kate often felt sorry that she had to leave them, but she wondered why they didn't just get someone in to take her place, even if it was only for a short time just to get some money in. There was no shortage of people looking for somewhere to stay and there was surely some girl like themselves who could use the room.

"No, thanks. I'll be eating with Tim later."

"How is he?" Sarah asked.

"He's good. He looks after me." Kate wondered had Mary already told Sarah about the letter. She assumed she would have done.

Mary dished up a bowl and handed to Sarah and then another smaller one which she handed to Kate.

"Just a little bit, so you don't feel left out," Mary smiled at her and Kate took the bowl with a thankful nod and smile. When she poured her own bowl, Mary sat down at the small table with the other two. There was silence for a few moments as they ate. Kate decided to break it.

"So what about this letter?" she said. Mary and Sarah looked at one another with concerned faces. "What? What is it?" Kate asked, fear evident in her voice. She didn't like the look they'd exchanged; saw something sinister in it and she was terrified now as to what the letter contained.

"It's nothing to be frightened of," Sarah assured her, taking her by the forearm.

"What did it say?"

"He said that he loves you. That he wants you to be with him."

"He loves me?" He had never said this to her before. Mary nodded.

"He said he is willing to make sure that Tim is looked after financially if you leave him."

"He wants to pay my husband for me!" Kate shrieked. She was furious, but instantly she felt embarrassed as she realised that he had paid for her many times over the last few years, and what he proposed was no different really to what had gone before. Neither of the women said anything to this. "He expects to be able to pay Tim and I'll just to him?" Kate asked in a calmer voice.

"That was the gist of it by my reading," Mary said.

"He said that Tim wouldn't have to work again if he was willing to go ahead with this," Sarah said.

"He thinks you don't really love Tim; that you feel you owe something to him," Mary went on.

"But I do love him," Kate said pleadingly, as though she needed to convince her audience.

"We know that," Mary smiled at her.

"What will you do?" Sarah asked.

"What do you mean?"

"How will you reply?"

"I'll tell him no."

"What if he goes to Tim himself and makes the offer?"

"Does he say in the letter he'll do that?"

"No, but what if he does?"

"Then Tim will make him regret it," Kate said triumphantly.

"And then Edwards will make him regret that in court," Mary said. Kate looked at her. She was right. If Tim struck Edwards that would all he needed to have him locked up or worse. She knew that Edwards had deep connections everywhere. He could arrange anything he wanted in a court trial.

"You have to find a way to say no gently," Sarah said. They were all silent again as they thought about a way to possibly do this, but they all knew but didn't say that this was not possible. It was a long time before anyone spoke.

"A man in love is a very dangerous beast," Sarah said.

"I've seen what they are capable of in the name of 'love' before," Kate said. It was true that a man in love, especially unrequited love, could do all sorts of things that you wouldn't think him capable of. It was like they were being denied air and they would lash out in the most unexpected ways, even to themselves it seemed. All logic would leave the benighted man when a woman he loved was unattainable to him.

"Are you going to talk to Tim?" Mary asked.

"I think I should, but I have no idea what I'll say to him."

"How do you think he will be?"

"Mad as hell!"

"Do you think he'd do anything?"

"It's hard to tell. You both know that Tim has fight in him, and I know he needs to let off steam from time to time. Maybe if I got him just after one of those times, it would be better."

"Send him out for a few drinks tomorrow night and then tell him when he gets home," Sarah laughed, and the two women giggled with her.

"I could do that, but maybe wait for the next morning," Kate said.

"How do you think Edwards will react to you saying no to him?" Mary asked.

"I know he doesn't like it when people say no. He not used to hearing it."

"You should probably try to appeal to his feelings for you," Sarah suggested, and Mary nodded in agreement. "Tell him that if he really loves you, he will let you be happy or something like that."

"Do you think that would do any good?" Kate asked. They both shrugged.

"You know him better than we do," Mary said.

Kate thought about this, and for a brief moment, she could imagine him backing away gracefully with a smile as she said this. Him telling her to look after herself and that he would always be around if she changed her mind. But this fantasy was short lived as she saw his evil sneering face, one that she had seen many times in the past. She knew him better all right. She knew how vindictive and petty he could be. How he always wanted his own way, like a child, and he got it which was worse. There was no happy outcome for her here. It was going to bad, it was just a matter of how bad. The stew in the bowl was warm, and it tasted good as he chewed.

"It's not going to be pretty, one way or the other," she said as upbeat as she could. "Now what's going on with you two?"

# Chapter 15

Sunday at three o'clock came, and Mary stood in this drizzle at the stall waiting for Colonel Spencer's carriage to collect her. She was nervous and almost hadn't come, but Sarah had reminded her about the money and said that she would probably be well fed there into the bargain. She also asked if Mary was not curious to see what his house looked like. She had left home with butterflies in her stomach, and it had almost turned to nausea now as she waited. She wore a plain black dress, the best that she owned, but she knew it was tatty compared to what even Spencer's maids probably wore. Her cloak covered her head from the rain, and she had washed her hair and her hand's as well as her face and neck before she came out. Sarah had dabbed some fruit water on her, and she could smell the light aroma from time to time as the wind drifted over her in weak waves.

A carriage appeared from the narrow lanes, two fine horses pulling a gleaming black coach. The driver pulled up and nodded to Mary.

"Colonel Spencer's?" he asked her.

"Yes." She was right about his being in the army so.

"Climb in, please. Do you need assistance?" the driver asked cheerfully. He was an older man, in his late fifties probably, and he too had the air of the military about him as Spencer had done.

"No I'm fine, I can get up." He leaned back and opened a door for her, and she hiked up her dress and stepped up into the back, and then they were off.

"Do you need to stop anywhere on the way Miss?" the driver asked.

"No, thank you." She didn't really understand why he had asked her that, but she assumed that this was what carriage drivers did. They were charged with looking after the people they ferried back and forth after all.

They wound their way back along the Liffey and crossed at Essex Bridge and travelled up Capel Street before turning right onto Bolton Street and then onto Dorset Street. After travelling on this for a little, they turned a final left onto Dominick Street where the carriage pulled up outside a large townhouse.

"Just up the steps madam; someone is waiting to let you in," the driver said opening the door and helping her out to the ground.

"Thank you," she said to him. She hadn't thought to take any money with her, and now she was unsure as to whether she was supposed to tip this man or not; if it was rude not to give him something. She rummaged in her cloak on the off chance that she might find something. She could feel her face go crimson and the driver looked at her, and he took hold of her hands.

"All taken care of Miss, you better get inside out of this rain," he smiled at her, and she couldn't help but smile back. He was such a genial man, and she could feel the warmth of his hands even through his gloves. She thought he must be someone's father and what a lucky child that would be.

"Thank you again," she said to him, and she started up the steps.

As she went up the steps towards the bright red door, it opened, and a maid with a smiling face stood there to greet her.

"Come in dear," she said pleasantly and taking her by

the arms. The house was warm, and as soon as she was inside, she could feel it infuse her whole body. There was a mat inside the door, and the maid took her cloak and hung it on a hook on the wall and beckoned her to follow. Mary wiped her feet and stepped of onto the softest surface she'd ever stood on. Deep red carpets lined the hallway and ran up the stairs, and she couldn't believe how soft it was and the comparison to even the mat at the door. She felt as though she shouldn't be wearing shoes on it, afraid that she would be getting it dirty. She took small steps on tip toe almost as she followed the maid.

She was brought to a room and told to wait and was then left alone. It was a large square room, the carpet was less thick here but still very soft and a brighter red than that in the hallway. The walls were covered in gold leaf designed wallpaper that shone with the light from the many candles in the chandelier. There were paintings on the wall of men in uniform, some who looked like Spencer and some battle scenes of which she had no way of even guessing at. There was a magnificent fireplace piled for a fire but not in use just then, it was white and clean, and there were ornaments of various birds on the mantle. There was very little furniture in the room. A couch and a chair side by side were all. Across from these was a wooden frame; she didn't know what it was called, but she knew people used them for painting. She had seen people in the street using them before. The maid came back in and said that the Colonel would be in shortly and asked if she wanted anything to eat or drink. Mary was too embarrassed to say she did so she declined politely.

She was left alone again, and soon Spencer came in with a large canvas under his arm and a leather bag in the other hand.

"Hello?" he said happily "I'm glad you came!"

"Hello sir," she said, and she completed and awkward curtsy.

"No need for such formalities, while you are in my house you call me Spencer, is that all right?" He was smiling a lot, and he looked at her a couple of times as he set up his canvas and set down his bag and began to go through it.

"Yes sir," she replied.

"Yes who?" he said laughing.

"Sp-Spencer," she said nervously, but his smile was infectious, and she let one slip of her own.

"That's it!" he said. "I like that you wore black; it's a perfect contrast to your white skin." Mary blushed at this feeling a compliment even though she hadn't heard one she understood. "We're just going to get things set up today, get you in a pose you find comfortable, and then I'll make a few quick sketches in my notebook," he said, taking this last item out of his bag. He looked at her for approval, and she nodded.

"Why don't you sit down?" he suggested.

"Where?" she asked.

"Try the couch first maybe." She sat down, her knees together and her feet planted on the floor. She sat upright and didn't lean into the back. "You'll have to get more comfortable than that," Spencer smiled. "Sit back, it's very soft and nice." Mary did as she was told and once more she was astonished by how soft and comfortable it was. It went so far back that for a moment she was afraid that she was going to fall through it and end out on the floor behind. But it stopped, and she felt the cool covering on her skin, and she liked it very, very much.

"How's that?"

"Nice."

"It doesn't quite suit the painting I have in mind, though," he said looking at her and then the couch as though he were trying to work something out. "Can you sit with your feet up and lean your side against the arm? Maybe hold your head up with your elbow propped on the arm and your fist under your chin?" he demonstrated what he meant as he spoke.

Mary was awkward doing this, but she slipped out of her shoes and put them to the side of the couch and pulled her legs up assuming the position he had asked. "Very good," he said, "Now can you look out towards the window, please?" She did this. "Perfect!" he exclaimed. She smiled at his enthusiasm. "Do you think you could hold that for twenty minutes at a go?"

"I think so. It seems fine."

"Great. Hold there for a bit so."

Mary stayed as still as she could. She could see a nest on top of a building across the road, and she focused on this for a time. Just out of the corner of her eye she could make out the movements of Spencer, but it was only a sense, and she didn't really know what he was doing. She could hear his pencils rushing over the paper, and every now and then she would hear a sheet be torn and hear it as it fell to the floor. Some of these sheets came into her view but of what she could see one seemed to be only her hair, and the other was the bottom of the couch with her shoes beside it. Every now and then he would make some noise in approval at something, or else scold himself for some mistake or blot he must have made.

"Nearly done for today," he said soon, and Mary was surprised at how quick the time had seemed to pass. She didn't know if she was allowed to move or reply so she let her eyes move to him for a moment and the looked back out the window. "You can move your head now, I'm just getting down something of the dress now," he said with a smile. She blushed at the thought of him studying her body so closely, and he would have to be if he was focusing on her dress.

"All done," he said finally. She stood up and stretched out her neck and hips.

"That was fast," she said.

"I'll try to keep all the sessions as brief as I can, I know it's not very exciting just sitting there."

"It was fine for me."

"Nice to near it. My coachman will drop you home or anywhere else you might like to go," Spencer said. He rummaged in his pockets and brought out some coins and offered them to her. She was about to put her hand out when he snatched them back suddenly. "How rude of me, dropping coins into your hands!" He went to his bag and took out a small change pouch and dropped the coins into it and tied the top and then handed it to her. "Terribly sorry about that," he said.

"That's no problem. Thank you," Mary said. She didn't look at the pouch, but she could feel the weight of the money and was excited by it.

"Next week at the same time?" he asked.

"Yes. Thank you."

"You have nothing to thank me for." She didn't know what to say to this, but he went on. "I have to get ready to go out now, so I'll get Hetty to call the coachman and see you out. See you next week," he said and with a wave and then he left the room at speed. Mary felt the money in her hand, and she couldn't wait to get home and show Sarah. She was delighted too that she was going to be taken home in the carriage as it was a long walk for her from here.

# Chapter 16

It was late in the day, and the dusk was still off by a little bit when the mob reached the graveyard. It had been no secret where Cleaves had been buried. Hundreds had turned out for his hanging, and many came to the site of the burial. It had been proposed that he be flung into a communal grave, but those with loved ones already in there raised concerns about them having to spend eternity with that monster beside them. Finally, the authorities, tired of hearing this, changed the location and Cleaves was given a dank pit of his own that was ordered to remain unmarked. The people cheered when he was buried, and it was known that people would often use the grave site as a toilet if they were caught short, on their way home drunk or just felt a little mischievous.

On this night they got to the grave, and their intention was morbid and out of fear. It had taken the men to drink a little before they could be cajoled into doing this deed that many thought sacrilegious despite the occupant of the grave. There was also the silly fear in some that they might find that they would be the ones to wake the actual Dolocher by digging him up. But most just had to know. They had to be sure that he was still in his grave and that there was no way it was really him, as he had been in human form going around and killing once more.

There was a brief discussion and disagreement as to the exact location but when this was settled three men set about digging. Having taken on a lot of alcohol, they were soon out of breath, and another two men took over for a time, and it was very slow progress. Women badgered from the side and jeered at the men for their lack of effort.

After about twenty minutes there was a general withdrawal from the grave, and one of the women let out a shriek.

They had uncovered a body, but it was not the decomposing and wretched body of Cleaves, no, instead in its place was that of a young woman, killed only very recently and buried in this spot. There was no sign of the Dolocher and the people around blessed themselves and looked about suddenly as though in terrible danger as the dusk began to settle. The women cried, and the men with shovels brandished them more firmly as all looked about as if expecting the Dolocher to launch an attack on them from any direction right there and then.

In a huddle they left, each afraid of their own shadow and all regretful that they had been so foolhardy to come and do what they had. Mullins watched them leave from his vantage point at the edge of the cemetery. He'd been at the graveside cursing his former friend to high heaven, in a fit of anger at Cleaves for turning out not to be the man Mullins had so liked. When he heard the crowd approaching he fled, not wanting to be seen at the grave in case he was mistaken for a mourner- that would be the last thing he needed. Now that they were all safely gone he approached the grave once more, curiosity being his lure now.

As he got closer, he saw the mounds of freshly dug earth that the men hadn't bothered pushing back in, and soon he was going to be close enough to see over it and into the grave. He braced himself for what he might see. He had never seen a body this long after burial, but he had no thoughts other than it being Cleaves in there, and in such a state that the people went scurrying off in revulsion. He closed his eyes as he stood on the mound and took a deep breath before looking in.

To his surprise, he saw the woman, and he knew straight away that she was not dead all that long. She had been the victim of a murder, and there were black stains all over the clothes that Mullins assumed were dried and caked blood. He wanted to jump in and take her out and dig down to see if Cleaves was underneath, but he knew in his heart that he was not down there. Now that he knew what was in the grave he knew he had to get away from here. Those people would bring back the first policeman or soldier they could find. The last thing he needed was to be caught near a scene like this.

He left quickly and travelled a few streets before stopping. There was terrible anger in him, and his emotions were so mixed. He had always been capable of self-deception when it came to Cleaves's guilt for all those murders. Even though he knew he had done it, Mullins couldn't help but remember the good times with Cleaves, the times he told stories to the children or when he helped out people in need. It was so hard to reconcile this with what had happened. He had countless hours of fond memories of his friend, but only those few minutes at the end of seeing him as the Dolocher. He'd wanted to visit the grave before now, but he hadn't dared for what people might think, especially with the rumours that flew around about his knowledge at that time. He felt tears on his cheeks, and he didn't know if it was for his lost friend, for the fact that someone had desecrated his grave and took his body somewhere, or because of the girl whose body he had just seen. He started walking again but with no real aim. He wasn't well known in this area, and he walked here in the hope that no one would recognise him.

Later in a coffee house on Fleet Street, he saw in his mind the wound on the woman's stomach and how large it was and how much blood there had been if everything he thought he'd seen had been blood. She had been savaged, a horrible way to die. It looked like a giant bite, but he knew that it must have been done by a person and so it must have been cut out of her. The place would be cordoned off by now and no doubt the Alderman would be there now. This was part of the new murders and the link to the Dolocher this time was not one of the sites of his murders but in the fact that his grave was used. He was sure too that Cleaves had been taken away so that doubt could be pressed into people's minds, that they could believe that he was back amongst the living. Whoever was responsible was interested in more than just killing, they wanted the fear and the paranoia that had been rife those two winters of 1788 and 1789. They wanted fear to reign and the streets to be emptied at night.

That whole time had been a terrible experience for anyone living in the Liberties and especially himself. Lord Muc's words came back to him; would Mullins be suspected again? He felt stupid now for going to the grave, and he wondered if anyone had seen him there. How could he have been so stupid! He wanted a drink, but he knew he shouldn't have one. He should go home and lay low for the evening. Cleaves was gone from his grave, what did that mean?

# Chapter 17

Alderman James climbed with distaste down the slopes that had been dug into the site of the Dolocher's grave. The mud slushed about, and he used his cane to balance, quickly feeling the stump of it grow heavy and slippery with mulch. There were foot prints of many other people here as he went down, no doubt they were the people who dug this hole and perhaps the first couple of soldiers who had been on the scene. He looked at the dead woman's face, not someone he recognised but he hadn't expected her to be. Looking at the face first was a habit he'd formed years before, there was always a chance that you might fleetingly have seen the person dead in front of you somewhere; crossing the road and nearly getting hit by a carriage, dropping something as they walked in front of you, who knew. That one thing could be a clue that would otherwise go undiscovered from the evidence of a case.

She was in her twenties, maybe mid-twenties he supposed, probably pretty while she was alive. Her clothes were those of one of the prostitutes who worked exclusively in one of the houses, not a street walkers get up. There was a massive hole in her abdomen, and he could see the jagged edges of the rim of it and the ripped and torn dress that clung thickly with blood to the skin. It was dark, and the lights of the lanterns were not enough for him to see inside the wound too well. He knew that the soldiers above would be watching, so he didn't want to put his hand inside the wound, who knew what rumours could come from something like that. He knew that this was another killing by the same person who had sent him the letter- who else would have dug up the Dolocher's grave, taken his body and replaced him with this fresh victim other than the new killer.

"Where is the cart to transport this woman to the mortuary?" he snapped looking up at the men. They looked around to see if it was in sight.

"It was called for about ten minutes ago sir," the officer said nervously. That meant it should be here in the next ten minutes, James thought. He stood up and began to trudge up the side of the embankment, there was no point in staying in the grave while he waited if he couldn't see anything properly. As he clambered out over the mound, he saw Edwards at the fringe of the graveyard, beyond the metal railing that ran around it. He was talking to some youths over at a street corner who looked like they had gathered to gawk at the military presence. He watched until Edwards looked over and he nodded in greeting. Edwards finished talking to the boys and made his way over to him.

"Did they see anything?" James asked, assuming that this was what Edwards had been talking to them about.

"They did. They said they saw a big man here earlier and they gave me a description."

"Did you recognise it?"

"Big, muscled, scar on his face," Edwards said looking at him in a knowing way.

"Lord Muc?"

"Try again," Edwards smiled.

"Mullins?"

"That's how it sounded to me."

"Definitely not Muc?"

"I asked a few more specific questions, and I ruled Muc out based on their answers." James nodded to this. The same names again, over and over. "Anything on the body?" Edwards said nodding at the girl and looking down at her.

"It's too dark to see, but I'm going to go to the mortuary when the cart comes."

"Do you want me to come with you?"

"If you can, yes." Another pair of eyes couldn't hurt, and Edwards had the kind of eyes that could see things both he and the doctor might miss.

"Do you think the blacksmith being here means anything?" Edwards asked him after a pause. James shrugged.

"I'm not sure."

"He could have been simply visiting his friend's grave."

"Possibly," James agreed, but even that was suspicious. He couldn't imagine visiting the grave of anyone he knew who turned out to be a lunatic murderer.

The cart came, and the body was lifted up carefully by the soldiers and loaded on to it. James was climbing up too when Edwards took him by the arm.

"It's getting a little cold Alderman, why don't you ride with me in my carriage, we can follow behind the cart and keep an eye on it that way." James hadn't felt the cold before but now that he had heard it said he could feel it inside him like he had been standing on damp ground for too long.

"Yes, thank you," he said, and they climbed on into Edwards plush carriage and followed the slow progress of the cart through the streets towards the mortuary.

"We have to hope that this body yields some clues," Edwards said.

"I have a feeling it will."

"Because of where it was found?"

"Yes, there will be something to this one. She is a girl from one of the brothels too, so the identity will be easy to establish."

"Perhaps I might know her then," Edwards said in a happy tone. He was doing this to rile James puritanical side, and the Alderman knew this.

"Most likely," he answered dryly.

"Was she killed in the same way?"

"I think so, but I'll have to wait to see properly. There was a huge section of her middle missing that was made to look like a bite."

"But you don't believe it?"

"You know I don't believe it, I was duped into thinking an animal might be responsible the last time against my better judgement, and I won't be drawn into that again."

They arrived at the mortuary to be greeted by Doctor Adams.

"I'm seeing too much of you Alderman James," the doctor said, there was some jest in the tone, but mostly it was serious.

"Far too much," James agreed. "Doctor Adams, this is Mr. Edwards."

"We've met, I believe," Edwards said with a smile, and the Doctor blushed and went inside after the body. James assumed that Edwards knew Adams from one of the brothels by this reaction and he thought no more of it.

In the same well lit room that James had been in with the last body, Doctor Adams ran over the woman with his hands, checking different parts as he went.

"This woman was killed by multiple stab wounds to the abdomen and the rest was cut away after or during death the same as the others," he announced standing back up to face the men.

"Do you know her?" Edwards asked, and Adams looked at him with shock.

"What?"

"She's one of the girls from Melanie's isn't she?"

"I don't know." James hid his smile at the awkwardness of the doctor.

"I don't know her name, but I think I recognise her face," Edwards said to James.

"We can call there later and find out," James said, "Is there anything else on the body?" he asked turning back to Adams.

"Not on the front. I'll turn her over." He did this in a careful and efficient way. The back of the dress was closed with strong lace ties, but straight away they could all see that there was something underneath the dress, something dark and coarse. Adams cut open the ties, and they saw that it was a cloth sack that was in there.

"Take it out," James said when Adams looked at him. The doctor did so carefully and placed it on a side table gently.

"It's very light," he said, and he stepped back to let James get to it. The Alderman took it by the sides and slowly opened the bag and looked inside.

"It's paper," he said, and he put his hand in and gently gripped the sheet and took it out. He held it out at arm's length so that they could all see it. It was a picture of a boy sitting down whittling at a stick.

"What's this?" Adam's asked, clearly confused at the idyllic nature of the scene.

"Is there something on the back?" Edwards asked.

James turned it, the only thing on this other side was the picture of a crude knife and a horizontal line drawn with a vertical one joining it at the edge.

"What do you make of that?" he asked, but Edwards just shook his head.

## Chapter 18

A man lay in an alley off Cutpurse, dead and white skinned as the June sun slowly rose. He was on his back, and his face was severely beaten, his left thigh was missing a large chunk, looking like a bite from some huge animal. He was found by a young boy who was running away from home, leaving by first light. The boy changed his mind when he saw the man and feared that whatever had done it was still close by. He ran home and told his father who alerted the guards at Newgate, who in turn sent a message to the barracks.

It was fully bright by the time James arrived, and Edwards was there ahead of him. The body was covered in a thick sheet and soldiers were not letting anyone hover in the area, moving people along as soon as they arrived in the vicinity of the body. Edwards was leaning against the wall of a tea room that had been forced to remain closed this morning, he smoked a pipe and looked about disinterestedly. James saw him from the carriage, and he sighed. Edwards was definitely involved now if he was showing up at the murder sites. James got out and went over to him.

"Alderman," Edwards nodded.

"Mr. Edwards," James replied.

"Another one made to look like a bite," Edwards said as James looked over at the sheet. "On the leg this time." They walked over to the sheet and James lifted it.

"He doesn't look so bad compared to the others," James noted. He leaned in and looked at the leg seeing the same marks and scratches the doctor at the barracks had shown him on the previous victim. There didn't seem to be anything inside the wound.  James stood up and looked about the ground.

"There's no sign that it was done here," Edwards said pre-empting him.

"That fits with our man," James looked back at the body.  "I wonder what this one died from?"

"The face looks pretty beat up.  That might have done it?" Edwards suggested.

"Maybe.  The doctor will look him over and let me know anyway," Edwards nodded and puffed on his pipe again.

"This wasn't one of the Dolocher sites was it?" he asked.

"It was.  The gaoler Brick was found here."

"Oh, yes.  That was the last murder," Edwards laughed.  "I think everyone forgets that one." James looked at him disapprovingly.

"So far they've all been Dolocher sites then, is that right?" Edwards asked.  James nodded.  "Are you going to put men on the other sites?"

"These killings are so far apart time wise compared to the others.  I've told the men and the parish watch to keep an eye out on the old sites, but the bodies are just dumped there, so it's been hard to spot them.  Any coach going by in the night could drop something, and no one would bat an eyelid in this place."

"Any suspects?"  James looked around to see that no one could be listening to them.

"None. Have you heard anything?"

"Afraid not."

James dropped the sheet back to cover the body and stood back up.

"You never did show me that letter and sketch that you

got," Edwards said.

"Can you come to the house now?" James asked.

"I'm at your disposal."

James left a note for the soldiers to take to the doctor when they brought the body to the mortuary that said he would drop by in the late afternoon.

Edwards joined James in his carriage so that they could talk on the way. James would have preferred to be on his own and Edwards in his own carriage, but he said nothing when Edwards climbed into his after him.

"Has anyone been questioned under suspicion yet?" Edwards asked.

"No. We've just been looking for witnesses so far, but that has turned up nothing."

"I think it might be time that you started getting at some of the old names."

"How do you mean?"

"Get the soldiers out and question people who were questioned last time."

"To what end?"

"Ruffle some feathers, who knows what you might turn up?" James mused on this for a moment and nodded slowly.

"Anyone in mind?"

"Well Lord Muc is always up to something and maybe that blacksmith, what was his name again?"

"Mullins?"

"Yes, that's the one."

"Why those two?" James asked with cocked eyebrows.

"Well, Muc for his violent tendencies. Don't forget that the gang fights have almost dried up completely now and he'll need to get rid of the violent energy somewhere."

"He's been brawling in bars on numerous occasions."

"That might not be enough for him. He always knew when he was going to be fighting. He almost made a religion of it from what I've heard. Then, of course, there were the tusks from that boar he uses; a paean to the Dolocher if ever there was one."

"And why Mullins?"

"He was a close friend to the killer. I don't think it is too much of a stretch to think he might be trying to emulate him."

"Maybe it's something worth looking into." James agreed. He didn't like the idea of questioning people randomly, but he supposed Edwards made some salient points about the two men and there were bound to be more people in similar circumstances that might be considered for questioning. Who knew what it might throw some light on?

When they arrived at James' house on Henrietta Street, they went straight to the study where James had the letter and envelope locked away in his desk.

"Sit by the window there, and I'll bring it over so you can see it better," James said. Edwards walked and leaned against the wall and looked out into the window at the street below. James looked to see that Edwards was not watching him and then took a small key on a chain from his waistcoat and bent to the drawer and opened it. He took the paper to Edwards and handed him the letter side up first. He watched Edwards face as he read the letter to see if he showed any kind of recognition of the handwriting or paper, but he didn't seem to. His eyes roved over the paper, and then he turned it to see the sketch on the back. At this, his eyes did light up.

"What is it?" James asked.

"Here is your clue Alderman," Edwards laughed. James looked at the sketch again, but he didn't see what Edwards was talking about.

"Where?"

"The sketch itself," Edwards was smiling at him as though the answer were completely obvious, but James had no clue what he meant. "This was done by a skilled and talented artist. This is as good as a signature!"

"How so?"

"This man will have worked for hire or commission before. No hobbyist is this talented."

"You think he is a professional?"

"I do, and there are not a million people in Dublin with this level of talent." Edwards sounded triumphant as though the case were solved.

"I think it's safe to say that Mullins and Lord Muc are in the clear on this one so," James laughed. Edwards stiffened.

"Not necessarily," he said, and James looked at him wondering what he could mean. "They may be working for this man, carrying out his dirty work." This didn't sound very convincing to James, and he wondered if Edwards had some kind of history with the two men he wanted to be harassed by the army. "Anyway, you need to be seen to be doing something in the Liberties," Edwards went on. With this James did agree, and he decided to go along for now and see what materialised.

"I'll send someone to question them both later today. How will we go about finding this artist then?"

"Ask your friends if they have had any artwork done recently and I'll do the same. We can then draw up a list and go and see what has been done and compare it to your sketch here."

"There are always many painters in the streets too, I will have them checked out as well."

"Good idea. Shall we meet tomorrow afternoon and compare lists?"

"OK, where do you want to meet?"

"Somewhere in the Liberties?"

"To be seen?"

"Exactly. How about that whiskey cabin we met in once. Do you remember the one?"

"On Cook Street, yes I remember it. Shall we say three o'clock?"

"Can we make it a little later, five maybe?"

"Of course."

"In case we need a little more time to get out information together," Edwards explained, but James felt it was so Edwards could sleep late after whatever he had planned for this evening.

"Five O' clock it is," James agreed with a knowing smile.

# Chapter 19

Kate stood to the side of the vegetable stall as Sarah dealt with a customer.

"Did you hear about Mary's fancy man?" Sarah asked looking sideways at her as she handed the customer their change and nodded goodbye.

"No, it's not the painter fella is it?" Kate said.

"No, no, he's a tavern boy, well man I suppose, around her age."

"Is he nice?"

"Nice on the eye anyway!" Sarah giggled, and Kate joined her.

"What's his name?"

"John something."

"And where does he work."

"In the same place she used to."

"Up on Wards Hill?"

"Yeah, he's not from Dublin, he's come up from Galway last year."

"What does she say about him?"

"She seems happy, she says he's nice, and he's picked her flowers a few times, I've seen them in glasses in the house."

"Young love," Kate smiled.

"Here she is now," Sarah said, "You can ask her yourself."

They looked and saw Mary coming across from the river side of the market. Her empty potato basket flopping at one side as she walked.

"I've heard all about you," Kate said mockingly.

"What?" Mary said coming up to the stall, her face

flushing in embarrassment.

"You know well what, men falling all over you," Sarah said taking up Mary's basket and starting to fill it again.

"John?" Mary asked innocently.

"Is he nice Mary?" Kate asked.

"He is, he's really lovely," Mary said, unable to contain her excitement. The other two laughed.

"It's great news, Mary," Kate said.

"Things have certainly looked up this year," Sarah said.

"How long do you think you will be going to the painter's house?"

"Hard to say, I don't get to see the painting, so he could be still at the start, or he could be nearly finished for all I know."

"Did he not say?"

"No, and I'm afraid to ask."

They all fell silent here, and Sarah passed the newly filled basket back to Mary so that she could go back up to the busy streets and try to sell some more.

"How have things been for you?" Mary asked Kate, and she knew that she was referring to Edwards.

"Quiet for a few days, but that only make me more nervous," she looked around to see if he was nearby, she felt that he was always nearby somehow.

"And Tim still knows nothing?" Sarah asked with concern. Kate shook her head. "You make sure it stays that way," Sarah said in warning.

"So tell us all about this John fella then Mary," Kate said happily, changing the subject back to the original topic. Mary blushed again but smiled.

"Well, he's from Galway, he's here alone. His family are on a small holding, and he is sending money to them.

They hope to be able to come here soon too."

"Where is he living?"

"He's living in a room above the tavern."

"Is it nice?" Kate said with a wink.

"I haven't been it!" Mary said with genuine alarm and shock and then hitting Kate's arm with a nervous smile when she realised that she was only joking. Sarah was laughing at them. "I'm seeing him tonight," Mary said with a wide smile.

"Where are you going?"

"Just for a walk along the river."

"Sounds very nice."

"Make sure he walks you home to your door," Kate said. There was no need to remind her that there was a killer about. As a group, they had not spoken of the fact that the killings were associated with the Dolocher and that two of them had been victims, albeit surviving victims, of those attacks. Kate had thought about the new murders a lot, and in a way that made her feel like a terrible person. She was happy when the identity of each person was revealed, and it was not someone who had been connected in any way with the previous murders two years ago. It made her feel less threatened, less like she was going to be targeted specifically as someone with a link to the Dolocher times.

"I will," Mary said quietly. Kate felt silly now for saying this, she knew that Mary would never walk the streets alone at night, had not done so since she was attacked near the very start of the Dolocher's run.

"I better get going," Kate said.

"Me too," Said Mary.

"Why don't you both pop over to the house tomorrow evening for a bit?" Kate suggested. The two women agreed, and Kate and Mary went differing ways, and Sarah was left behind attending the stall.

As Kate walked towards the blacksmith shop, she could feel that Edwards was about to appear and she was not surprised in the least when he did. He emerged from a coffee house just as she was passing and for all the world it looked like a complete coincidence, but she knew better.

"Hello Mrs. Mullins," he said politely.

"Hello," she replied sullenly.

"I never did hear back about that letter I gave you," he said, his voice false with mock hurt.

"That should be answer enough," she said, happy with this flippancy. He looked at her, but his face didn't betray any real emotion. He looked about the street and sighed.

"Is this place what you really want?" he asked. She didn't answer. "The streets here are not safe Kate. Especially for you."

"What do you mean for me?"

"Have you not heard that someone is copying the Dolocher's murders?"

"Of course I have!" she snapped.

"That would put you in danger."

"Why?"

"What do you mean why? I know you haven't forgotten that night when he attacked you." He was angry now.

"I haven't forgotten anything, but no one that has been killed so far has had anything to do with the Dolocher."

"And you think that will last?" he was looking at her intensely, and she thought she could see fear in his eyes at her recklessness and she felt foolish for thinking that she was safe.

"I have to go," she said.

"Kate, this killer is more dangerous than the Dolocher was," Edwards warned. She didn't want to ask why, to make this meeting last any longer than it already had. She looked up the road fearful that for some reason Tim might be coming down this way on some job or errand and would see her talking to Edwards. "This man is smart, and he won't be caught any time soon," he said, a note of finality in his voice that scared her, though she didn't know why.

"I have to go," she said again backing away. "I'm sorry, I have to go."

As she walked away, she was trembling, and she felt that if he was watching her he would be able to see it in her gait. She felt as though she had been threatened that the killer had sent Edwards as some warning to her.

"I can protect you, Kate." His voice carried the twenty feet that separated them now, but she didn't turn around but just kept on walking towards the shop where Tim would be.

# Chapter 20

Mullins sat outside the blacksmith in the afternoon sun. Scally was on his small stool beside him cleaning some dried flaking off an old halberd that looked like it must have been in a fire somewhere. Mullins didn't bother asking where he'd gotten it or what he intended to do with it. It had been a slow morning, and Mullins wasn't in the mood to work on one of his private projects.

"You heard about the murder down the road?" Scally said to him, not looking up but still flaking away.

"I did."

"They think it's some animal. There was a big bite mark out of the leg."

"A bite mark?"

"Yeah."

"Where did you hear that?" Mullins hadn't heard about this part.

"I heard the soldiers who took the body away talking about it. They said there was another woman who had a bite taken out of her stomach." Mullins saw for a moment the flash of the metal teeth Cleaves had fashioned and held fast to his forearms that everyone who saw him thought was the vicious mouth of the Dolocher. Was there someone else out there doing this same thing? Could it be someone he knew again? Faces of people he knew whisked by, and he shook his head to dispel them and these thoughts he was having.

"Is there talk of the Dolocher?" Mullins asked, people generally didn't mention this subject around him, but he knew it was mentioned from time to time.

"Yeah, the murders are in the same places."

"People believe Cleaves is back from the dead?"

"I don't know about that, but they talk about the Dolocher as some animal. I think some people think Cleaves wasn't it, that it was never caught." It was heartening to hear that others found it hard to believe that Cleaves was the killer too. He wanted to question Scally more on this, but he knew that the answers he'd get would dissolve this myth if he poked any further at it.

Then he had another flash; he saw the teeth shine in the moonlight and then he saw something else, something different but yet something he knew he had seen before. The colour of bone but what was it? He closed his eyes to try to see it better.

"Are you alright Tim?" he heard Scally ask.

"I'm fine," he replied, and then he saw clearly what it was. It was the tusks of the boar, the ones Muc had used in his fights. Now he was seeing them as the silver of metal, and he opened his eyes. Someone must have made those tusks in steel as he had wanted Mullins to do. That was what was causing this injury to people that everyone thought were bite marks.

It was Lord Muc, he was going around killing in the name of the Dolocher. Had he not basically told Mullins this very thing on the night in the cabin when they both went home bruised? It all made sense, Muc was nothing without his gang and his fights, and he couldn't take life like that. He had found a way to be more than that and still get rid of all that vicious energy that mashed around inside of him. It had to be him.

Mullins was suddenly aware that Scally had stood up hastily and he looked up to see the Alderman and two soldiers standing in front of him. Mullins stood up.

"Can I help you sir?" he said, taking his cap off and holding it down low in front of him.

"Can we speak inside?" the Alderman asked.

"Yes, come in." Mullins held open the sheet at the door, and Alderman James walked inside. The two soldiers stayed where they were, and Mullins went inside and let the drape fall shut behind him. Mullins wondered if he had been seen at Cleaves grave, he knew he shouldn't have gone there, it was a stupid thing to do.

"I'll be brief Mr. Mullins; I'm sure you have heard about the recent murders in the area?" Mullins nodded that he had. "I need you to tell me where you were on the night that each was committed."

"Where I was?" Mullins was instantly scared. "I was at home for the three of them."

"You have someone who could vouch for you on that?"

"My wife." James nodded.

"You're married now?"

"Yes, for about a year now."

"Congratulations."

"Thank you."

"Have you seen or heard anything about the murders that we might not know about?" James asked. Mullins shook his head, but he slowed as he did and he recalled what he had been thinking just now outside. "What is it?" James asked, and Mullins knew that his face had betrayed him. He wondered should he say something. He decided he would, he wouldn't be able to live with himself if he was right and more people had to die. If he was wrong, he might make a little trouble for Lord Muc, but he deserved it.

"There is something I have just thought of," he started.

"Yes?"

"A while back Lord Muc came to me and asked that I make steel replicas of the serrated tusks he used in the gang fights."

"Did you make them?"

"No, but I've just heard this minute from the boy out there that there are bite marks made in the dead people."

"From the boy out front?" James asked, and Mullins cursed himself, he had probably just got Scally in trouble somehow.

"Yes, but I was thinking that maybe someone did make these things for him, and that is what is used for faking the bites," he spoke fast to try to make the Alderman forget Scally.

"You think the bites are faked?" James said interestedly.

"Yes, I think some sick person is trying to pretend to be the Dolocher." James looked at him for a while without speaking. Mullins stood there not knowing if he should say something else or remain silent.

"Do you think Muc is capable of this? I know his reputation for fighting but doesn't he revel in the fight itself and not the slaying of people?" This was true, Mullins has to agree, and he nodded to this. "Still, he is very violent, and there has been less opportunity for him to fight since the rival gangs broke up."

"That's what I was thinking."

"You were in that gang too as well were you not?" Alderman said, his tone accusatory.

"No, I fought once in exchange for help in finding the Dolocher."

"What help did he give you?"

"He had some of his men search the streets on the same

nights that I was out."

"But not the night you caught him?"

"No, they only helped for a couple of nights."

James looked about the shop and fingered some of the tools.

"You can see why I came to talk to you?" he asked.

"No sir," Mullins answered.

"Cleaves was a good friend to you." Was he going to mention being at the grave now? Was this what he was leading up to all along?

"He was, but I had no idea what he was up to."

"I don't doubt that for a moment, but I also know that people have a tendency to make saints out of the dead."

"What he did was unforgivable, and it will be hell where he has gone for it," Mullins said. James nodded in agreement.

"I'll speak to Lord Muc too, your name will probably come up when I mention about those steel tusks he wanted."

"That's alright."

James made to leave, but he stopped and turned to Mullins one last time.

"You should probably try to be home at night until we catch this man." Mullins understood what he meant by this.

"I will," he said, and James left, taking his soldiers with him, seeming to have forgotten about Scally altogether.

# Chapter 21

After James had spoken to Mullins, he went in search of Lord Muc. He'd not said anything to the blacksmith of the artist slant that had been put on the investigation as for now he was simply following Edwards' idea of rustling a few feathers. He had no intention of mentioning it to Muc either. He went to Muc's home on the outskirts of the city, but he was nowhere to be found. None of his neighbours that James had spoken to had seen him so far today. They suggested that he might still be in bed, as some days he up with the lark and others it could be anytime when he surfaced. This added to James' suspicions; did he sleep late after killing someone and transporting their body in the night and dumping it? It was just as possible that he slept late the days after heavy drinking sessions which he was well known to engage in. Could he have the patience to kill and then carry a body to a specific site and dump it? James hadn't spoken to Muc in over two years, but he knew he would get that same vibe from him as before when they met; the violence inside waiting to get out, looking for an excuse or an opportunity.

While he was at the old farmhouse where Muc lived, he looked about the yard and sheds. The sheds were locked up, but he could see inside and saw the old arsenal of weapons from the gang days. He looked at the cart under an awning, searching inside to see if there were any traces of blood or anything else that might look out of place. There was nothing he could see.

"Wait here," he said to the soldiers who were with him. "If he comes back leave a message for me in the whiskey cabin on Cook Street. I'll be there from five."

He left them there and walked towards the Cook Street area. As soon as he was out of sight of the farmhouse, a voice startled him from behind.

"You looking for me?" James turned as faced Lord Muc who stood at an alleyway entrance. He had marks on his face from a recent fight, bruising and a cut.

"I was," James said looking him over with disdain.

"Let me guess why."

"Go ahead."

"You want to ask me about the murders. You have no suspects, so you are going back over old ground?" Muc was sneering, but James didn't say anything. "Have you spoken to the blacksmith yet?" Now his smile was as broad as his face and James felt idiotic and caught off guard.

"I did," he said controlling his composure, "and he had something very interesting to say about you."

"Oh yes?" Muc seemed keenly interested in this.

"He told me about the tusks you wanted to be made of steel."

"Did he now, did he also tell you that he wouldn't make them?"

"Yes. What did you want then for?"

"To commemorate my many victories," Muc laughed.

"Did someone else make them for you?"

"No. He is the only one who would be able to do what I want. His work is good even if he is not."

"Why do you say that he is not good?"

"He's a violent man, but he hides it. He did this to me," Muc thrust his face forward to show the marks.

"Why did he do that?"

"I don't know. He was drinking and who knows what

goes through a man's mind when he has a drink in his belly?"

"About the murders," James changed the subject, he had no interest in Muc and Mullins drinking and bar fighting exploits. Both were well known to him.

"Go on."

"Where were you when they happened?"

"I have no idea when they happened."

"We'll one was only a few days ago, where were you last Thursday night?"

"I was either at home or in a tavern."

"Which was it last Thursday?"

"I don't know. Ask around Alderman, someone will tell you where I was on all the nights that anything happened. I'm hard to miss, people generally remember if I was in their company on a certain night." Muc was smiling again with a sardonic look on his face. James felt that he was trying to goad him into arresting him without the help of the soldiers.

"I will be asking around, and I hope for your sake you're right. Someone is going to hang for these crimes, and your neck is as good as any other to me," James said as roughly as he could. To his surprise, Lord Muc burst out laughing.

"Good man!" he said between fits, "Now we're talking!" James was at a loss as to what he was getting at. "That's the good old Level Low coming out in you!" Muc burst out laughing afresh. James saw red and smashed the handle of his cane up into the nose of Muc and sent him sprawling back against the wall. He regretted it instantly, and he turned his back and began to walk away from Muc, expecting to hear his rushed footsteps coming after him any second. But they didn't come. Instead, all he heard was his voice calling after him. "Level Low! Level Low!" and more laughter.

James stopped and turned and looked at him. Muc spat some blood out onto the ground and sneered at him. His face said he wanted to fight and James clenched his fists and was tempted to oblige him. He would lose, there was no doubt about that, but if the soldiers heard the commotion and came to his aid they would kill Muc and, though the savage was disliked in all quarters, if James was the cause of his death Lord Muc would quickly become a hero and James would never get these people back on his side.

"Keep your nose clean pig!" James said, and he walked away.

As he walked, he couldn't stop images of the weaver's riots coming into his head. This was where he had received the moniker 'Level Low' when his soldiers had fired above the heads of the weavers who refused to desist. James had used his cane to lower the barrels of the guns of the men closest to him and when they fired the next time men piled up dead. The riot ended, but that was not the end of it for James. One of the men he'd made kill those civilians tried in turn to kill him and failed. James had him court martialled, and he was put to death. This was the shame that James carried around with him every day. It was something that he couldn't get rid of, and he remembered it at the oddest moments sometimes. No matter what he was engaged in it was never far from his thoughts. So many nights he'd woken to either the bodies falling down or the soldier trying to kill him.

This was the first time in years he'd heard it said out loud, had heard someone call him it to his face. He felt weak now for not arresting Muc despite his knowing what would have happened. He rounded the corner and came onto Cook Street. He decided he would go for a drink before he was due to meet Edwards, something to calm him so Edwards couldn't jeer at him and make a laugh of this whole thing.

# Chapter 22

When James came into the whiskey cabin on Cook Street he was surprised to see Edwards was there ahead of him sitting at the very table they'd sat the only other time they had been in this establishment. Edwards raised a jug to him and beamed a broad smile at him as he entered the stuffy and hot room. He saw Edwards motion to the barman for another for James as he made his way through the crowd. It never ceased to amaze James how busy these types of places always were. No matter how little money people might have, they would always have money for taverns and cabins and the like.

"Good afternoon Alderman," Edwards said standing to shake his hand when he was close enough. "You probably don't remember too much about the last time you were in here," he continued with a laugh. James could feel himself blush, but he affected that he had not heard this remark. The last time he was here he was in the depths of depression about the elusiveness of the Dolocher, and he'd had too much to drink. It was a hazy memory to him, but he knew that he had gone on something about the inherent goodness in man. He sat down, and a jug and cup were placed in front of him.

"Have you any news?" James asked, getting down to business straight away.

"I've been to few people who have new art either in progress or recently finished but none match what we have in that sketch."

"I'm the same, and so far there has been nothing from street artists either."

"So we are back to where we started."

"Seems so."

James poured and took a sip of the whiskey and recoiled from it. Edwards laughed.

"I'm surprised that you were able to forget that part of being here!" The rancid taste of what passed for whiskey here filled his nostrils, and he coughed.

"Terrible stuff eh!" he said laughing himself now.

"What's this?" Edwards said suddenly grabbing at the cane James had leaned against the table. The Alderman could see straight away that there was a smeared sheen of blood on it and some had run a little towards the wood.

"I don't know," he said looking at it with screwed up eyes.

"I think I know what it is," Edwards said looking at him. "Someone close by, I'd guess." James decided that there was no point in lying, but also that he was not going to say anything more about it. He shrugged disinterestedly. Edwards grinned and put the cane down, looking at it once more before going back to James.

"Where do we go from here with the artist thing?" James asked.

"I suppose we just keep on looking there. The word will get out among them, and hopefully, that will cause him to do something rash, and we'll have him."

"It could always be someone who is just a very talented artist but has kept it to themselves for whatever reason."

"If there is one thing you will learn about about people with talent, it is that they can't keep it to themselves," Edwards said, his tone and manner sagacious. James didn't have anything to say to this.

"Did you find out anything about the amulet?" he asked, casually wiping the blood from his cane with a handkerchief.

"No, I'm going to need to show it to someone." James didn't really want to give him the amulet, to have it out of his own safe possession.

"Who?"

"I can't tell you that."

"I take it then that you wouldn't allow me to accompany you to see him?"

"That's correct."

"Can I have your assurance that I'll get it back as I give it to you?"

"You can have my assurance that you will get it back as I get it back from him" This wordplay of his, his way of going around in circles and making light of everything that was serious to James rankled him deeply. He was still flushed from his encounter with Lord Muc; that was why he had come her early and wanted a drink alone before Edwards came.

"Where will you be later? I'll send a messenger with it to you." Edwards looked as though he were thinking seriously about what he should do later.

"I suppose I can be in the house on Francis Street, you're welcome to drop by if you want instead of sending a boy."

"No, I'm in court tomorrow, and there are papers I need to go over tonight to be prepared properly for that."

They were silent again for a time, both forcing the terrible concoction into their bodies.

"What did the two suspects have to say?"

"What suspects?" James asked. He knew full well who Edwards was talking about but didn't like this choice of word.

"You know who," Edwards smiled, "the blacksmith and

the brawler."

"They both pointed to the other."

"Really?" There was a look on Edwards' face that James thought was mild scepticism.

"Does that surprise you?"

"My first thought is that they might be cleverer that we gave them credit for."

"How do you mean?"

"What if they were working together?"

"Why would they?" This thought hadn't occurred to James, and in the split second he had to think about it he still couldn't see it as a possibility.

"The blacksmith could be avenging his friend and Muc will get the thrill of violence out of it." This seemed very fanciful to James.

"Then why would they point to the other?" he asked.

"To hide that fact. They must know that there is no evidence against them."

"They know they are under suspicion."

"If they are that clever they would have expected that," Edwards said. James recalled that Muc knew exactly what he wanted to speak to him about. The blacksmith, though... "This may be getting more interesting," Edwards said with glee rubbing his hands together.

"No this wouldn't explain the letter or the drawing. I don't know if either of them can even write, but I'm sure neither of them can draw."

"I don't know," Edwards said looking as though something had just struck him, "I suppose the blacksmith might consider his work something of an art form, perhaps he has some other artistic talents that he keeps at home."

"That's true, I have seen tradespeople draw things in the

past to ensure they are going to do what the customer asks. He probably does this too," James said, a spark of excitement welling in him.

"There could be drawings in his shop or at his home," Edwards suggested.

"Maybe," James said. "There are some soldiers meeting me here soon, I'll get them to go look when they get here."

"That might be too late."

"Why?"

"If you saw him today he might panic. He could be burning everything in the fire in the shop right now," Edwards said.

"We better go look," James said getting up, this possibility raging through him all of a sudden.

"Right behind you," Edwards said, finishing his glass as he stood and throwing a cloak over his shoulders.

They marched with intent along Cook Street to the blacksmith. They came into the shop to find Mullins bent over some white hot piece that he was trying to straighten with metal tongs. He looked up as they came in and seemed confused at their appearance. James was slightly out of breath. Mullins stood up and regarded them with a questioning gaze.

"Is there something else you want to ask me Alderman?" he said, looking at Edwards as though trying to figure out who he was. "I know you from somewhere," Mullins said.

"You know me from prowling the streets late at night a few years ago," Edwards smiled at him. Mullins nodded as the recollection must have come to him. "You told the Alderman here that I was the Dolocher," Edwards laughed.

"I'm sorry about that. It was a very confusing time, especially that night."

"I should say so, you witness a murder, and then you are the one arrested for it."

"I didn't witness it."

"What's that?"

"I came on the scene just after it happened. I heard the girl scream, but I was too late getting there."

"Oh, I see," Edwards said with what James knew was insincere understanding.

"I wanted to ask you do you do any artwork for your customers?" James said, getting to the point as to why they were there.

"I can make some fancy things, but I don't know if you would call it arty."

"No, I mean do you sketch things out for people, to give them an idea of what a piece will look like?"

"I normally just fix everyday things."

"So you never have to draw something?"

"I get the boy to draw something sometimes, he's very good at it actually."

"Do you have any of those here now?"

"No we don't keep them, I know what I'm doing. It's only for the customer, I don't need it."

"So what do you do with them?" Edwards asked.

"Just dump them in the fire, unless the customer wants to keep them."

"Is the boy here now?" James asked.

"I think he's out the back," Mullins said, and then he called out, "Scally?"

"Yeah?" a voice came from out there.

"Can you come in here a minute?"

A few seconds later Scally came in and looked at the assembled group in front of him. James noticed a shift in Edwards, and he looked at him from the side. Edwards looked like he'd seen a ghost, but he hid it almost instantly.

"I want you to draw something for these men," Mullins said to the boy. They watched as he went to a desk and took up a loose sheet of paper and then some charcoal that was beside it.

"What do you want me to draw?" Scally said looking up at Mullins who in turn looked at the Alderman.

"Can you draw people?" James asked. Scally looked at him confused.

"Like a statue?"

"Well, I suppose yes."

"Is it for a gate or something?" Scally asked.

"Yes why not," James said. Scally looked again at Mullins who nodded that he should go on. The boy shrugged and went to the desk and began to draw. When he was finished, he came over and handed it to James. He held it out so that Edwards could see at the same time.

"This is very good," James said, genuinely impressed with the drawing.

"But not what we are looking for," Edwards said dolefully. James handed the picture back to Scally.

"You can keep it if you want, it'll only go in the fire otherwise," Scally said to him, his smiling face showing pride that these two men had liked it.

"Thank you, I think I will," James said, rolling it up and putting it inside his coat. We won't take any more of your time, goodbye," he said, and they left.

When they were a distance from the shop, James looked over at Edwards.

"You looked quite aghast when you saw that boy?" he said, thankful for having something over him for once.

"I thought he looked like the son of someone I used to know."

"Who?"

"Not someone I'd like to see turn up in Dublin."

"Why is that?"

"Don't worry Alderman, he's not someone who would be going around killing, and besides I had a closer look and that boy isn't his son," Edwards was laughing now, and he walked off ahead of the Alderman. The alcohol and then the heat of the blacksmith had made James feel tired, and he stood there for a moment before he followed.

# Chapter 23

Mary arrived at Spencer's house on Sunday a little after three as planned. Once more she was shown into the same room as before by Hetty. Mary was much more comfortable here now, and she was even able to sit down on the chair before being asked, as she waited for Spencer to come. The painting was on the easel in front of her, and she so often wanted to take a peek to see how it was coming. She was too terrified, however, that she would get caught and Spencer would be angry and cancel the whole arrangement. She couldn't afford that, the money for this sitting had been a godsend; it enabled Sarah and her to keep their heads above water financially.

Spencer came in after much less of a wait than usual, and she was glad that she hadn't tried to look at the painting today.

"Miss Sommers, how are you?" he said with a smile.

"I'm very well thank you," she said standing up. He strode across the room and pulled the sheet from the canvas and looked at it. He glanced at Mary and then back at the painting.

"Have you been offered anything to eat and drink?" he asked.

"Yes, but I said I was fine." Spencer was making a face at the painting, and she was not sure he'd heard her.

"I think I have all I need on this one," he said after a long pause. "Would you be interested in sitting for another, in another room of the house?" Mary hadn't realised he was close to finishing and she was glad that he offered another.

"Yes, I'm happy to do whatever you want," she said.

"Come with me," he said.

Spencer led her out of the room and towards the front door and then up the stairs. Mary looked at the paintings on the wall on the way up and wondered if the Colonel had painted any of them. They got to a long landing and then went up a smaller wooden stairs into the attic. It was dark up there, lighted by candles and a single skylight. Many of the corners were in complete darkness, and she was sure there would be spiders crawling everywhere that she could not see. The temperature was much cooler than the rest of the house but not uncomfortably so.

"Is this setting too grim for you?" Spencer asked holding a candle toward her.

"Not at all," she said, though she much preferred the room downstairs. "Where do you want me to be?" Spencer looked around and pulled a chair to the centre of the room, a little to the left of the slant of light let in by the skylight.

"Can you sit there for a moment?" he asked, and she did. He stepped back a few paces and looked at her. He nodded in satisfaction and then adjusted some candles to the place he was standing before setting up his easel. Lastly, he took a blank canvas from a pile of them on the floor near the door. Spencer then took his notebook from his jacket pocket and began to make furious sketches as he had on that first day, once more he letting the sheets fall about him as he finished with each one. The light outside was waning, and the candles grew warmer.

"That's the sketches done!" he said with a smile after about half an hour. "Do you want to stretch your legs and back a little before I start on the paining?"

"I can go on sitting like this if you like?" she answered.

"No, get up and take a rest from it. I have something to do, but I will be back in about fifteen minutes. Do you want anything sent up?" Mary shook her head, and he left the room.

Once alone in that attic, it took on a whole new persona, and Mary began to feel apprehensive after only a minute on her own. The lights flickered from various breezes that smuggled their way in from different apertures, and the shadows danced and took on forms that scared her, like something living just beyond the light, something that could pounce on her and kill her. Something like the Dolocher. She'd heard all about the new murders and the rumours, and she hadn't slept well at all since. She tried to calm herself, telling herself that it was all in her imagination, that Spencer would be back any minute and all would be well again.

She stood up and looked out through the skylight, it was dull now, but she could make out the roofs of some of the buildings nearby, and it was a beautiful sight that she hadn't expected or seen before. She moved around the room carrying the candle he'd given her, and she lit up old objects and trunks filled with clothes and silver and some children's toys. She came to the pile of canvasses, and she lifted one to see that they were all blank. Dust rose as she did this and she stepped away from them. She went to a corner of the room that was in complete darkness and suddenly saw that the room was much larger that she had imagined, only about a third of it had been lit up by the candles.

Down this end, she saw military things, muskets and sabres, and uniforms, but there were also other things that she didn't recognise, things that were sharp and metal and looked dangerous and large enough that they might be some sort of torture devices. There were sharp metal teeth on some that reminded her once more of her attack. Mary recoiled at the cold touch she gave these things to convince herself she was safe from them.

She looked away and towards the back wall, and she saw that there was a large drop sheet on the wall and what looked like the shape of a picture frame underneath it. She crept closer and looked back towards the door and listened to see if anyone was coming. There was no sound. She lifter the corner of the sheet but she could make out nothing decipherable, just fire coal red and dark patches. Lifting the sheet higher, she could see more colours but still not what was depicted. Finally, she lifted the sheet above her head, and the candlelight fell on a vicious and terrifying face of some crazed and wild creature. Teeth flashed at her, and wild red eyes showed rage and menace, and she fell backwards, pulling the sheet of completely and dropping the candle causing it snuff out on the floor. In this new dark, all she could see were those eyes and those teeth, and she knew that it was coming for her, that she had unleashed something terrible. She cowered and tried to defend herself, and she screamed as she heard shuffling and felt things move around her.

And then there was light again, and she heard someone calling to her. She looked up and saw Spence standing there, a look of terrified concern on his face, he was saying something but she couldn't make it out.

"Miss Sommers!" she heard finally before the dark took hold of her once more.

## Chapter 24

When Mary came to the room was cold and wind whipped through it. There were more candles lit, and Hetty was there now as well as Colonel Spencer. Mary didn't know for a few moments where she was even though she knew who the people were around her straight away.

"What happened?" she asked, wearily as she tried to sit up.

"You fainted," Spencer said helping her. As she sat up, Mary saw the wall, and she remembered the face she'd seen, was something coming after her? What was it?

"Do you know what happened dear?" Hetty asked. Mary shook her head. She remembered finding the larger part of the room and seeing those machines, she looked about and saw that they were still there. She'd been afraid, she could feel the ghost of that fear still inside her. She'd been thinking about her attack, and she could feel that nausea too. She was suddenly aware that she was in a part of the room that she shouldn't have been and she looked up at Spencer in apology but didn't know what to say.

"Are you feeling alright now?" he asked.

"Yes, thank you. I'm very sorry about this," she said.

"Nothing to be sorry about," Spencer said with a smile.

They helped her up and back across the room to the seat she'd been in before.

"She's fine now Hetty, but I think we'll call a halt to our sitting for this week. Can you see Mary out to the coach, please? There is a purse in the dining room on the table that Mary should take with her," Spencer said.

"I can still sit if you want to go on?" Mary said feebly.

"Not at all, you've had a little turn, best that you go home and rest and we will continue on next week."

"I'm very sorry, Sir," Mary said again, but Spencer waved her away with an affable smile as Hetty took her by the arm to indicate that it was time to go. As she was leaving the room, Mary had one last glance, and she remembered the painting on the wall, an evil presence there, a depiction of something so terrible it could have been nothing but the Devil himself. Spencer was facing away from her, and she wondered what had become of the painting while she was unconscious. Why would it have been moved? She felt a chill run down her spine as she saw those fiendish eyes in her mind.

## Chapter 25

Edwards passed the sentries at the entrance to the hunting lodge at Montpelier Hill. He could hear from there that the revelry inside was already in full swing and he was glad he'd been drinking on the way. The carriage let him out at the door, and his coachman saw to the animals and parked the carriage out of sight at the rear. Edwards took a final slug from his brandy bottle before dashing it against the wall across from the doorway to mark his entrance.

Edward's swaggered inside to cheers and whistles and men came to greet him as he made his way to the table. The whole contingent of the club was here tonight, all twenty of them. The table was covered in platters of food, bowls of scalteen and jugs of various liquors. Some of the chairs were occupied or showed signs of having been, all except the one reserved for the special guest should he ever deign to come to one of these gatherings. Edwards always smiled at this, it was one of the few rumours that went around about the club that was true, but people didn't understand it at all, didn't understand the Hellfire Club at all. They all thought it was about Devil worship but it was nothing of the sort, none of the men here held any more belief in the Devil than they did in God. That was the part that Edwards never understood of the public perception of them; if it was clear that they did not believe in God why did they think they would believe in the Devil?

"There's the man of the hour!" he called out on seeing Spencer. The Colonel looked up and saw him and got up to shake his hand.

"Good to see you!" Spencer said.

"Are you happy with it?" Edwards asked nodding to the covered painting hung on the wall.

"More than happy. It had its first viewing a few days ago by accident, and it caused the viewer to faint!" Spencer's smile of pride at this was impossible to hide.

"I better be sitting down when it is unveiled then!" Edwards laughed as he took up a tumbler and scooped some scalteen in and drank from it. It was a powerful and not altogether tasty beverage that Edwards mostly drank early so as it didn't get shoved at him later if by some accident they ran out of everything else.

"I think everyone here will be alright," Spencer laughed, "We've all seen worse things than a painting."

"What do you think the God fearing of Dublin will think when they hear about this?"

"They probably expect that there is something like it here already." They drank, and both were looking at the dust cover.

"Did you draw on yourself for inspiration?" Edwards asked, and he felt Spencer sour a little and look at him.

"No, I used you," he said. Edwards smiled.

"The Alderman has a few leads on these murders in the city," he said casually.

"Oh yes? About time."

"Yes, but his leads are all wrong."

"Same as ever then."

"I feel sorry for him really. He cares so much about those people."

"He'll never be happy if that's true," Spencer opined.

"He'll be happy when he catches the killer."

"If."

"No, he will catch him." Again he could feel the eyes of

the Colonel on him and could feel the charged atmosphere.

"Why do you think that?" Spencer asked.

"Just a feeling. It may not be the Alderman himself who catches the killer, it could be someone else, like when the blacksmith caught the Dolocher." Edwards still didn't look at Spencer. "Little clues go a long way, but pure luck also plays its part in these things. Who did you say saw this painting?"

"No one important."

"What's going on here ladies!" Buck Whaley said dropping in on them from behind. "Something serious?" he was laughing, and Edwards looked at Spencer,

"Not at all, just sorting out a little mess," Edwards said. Spencer looked at him curiously.

"Time to unveil the painting," Whaley said aloud, and a cheer went up, and everyone began to gather around the table. Edwards stepped forward and took the rope and hushed the assembled crowd.

"Gentlemen, our esteemed artist has given us something to be truly thankful for. Something beyond what we could have expected. I'm not going to make any speeches here, but I know that the subject of this picture will be as happy with it as we are!" and with that Edwards pulled at the rope harshly and let the droop sheet fall to the floor to unveil the painting that had until recently sat in Colonel Spencer's attic.

There was a general gasp at the sight, and Edwards stepped away from it so that he could see it better. It was a large sized painting of the face of the Devil up close as though he were coming out through the canvas, his eyes were fiery red and seemed almost to have the quality of liquid in them. His teeth white and sharp and framed by a crooked mouth and inside that mouth the outline, if you looked closely, of spectral bodies, souls being devoured Edwards supposed. Dark red skin covered the face and scars ran deep with more limbs trying of escape from the crevasses, the horns were dark and short but pointed and held the threat of stabbing. Behind the Devil was the coal fires of hell and his body, what there was of it and neck were also made of coals burning so hot. They looked almost too hot to touch even for a painting. It really was a masterful work, and Edwards looked at Spencer who was receiving slaps on the back and having drinks thrust into his hands. Spencer looked at him, and in his eyes, there was something of not only fear but hatred for Edwards. Edwards smiled and raised his glass to the artist who nodded and then went about taking the compliments of the men around him.

Later when the people thinned out, some having left and others passed out on various chairs and couches, Edwards sat alone at the table looking at the painting in the weak light of the fading candles. Spencer arrived in front of him, also looking at the painting. Everyone had spent some part of their night contemplating the painting like this, and no one has been able to look away from it for too long.

"It's truly great work," Edwards said to him. He could feel the weight of the alcohol on him, and he was tired. Spencer looked worse for wear too, and he sat down without answering the compliment.

"What do you think I've done?" Spencer asked after a long pause.

"I don't suspect you of anything," Edwards said. He could tell that Spencer was badly rattled.

"What was all that about, then, earlier on?"

"Spencer," Edwards started in a fatherly tone, "If you've done something to be ashamed of you don't have to confess to it. That's one of the great things about being a non-believer."

"I haven't done anything," Spencer protested.

They were silent for a time. "Normal people believe in this," Spencer said nodding towards the painting.

"I know, that's why they are so afraid all the time."

"That must be an awful life."

"All lives are awful." Edwards looked at Spencer, and he could see that the Colonel was badly in need of sleep.

"Not all," Spencer said, and there was a hint of defensiveness in his voice, as though he alone were the only happy man on earth. Edwards wished that he was looking at him now eye to eye so that he might see something of what the Colonel might be thinking, but instead, he could only look up at the painting. It really was terrifying, the most nerve racking thing he'd even seen, so life-like and angry and portentous. It gave off the feeling of something of the future somehow, even to his disbelieving mind.

# Chapter 26

That night, Kate lay in bed and listened to the light breaths Tim took in the cold dark as he slept. She could see the embers of the fire, and they looked inviting, but she knew if she got out of the bed she would feel chilly all over. It was odd that it was so cold on this night so early in the year, this type of night was more like what Dublin would expect in early November. She looked at Tim and smiled; he was never too bothered about the cold.

She'd been happy to get to his shop that afternoon after seeing Edwards. She had to hide how she was feeling, but he hugged her as she knew he would, and she felt safe and concealed in his huge arms. He was always so happy to see her when she dropped in and surprised him. Today she didn't stay long, not wanting to hold him up in his work and she wanted to get home to prepare their dinner. The short walk home was a nervous one, and she was glad when she was finally inside the door to this little home.

Kate's fear, unfortunately, did not end there, and every noise that she heard in the neighbours on either side or from above, jolted her. Once, the children's football crashed against the front door, and she shrieked, dropping the bowl she was carrying, and it shattered on the floor. She went to the door and set the boys who were running away a tongue lashing to chase them. Her hands were trembling as she picked up the broken crockery pieces of the bowl. She looked at her hands, and she couldn't fully understand why she was like this. She went to the fire to warm them, trying to convince herself that she was just cold. The heat was pleasant, but it didn't stop her hands shaking.

Kate recalled all this vividly as she lay there. She rolled on to her back and looked up at the ceiling. Fear was still gnawing at her, and she knew it, too afraid to close her eyes. Earlier when she had tried, she saw the vision of the Dolocher rising up from Mary's body as she had imagined it during her Absinthe hallucination a few years ago. This image hadn't come to her for so long, and the image was as clear in her mind as when she had first thought she'd seen it. Her heart was racing. Tim shifted his weight and let out a contented sigh.

Kate looked at him for a while until she knew he was asleep properly again, his breathing regular. She was afraid that he might somehow figure out what she was thinking if he was even somewhat awake and she didn't want to burden him with this. She ran a hand over his leg and felt the scars he'd gotten when he fought for Lord Muc's gang. He'd done that so he could get their help in tracking the Dolocher at night, something Kate herself had asked him to do. They hadn't even been together at the time, hardly knew one another but still, he had done it for her. Not just for her, though, he did it for Mary Sommers too and also at the time he thought his best friend had been murdered by the Dolocher. Who knew that this best friend was who the Dolocher would have turned out to be?

What had set her like this today? Edwards; it was when he was talking to her that she started to feel this way, it was something he said that unnerved her but what? He had gone on in a normal way, hadn't he? Not as abrasive as usual but still normal. Kate tried to remember his words and she found that she could and quite easily, but it wasn't those that did this to her. Was it the way he said them? Again she didn't think so. His facial expressions as he spoke?  She pictured his face and even as she poured into them and exaggerated in her mind each twitch and fold of skin or movement of muscle she couldn't make it a sinister or threatening face.

And then she realised what it was! It was her, a feeling that she had gotten as he spoke, nothing in what he said, how he said it or how his face reacted to it. It a feeling of fear that she got from him, she thought at that moment that he was the killer, even if she had not realised this at the time she knew now for sure that this was what it was. Edwards was the one going around killing these people in the name of the Dolocher!  She sat up trying not to wake Tim.  Could this be all part of his plan to get to her?  She shook her head, no, this couldn't be right.  Edwards was many things, but he was not a killer.  She thought back to her days in the brothel, and she could remember no times when he had ever resorted to violence with any of the other customers, which was something that happened a lot. It couldn't be the case, could it?

By the time she'd fallen asleep that night she was no clearer in her head as to what she really thought.

# Chapter 27

Mr. Edwards stepped over the threshold and into the almost dilapidated building. The place was so run down that the walls seemed to slant in the corridors like the building might collapse on one side at any moment. There was creaking everywhere as people moved about, making it seem as though the whole structure was breathing wheezily, taking its last breaths. He found the door he was looking for and knocked lightly on it.

A woman answered, and she peered out at him through a distrustful thin opening of the door, her weight behind it in case the caller might try to force his way in. She didn't say anything but just looked at him, with crooked eyes waiting for him to explain himself.

"Mrs. Scanlon, I'd like to help you," Edwards said in his most charming voice.

"I don't need any help!" she snapped back, still wary and ready to close the door on him at the slightest movement. He took his hand from beneath his cloak and held up a large purse, and he let the coins jingle and rub off one another to let her guess how much might be in it. Her eyes betrayed her amazement at the sight. "What do you want?" she asked.

"I want to talk to you for a few minutes, that's all."

"What about?"

"Your son."

"Is he in trouble?"

"No, and I am to insure he doesn't get into any." Edwards flashed her a smile, and she seemed to warm a little. She edged back from the door and let it fall open and motioned for him to come in. When he was in the room, she looked up and down the hall to see if any of the neighbours were watching and then closed the door hurriedly and came about to face Edwards.

"Sit down," she said, "I'll make some tea." He threw the coins on the wooden table, and they made a ringing noise that was pleasant to the ears.

"I don't need tea, thank you," he said sitting down. She looked at the coins and then looked at him.

"Do you want something stronger?" she asked conspiratorially. The idea of what she might have that she considered alcohol made him shudder.

"No thank you, I'll not take but a minute of your time, please sit down," he said jovially. She sat across from him. "What is your son's name by the way? I've only ever heard of him being referred to as 'Scally."

"His name is Stephen."

"Stephen Scanlon," he said out loud, "Nice strong name."

"Thank you."

"Where is his father?"

"Passed away."

"I'm sorry to hear that. Is he long deceased?"

"A few years now, but Stephen never had anything to do with him. He left before the boy was even born."

"Did they ever even meet?"

"No."

"And what does Stephen know about his father?"

"Nothing."

"Does he know how his father died?" She looked at him now with a scowl as though he were being disrespectful.

"I told you, he knows nothing about his father." Edwards could see that she was starting to regret letting him in.

"Why is that?" he asked with a smile.

"I thought you said you wanted to help my son." She was nervous now and getting agitated.

"I do, I do," he assured in a reassuring tone. "I'm just trying to figure out the best way to do that." She was silent, and she looked at him. He wondered how best to go on. "Did you go to the trial?" he asked, and her face went white, and her hands began to tremble on the table top.

"What?" she said, denial in her voice but the futility of doing so in her tone.

"Thomas Olocher's trial, did you go to it?"

"No..." she muttered.

"Does anyone else know that he is the father of your child?"

"He's not!" she said weeping, the lie ridiculous. She had obviously thought that name would never come up again in her life and she was devastated and in shock that it had.

"Don't worry, this information will not go beyond this room," Edwards said soothingly.

"How did you know?" she asked, staring at the table, her mind distant.

"I've met Olocher many times, I can see it clearly in the boy."

"He's nothing like him!" she said crying more.

"I've no doubt he's a fine lad," Edwards said. "He works with the blacksmith?"

"Yes, Mr. Mullins."

"Did you know that Mullins was good friends with the Dolocher?"

"I'd heard that he knew him."

"Did you hear that some people suspect him of these

new murders?"

"No," she looked at him in shock.

"It's true I'm afraid," he nodded. "Perhaps this is not the best environment for young Stephen to work?"

"Mr. Mullins has been very good to us."

"He may be going to the gallows soon if the rumours are true; he won't be any good to you then will he?" She shook her head, conceding this point. "I would be able to find something more suitable for him," Edwards went on.

"That would be fantastic," she said, she had aged ten years since he came in and she looked like she could fall asleep right there at the table.

"Let him work at the blacksmith's until I get him something better. I'll see that he is paid well enough for both of you."

"Thank you, sir," she said. He wondered, as he looked at her and saw the effect the mere mention of Olocher's name had on her, whether she had been a victim of his wild and bestial ways, or if it was possible that at one time they could have been lovers. She was not an unattractive woman, and he could see many men with lower standards than his own falling for her in the past. The boy was about thirteen now, maybe younger. He tried to picture her in her twenties, and he could see that she would have been something to look at. Still, he couldn't picture Olocher in a relationship, he was too wild, too restless for something as day to day and trivial as that. It stood to reason that this woman was lucky to be alive.

"Think nothing of it. There's no need to treat the son in the same way as the father," he said smiling at her.

"Please don't ever tell him," she pleaded in a weak, pathetic voice. He saw that she was about to reach out and touch his hand but thought better of it.

"Stephen?"

"Yes, it's not something a boy should have to deal with."

"Someday he'll want to know who his father was and he will know if you lie to him."

"That's for me to deal with if it comes up."

"Something like that will always come up."

"Maybe."

"He'll be fine," Edwards said.

# Chapter 28

It was growing dark as Mullins walked up on Ash Street and looked for Croslick Lane. Scally had come in earlier with a note from a gentleman who needed some work done up in his yard there. The customer said he was busy during the day and asked that the blacksmith come in the evening when he would be home. There was an address and some money up front, so Mullins had felt obliged to do it. Now as he looked for the place he felt put out and annoyed that he was here. Though it was not far from where he lived, it had been a long time since he was on any of the streets here. His bag was heavy, and he grew tired after a full day working, and now this walking around lugging it with him. Finally, he found the address and knocked on the gate at the rear of the house.

There was no noise from within, and Mullins could see no light from there. He waited for a moment and then knocked again heavier this time. Still, there was nothing. He looked at the address once more and assured himself that he was in the right place. He called out,

"Hello, it's the blacksmith." But still there was no noise and no sign of any light coming. He wondered should he go around to the front of the house and enquire, but he knew that people could be prickly about that and could get upset and cause problems for him. He looked up and down the lane; it was very quiet with no other soul around. Mullins walked to the end of the lane the way he had come in and looked up and down the street in the hope that he would see someone coming.

He hated the way he was sometimes treated. Men with trades were always treated like this, and tonight was not the first time that Mullins was left waiting for a customer, especially a well off customer. Mullins imagined the man was probably having a brandy in his club somewhere, or dinner at some fancy place. He wouldn't give a damn about any inconvenience that he might be causing for Mullins. It was such an unequal society, and those who were deemed to be at the top were the least polite or considerate. It made no sense to Mullins.

The blacksmith walked back down to the gate. There was still no sign of light, but he knocked again anyway. Nothing. He waited for over half an hour, walking the lane to both ends and looking around. He checked back at the gate a few times and finally decided that he was going to have one walk around the block, by the font of the house and then he was going home. As he passed the front of the house, there was no sign of life inside. It was dark and foreboding looking, and for all he knew no one had lived or worked there for many years. He came back around by the lane and knocked once more, knowing that no one was going to answer. He thought about putting the enveloped with the money through the fence or else back around through the letter box but he decided against this, thinking it better to send it with Scally the next day and have it delivered by hand; it would be just like these rich folk to pretend that they never got the money back and come looking for it. It was a miserable walk through the lonely streets home.

The aroma of vegetable stew and the sound of Kate humming as he stirred it, greeted Mullins when he got home.

"Done already?" she asked in surprise when she heard him come in.

"Customer wasn't there. I waited and checked around, but he didn't show."

"What a waste of an evening," Kate said with a sympathetic look on her face as she put a hand on his arm.

"I know, and it's cold out there now too."

"Well, this will warm you up. It's ready now, I was just keeping it warm."

"Great." Mullins dropped his bag by the door where he would see it on his way out in the morning and not forget about it and sat down at the table. Kate poured a large bowl and brought it over to him.

"There's a little bread," she said nodding to it. He took it up, and it felt as hard as stone, he broke strips from it and dropped it into his bowl where the liquid would be absorbed and make it more palatable. He tore more strips and put them down where he knew Kate was going to sit. She came over with her own food and put a hand on his shoulder in thanks when she saw the bread.

"Do you think he'll come back to you again?" she asked when they had both eaten a little.

"I still have his money. I'm going to send Scally back with it tomorrow. He might still want something done."

"Try to tie him down to work during the day if he does. I don't like the idea of you walking the streets at night with these murders going on again."

"I don't get to decide love, you know that. I have to take the jobs as they come."

"I know, it's just that I worry."

"I know love, I don't like it myself." He knew she was very much afraid of the fact of these murders, afraid that he would be killed. He didn't have this fear, his size had never let him fear violence really, but he did have a fear of being in the wrong place at the wrong time and ending up in 'The Black Dog' again. He hated the idea that this killer was in the same area as the last time. Why could he not kill over on the north side somewhere, it was a big city, and there were plenty of places outside the Liberties were he could go.

"The shop is doing fine isn't it?" Kate asked, "Can you not afford to turn down jobs in the evening?"

"I can at the moment Kate, but things can change very fast, and there could be times when there are no customers for days at a time. That's why I need to take anything that comes my way when it does, to have money saved for quieter times." He could see that she knew he was right but her worry wouldn't let go and she couldn't say so. "How are Mary and Sarah?" he asked, hoping to lighten her mood.

"They are good. Actually, a man, a Colonel in the army is paying Mary for her to sit while he paints her."

"Really?"

"Yes, over in his house somewhere across the Liffey."

"What does she have to do?"

"She just sits there, and he paints her."

"I've never seen a picture with a woman with scars in it."

"Neither have I, but apparently he says that she has a unique face."

"She does I suppose."

"He's paying well too."

"Odd." Mullins leaned back in his chair as he spooned up the last of his bread. "Is there water for tea?"

"I'll make you one," Kate said with a smile.

While she was at the pot, he looked out the window and

saw that it had started to rain. He was glad he was inside before that came down. Paying a woman with a scarred face to paint her, now he had heard it all. What could he be doing it for? He recalled feeling a little odd about being where he had been tonight, and now he knew why, now that Mary had been mentioned and more specifically her scars. He had been in the very spot this evening where she had been attacked by Cleaves, the place where she had almost lost her life. She had been one of the lucky ones, some local men had heard her screams and came to her aid. He had been there tonight, had probably stood in the very places that her blood had spilled. She had been so lucky to escape that night, and he was glad that she was finally getting some luck in relation to it come her way. She was a nice young girl, and she deserved it.

# Chapter 29

Kate stood at the corner of Henrietta Street and looked at all the houses. She had been in this area before, but she had no idea which house belonged to the Alderman. She had tried to ask a couple of passers-by, but they had just ignored her, assuming she was begging or something like that. Understandable considering her clothes were so tatty, and she looked so poor compared to everyone else in this part of the city. Finally, she caught an errand boy on a message, and he told her which one was the Alderman's house.

She climbed the steps of the imposing house and stood at the door. She looked around to see if anyone was watching her. Kate worried that she would just be sent away and that she would have made a wasted journey. She teetered between knocking and seeing what would happen and just turning around and leaving. Perhaps she could try to talk to the Alderman the next time she saw him in the Liberties. But she knew she couldn't do that. Edwards was always with him when she saw him. She knocked as hard as she could and stood back a step to wait.

A man answered, not elderly but getting there and he looked at her with disdain but answered politely.

"Yes Miss, can I help you?"

"I need to speak to the Alderman."

"Is he expecting you?"

"No," she thought better of lying, "But I have some information that he will find very interesting."

"The Alderman is very busy. If you would like to leave a message, I will ensure that he gets it?"

"No, I need to talk to him myself. Can you tell him it is

about the identity of the murderer he is looking for?" The man stiffened at this.

"Wait here," he said, and he closed the door.

About four minutes later, which felt a lot longer to Kate, the door opened, and the same man ushered her inside.

"The Alderman will see you in here," he said leading her into a room just off the hallway.

The Alderman came in with a flourish and greeted her a few minutes later.

"Hello, I am Alderman James," he said extending his hand for her.

"Mrs. Mullins," she introduced herself warily as he shook her hand.

"Is your husband the blacksmith?" James asked with a look of recognition in his eyes.

"Yes."

"And you have information about the killer?"

"I think so."

"You thinks so?" he suddenly seemed to have an air of irritability.

"Yes," she said meekly, she was worried now at what he might say to her and if she could get in trouble for what she planned to say. He was looked at her with questioning eyes, and she couldn't match his gaze.

"Well," he said gruffly, "Out with it."

"Sir?" she was flustered and didn't know quite what he meant.

"What did you come here to tell me?"

"I think I know who is going around doing all these murders."

"And who is that?" She hesitated now, afraid to say the name but knowing that she had come too far now not to.

"Mr. Edwards," she said after a pause in which he poured into her with his eyes, making her feel doubtful about everything she had to tell him. She saw his face change but not angrily and not quite in shock either she felt. He looked away from her and walked over and peered out the window.

"What makes you come to this conclusion?" he asked dryly. There was no sense of anger or bitterness in his voice, and it gave her the temerity she needed to go on talking.

"He's spoken to me a few times, and it's in the way he says things."

"Has he admitted to anything to you?"

"No, not exactly," she felt her voice tremble and her visit becoming useless.

"What does that mean?" he asked looking at her again. He looked tired.

"He wants me to leave my husband and go to him," James raised an eyebrow in surprise at this, but she ploughed on, "He speaks to me sometimes in allusions to the people who have been killed. He seems to know a lot about each one."

"He does know a lot about each one," James said in a matter of fact tone.

"I don't mean in the way you know a lot about them, but, as though he was the one doing the killing."

"I don't understand how you come to this answer."

"It's a feeling I have like he is threatening me with their fate." The Alderman sighed.

"This information is of no use to me Mrs. Mullins. If you have something else, please let me know, but I can't do anything with your 'feelings' about Mr. Edwards."

"Please!" she said grabbing his sleeve, she could sense that he was ending their conversation and that nothing was going to be done. She looked him in the eyes deeply.

"Mrs. Mullins, please!" he said taking his sleeve away from her grasp. She felt the tears come and his angry face softened at the sight of this. "Sit down," he said motioning to a seat by the window guiding her to it. "Don't cry," he added softly.

"I'm sorry Sir."

"Have you been having an affair with Mr. Edwards?" the Alderman asked when she had composed herself.

"No!" Kate cried, she wondered what he thought, should she tell him the truth? He probably already knew about her past. "I used to work in Madam Melanie's house, and Mr. Edwards was a customer there."

"I see," James said, his face unable to hide a little disdain for her former life.

"I don't work there since I was married, but Mr. Edwards has stated that he wants me to go back there."

"And you said no?"

"Right, and then he sent me a letter telling me he loved me!" Again the Alderman's eyebrow raised, "And that he wanted me to leave my husband and go live with him."

"Extraordinary," James said like a fish wife who'd just heard some shocking gossip. She waited for him to say something else or ask a question. "What does your husband say to all this?"

"He doesn't know anything about it," she said shamed, "and he can't find out about it."

"I know your husband," the Alderman admitted.

"He's a good man, but he can have a temper, and I'd be afraid what he'd do if he found out." She must have sounded scared because he then said,

"Well, he won't find out from me Mrs. Mullins."

"Mr. Edwards scares me," she said, feeling that they were getting off track.

"What is it he said that leads you to believe he is a killer?"

"I know you know him Sir, but there is a dark side to him that you may never have seen. Any of the women at Melanie's will tell you the same thing. He can get angry, or cold and bitter and there is no reasoning with him."

"I have to admit I've never seen anything like this in him."

"He stops me sometimes when I am coming home, or on my way somewhere, and he asks me to go with him. When I decline, he starts taking about how unsafe it is for me to walk the streets alone with all the killing going on. He always mentions the most recent killing and describes to me in horrible detail how they were killed."

"That does sound odd."

"I'm very frightened of him. I've known him for years, and even at his worst, I've never felt afraid of him. Not until very recently."

"And this feeling you have is why you think he is the killer?"

"I know it sounds pitiful," she knew it did, "But I'm almost sure of it." The Alderman looked out the window once more.

"Every piece of information is precious in some way or another," he said after a pause. "I'll keep an eye on Mr. Edwards, I'll find out what I can, but that's all I can do for now."

"I understand," Kate said nodding. "Thank you."

"For what?"

"For listening to me."

"I'm sorry I can't do anything about your other problem."

"That's my own concern, and I just have to hope he give up soon."

"I think you're right not to tell your husband. Most likely that is what Mr. Edwards wants you to do." She thought about this for a moment and understood what he meant by this.

"I see what you mean," she nodded. "I know it is him, Alderman. You have to stop him." She was more sure of this than of anything else in her life.

# Chapter 30

Edwards stood in the dark of the alcove at the square that led from Christchurch Cathedral to Hell. He looked in the dim light at the carved statue of the Devil that resided there. The torches in this alcove were always extinguished, nothing supernatural but people pranking the whole time, thinking it funny that others should be wary of entering by this way. It was long dark now as he waited. That afternoon Edwards had gone to the blacksmith's to Scally and asked him to bring a message to Lord Muc when the workday was over. It was Lord Muc he awaited now in this most auspicious place. Few people passed tonight, and those that did could probably see him the alcove and avoided it, not knowing who he was or what his designs were. There was a killer at large after all.

He saw Muc coming from a distance, his hulking aggressive frame unmistakable in the shadowy light. Muc looked directly ahead, not caring what was to either side of him until he got to the alcove. Edwards was about to speak when Muc grabbed him by the throat and shoved him up against the wall, directly under the statue. Edwards couldn't breathe for a moment, but he kept his cool, stopping his hand from clutching Muc's wrist.

"What do you mean by sending some boy to my house and summoning me here at this hour?" Muc said through bared teeth, his warm spittle and alcohol tinged breath flushing Edwards' face. Edwards didn't try to talk, knowing that he wouldn't be able to if he did. He looked passively at Muc as if trying to convey boredom at his antics. Muc pressed in harder on his windpipe and then eased up suddenly. When he was free Edwards fixed his collar and smiled at Muc.

"Thank you for coming," he said in a friendly tone as though nothing had just happened.

"What do you want?"

"I want to give you some money."

"In return for what?"

"Following a couple of people."

"A couple, how do you propose I do that?"

"Not at the same time of course."

"Who?"

"The blacksmith Mullins and a Colonel."

"I don't know any Colonel's."

"I'll point him out to you, he frequents the bars and coffeehouses in this area some of the time."

"Why?"

"To see what they are up to?"

"What do you think they are up to?"

"Best you don't know that."

"You think they're involved in these murders?"

"It's possible," Edwards answered. Muc looked around to see if anyone was watching them.

"Do you have someone following me?" he asked.

"No, this is not your style." Muc smiled at this.

"So you think I have style."

"I think you have 'a' style," Edwards clarified. Muc was silent for a bit as he seemed to be thinking about it. Edwards followed his distracted gaze to the statue of the Devil.

"Who made that?" Muc asked nodding to it.

"I have no idea," Edwards answered truthfully.

"Thought you might know seeing as the crowd you go around with," Muc said, and this surprised Edwards a little. This was an allusion to his Hellfire Club membership, not something he would have thought Muc knew anything about. They were silent again, and Edwards waited for him to say how much he would want for such a task as this.

"You know there's danger in this for me?" Muc said finally. "If I'm seen out on the streets on the night's murders happen I'll be suspected again. I've already had the Alderman breathing down my neck about this."

"You can leave the Alderman to me, you won't have to worry about being a suspect."

"Tell me first what you suspect of the blacksmith."

"He's been seen in places near where the bodies were found. We know he is strong and able and he was a good friend to the Dolocher."

"You think he's trying to avenge him?"

"Maybe."

"It has nothing to do with you wanting his wife for yourself?" Muc face wore a malicious sneer now, and Edwards was genuinely shocked that he knew anything at all about this. Muc's informants seemed to be every bit as good as his own. He didn't like being on this end of the information tree.

"There are plenty of other lowlife's I can get to do this if you are not interested!" Edwards snapped. He regretted this instantly when Muc laughed.

"Very touchy," Muc said. Edwards made a move to leave, and Muc grabbed his arm. "I'll do it," Muc said making his face serious again.

"You haven't asked about payment."

"That's because you don't know what it is." This confused Edwards, but he put his hand in his pocket all the same and coins jingled as he felt for the proper coin sack. Again Muc took his arm, "It won't be money." Edwards looked at him.

"What then?"

"I want you to take me to that house you have in the mountains, where you all meet up."

"I can't take you to a meeting..."

"I don't want to go to a meeting. I want you to take me up there one night when it is quiet. I want to see it and what is inside of it."

"It's not what you think."

"I still want to see it," Muc insisted. Edwards shrugged, this was a much lower price than he had set out to pay this evening.

"If that's what you want for payment then fine, but you will be very disappointed that you didn't take the money," he smirked.

"You let me worry about my disappointments," Muc said.

"I need you to start straight away. Come to the Eagle on Cork Hill tomorrow night about eight, and I'll show you the Colonel, his name is Spencer."

"What about the blacksmith?"

"You can follow him after a couple of nights of watching Spencer."

"Are you expecting me to witness a murder?" Muc asked with seeming glee at the idea.

"No, but you can keep tabs on the people they meet, the places they go, that sort of thing."

"If it's worth anything to you, I don't think the blacksmith has it in him to kill anyone, not on purpose anyway."

"Well, then you may help to take him off the suspect list then."

Someone coughed, and they both looked at the man shuffling past, wrapped up against the cold.

"Do you know who I think is behind all this?" Muc said with a sly grin.

"Who?" Edwards asked, thinking it as well to humour him.

"The Alderman."

"That would be a quite a scandal," Edwards said, not able to stop himself from laughing.

"It's not as funny as all that. He's often been prowling the streets alone at night. He has the opportunity to do what he wants and the kind of friends who would probably give him an alibi whenever he asked."

"Do a lot of people around here share your ideas?" Edwards asked; Muc seemed very confident in his assertion.

"I don't know, but I'm sure some have thought of it just as I have."

"There might be something to it," Edwards said not able to control his mischievous side. "It could be true I suppose."

"Maybe you should have someone follow him too?" Muc suggested.

"Maybe I should," Edwards said, his tone serious though inside he was still laughing. If only these people knew how much the Alderman wanted to protect them. It would kill the Alderman to know that he was a suspect in this case. Edwards knew that it was a fool's errand, on the Alderman's part, in the first place, to ever seek the forgiveness of the people of this area. They were incapable of it as far as he could see. The Alderman thought of them as if they were the same as himself, but these were different creatures entirely. He thought for a moment about letting the Alderman know this little nugget of information, but he decided against it. It was hard enough for the Alderman as it was without adding this to his worries.

# Chapter 31

Scally leaned into the shop with a look of concern on his face.

"What is it?" Mullins asked.

"That man who was here before is back, and he has some more soldiers with him." Mullins looked out through the small gap in the curtain that Scally made as he held it up. He walked to the door and Scally backed away to let him come out. Alderman James was coming across the road with five soldiers, and he had a resolute and angry face. His eyes bore into Mullins.

"What can I help you with, Sir," Mullins said when they were close enough.

"I have one question Mr. Mullins," the Alderman said sharply. "Were you on Ash Street two nights ago; in the vicinity of Croslick lane?" Mullins felt his stomach lurch, and he knew instinctively that there had been another murder. Could he lie? No, there was no point. It was a case of mistaken identity, it had happened before. He would spend a few hours in prison and then be sent on his way. If he lied, he would only draw suspicion on himself.

"I was."

"Then you must come with us." The soldiers came forward and took him by the arms. The Alderman had already turned and walked away heading for the front gate of Newgate gaol across the road. Mullins didn't give any resistance as he knew where that would get him.

"Lock up and go home Scally," he called out trying to look over his shoulder. Alderman James was at the gate of the 'Black Dog' now and knocking with his cane. The gates were opened just as Mullins and the soldiers got there and it didn't interrupt their step.

They came to a halt and stood in the courtyard for a little while, no one saying anything and none of his captors looking at him. Then a man Mullins recognised as the new gaoler, whose name escaped him just then, appeared from the back rooms and greeted them.

"Where do you want to put him?" the gaoler asked

"Any quiet room for a chat will do, Mr. Cabinteely," the Alderman said.

"This way so," the cheery gaoler said leading them back the way he had come. They passed along a corridor with heavy wooden doors locked on either side. Someone said something from within one as they passed but the gaoler barked at them to be quiet, and no more sound came forth. Mullins was finally led into a small room at the very end of the corridor. It held one small pile of hay and nothing more. There were no windows, and no candle, bar the one Cabinteely carried, lighted the room. "This do you?" he asked the Alderman who nodded that it would. Cabinteely lit a lantern by the door and one inside the room and left.

"Put him in and wait outside," the Alderman said to the soldiers. They did as commanded and the Alderman came in and closed the door so that he and Mullins were alone in the room.

"We've been here before," the Alderman said, Mullins was glad that he remembered.

"Yes, Sir."

"Why are we here again?" He seemed to be genuinely asking, and Mullins didn't know what to say in response. He stayed silent. "You've heard about the latest murder?"

"No," Mullins said, terrified now that he knew he was right about his feeling before.

"It was on Ash Street, the body found just off it, in the alleyway."

"The night I was there?" Mullins asked, already knowing the answer. Alderman James arched his eyebrows at this.

"Yes," he said.

"I'm sure you know that I'm no killer?" Mullins said hopefully, remembering the Alderman's faith him in two years ago when in the same situation.

"I don't know anyone anymore." The Alderman was cold in tone, and this certainly was not the answer Mullins had hoped to hear.

"I didn't do it," he said in a panic.

"What were you doing up there that night?"

"I was to do a job for someone."

"Who?"

"I don't know, they weren't at home?"

"You don't know?" the Alderman sounded incredulous.

"Someone gave my boy at the shop some money and the address, and asked me to come after hours for some work at the back of the house."

"And you don't know who this person was?"

"No, no one was there on the night, and I've sent the boy three times to the house to return the money, but he hasn't gotten an answer yet either."

"Do you often do jobs like that?"

"Not often but sometimes, I have to take the work as it comes."

"You were seen in the area on that night, by numerous people."

"Yes, I walked around as I waited for the person to show up."

"Did you see anyone else around?"

"No, it was very quiet, I don't think I saw a single person at all." He was trying to remember if he had or not but no one was coming to mind.

"A woman was killed." It sounded as though it were an accusation but the Alderman's face didn't betray anything.

"I didn't see any woman," Mullins reiterated. He could feel the sweat in his palms, and he rubbed at them to try to dry it off, shaking them lightly in the air by his sides now.

"If this was a once off thing I could think of forgetting about it, but this is a lot of times when you have been in the wrong place at the wrong time."

"I was only here once before, Sir," Mullins said in defence.

"You were at Cleaves grave a while back too, were you not?" This stunned Mullins into silence, and he looked at his inquisitor with pleading eyes.

"I heard people say they were going to dig it up to see if he was still in there. They were afraid of the Dolocher," he mumbled

"Why were you there?"

"I needed to see for myself that he was still in there."

"And was he?"

"No."

"But you already knew that didn't you?"

"No!" this time he raised his voice in passion.

"I have witnesses that say you were at that graveside a few nights before acting suspiciously when people passed by."

"No, I was only there the night they dug it up! Never any other time!"

"This does not look good for you Mr. Mullins."

"But I didn't do anything."

"It is not for me to decide."

"I swear to you that I'm innocent," Mullins pleaded. The Alderman was silent for few moments and looked to be in deep thought.

"You drank and conversed with Cleaves the whole time he was killing your neighbours, up to when he faked his own death and who knows maybe after that."

"No, I was the one who caught him?"

"Did you, though? Or was he a loyal friend to the end, one that was willing to lay down his life that you be spared yours?" Was he actually saying this? Did he really believe that Mullins had been the Dolocher all along and had let his friend go to the gallows in his stead?

"I've never hurt anyone in my life," he said plaintively.

"There is many a man in the local taverns who will say different."

"I've been in fights from time to time, I freely admit that, but I'm not capable of anything worse than that."

"Did you think Cleaves was capable of what he is accused of?" This silenced Mullins, and he thought about this. He hadn't thought Cleaves capable of anything like what he had done. Right now, however, admitting that made him even more suspect.

"No," he said, the lie not coming to him with enough force to go through with it.

"So you can see how things might look to me right now?" Mullins didn't want to answer this, but he nodded slowly.

"I swear to God I didn't do this, any of this," he said looking deeply into the Alderman's eyes.

"It doesn't look good for you," The Alderman said, and

he knocked at the door for the soldiers to let him out.

# Chapter 32

Kate stood dejected and in tears at the gates of 'The Black Dog.' She had come here as soon as Scally had come to the house to let her know that Tim had been arrested. She came straight to the gaol and banged at the gates. As she stood waiting for someone to answer her, she thought of how odd life was. She had been a prisoner here, in the 'Nunnery' when she worked the streets, and she had wanted so much to get out of its stinking wretchedness that she swore that she would never go back there. The guard came to the slot,

"What is it?" he barked.

"My husband is in there."

"No visitors for any prisoners."

"But he's innocent!"

"No visitors, don't knock on the gate again." And with that, the slot shut and she was left standing there. Kate didn't know what to do, and she felt so hopeless and alone. There was no one she could turn to; the only person she could think who might be able to help was the Alderman, but Scally had told her he was the one who had arrested her husband. Everything seemed so helpless, and there was a sick feeling that Tim would be locked up for good. She had no doubt that he was innocent but that meant nothing to the judges, all they wanted was someone they could blame, and they had that in Tim. He had been arrested before, at the very scene of one of the Dolocher's murders and he had been a good friend of the man who turned out to be that crazed killer, the man who had tried to kill her that night by the docks. They could hang this on Tim easily, and there was nothing she could say or do that would be of any use to him. These facts jumbled around in her head and images of Tim's temper came to mind. Before she knew what was happening, Kate realised she was entertaining thoughts that perhaps Tim could be the killer this time round. She shook her head, regaining her sense, she knew he couldn't be, she just knew it, didn't she? A harsh clacking of wooden carriage wheels and the creaking of the axles met her ears.

"Kate?" a voice that she knew too well said softly. She looked up to see Edwards peering out the opened door of his coach.

"What do you want?" she said sharply, her anger overriding her fear at that moment.

"I want to help you," he said and then after a brief pause "and your husband." She looked at him suspiciously but there was something in the way he spoke, and in her desperation and desire she answered,

"How?"

"Come with me, and we'll talk some," he offered his hand to help her into the coach.

"Why can't we talk here?" she asked.

"Because I don't want to," he said humourlessly. Kate didn't know what to do; she looked at the coachman and wondered would he say anything if he ever found out that his master was a killer "Do you want my help or not?" Edwards asked impatiently. Kate hesitated for a moment but looking around and seeing nothing that might in any way help her she took his hand and climbed up into the black box.

When she was inside, sitting across from him, he covered her lap with a thick, soft blanket, and she didn't try to stop him. The carriage moved off, and she looked out the window just for a general sense of the direction they were heading.

"You were not able to talk to your husband?" he asked after a time. She shook her head. "Have you been told even what he has been arrested for?"

"No."

"There was another murder a couple of nights ago, a woman up on Ash Street." She immediately knew that Tim had been arrested for this, she remembered that he was in that area the other night waiting for a man who never showed up.

"He didn't kill her."

"I know that, and you know that, but it does not look good for him."

"Why, just because he was out that night? He can't have been the only person in Dublin out."

"He was seen all around the area where she was killed, but that is not all."

"What else is there?"

"There are many witnesses that put him in the vicinity of the other murders as well and..." he stopped as if he were searching for the right way to express his next thought.

"What is it?"

"He has been seen around the Dolocher's grave."

"What?" this she did not expect to hear.

"The Dolocher is missing from there, did you know that?"

"Yes, I heard that; everyone has."

"Your husband is suspected of digging him up and moving him and replacing him with the dead woman who was found there."

"There's no way he would do any of this." She was crying now, and she looked out the window in an attempt to hide this fact. "What can you do to help then?" she said after a while remembering that this was why she had gotten into the coach with him in the first place.

"Well, one way really."

"Which is?"

"There are a lot of witnesses in this case, and all of them put your husband where he should not have been," he started, and she could see something wicked come over his face. "Witnesses are fickle beings, they can disappear as quickly as they crop up." She looked at him, and his smiling face sickened her as it dawned on her what he had done.

"You hired them all to say he did these things!" she spat at him.

"I don't know what you can be implying," he replied, but she knew by his almost mocking face that she was right. He had played a master stroke against her, and now the life of her very husband was hanging on whether she would leave him and go with this evil man.

"How can you do this?" she asked, her voice searching for something in him, some conscience.

"I'm offering to help you?" his tone affected injury.

"And what do you get from this?"

"Your gratitude I hope."

"And in what form should my gratitude come?"

"You know what I want. I want to make you happy."

"You want me to make you happy you mean."

"They are one and the same thing."

"Not to me."

"The choice is yours, Kate. I love you, I want you by

my side. If you agree to leave your husband and come to me, I will ensure his release." She cried again, this time it was in defeat. She knew that she couldn't let Tim stay in that place and then go to trial. She knew in her heart that she was going to have to leave him to save him. She searched for something else she could do, some other way that she could save him but there was nothing, nothing that Tim would ever go along with."

"What if I came to you a few times a week?" she offered, ashamed of her voice as she said it.

"That won't be enough."

"How can do this to me?"

"You don't see it now, but in time you will see that I am saving you." His look was almost convincing, and she had to wonder if he actually believed in what he was saying. She looked out the window again. There was no way out for her. She was going to have to do what he wanted.

"Why does Tim have to suffer for this?"

"No one has to suffer at all," he said. She looked at him coldly, his eyes darkly merry.

# Chapter 33

Kate stood on the doorstep of the house. She had been here once before, but she never thought she would be back. Kate knocked and waited for someone to let her in. Though the staff wouldn't know it, they were going to be showing in the new lady of the house. The idea of this title didn't even raise a smile in her, not for the fact of it or for its irony. The door opened, and a maid she vaguely recognised from her last visit here answered timidly.

"Can I help you?" she looked over Kate, clearly not expecting someone like her to be calling, or perhaps she remembered Kate too, knew what she had been in a previous life.

"I'm here to see Mr. Edwards, he's expecting me."

"He's not at home right now."

"Can I come in and wait?" Kate asked when a long enough silence passed that she knew that maid wasn't going to invite her in. The maid looked nervous at the thought of this, and she looked behind her, but there was no one there she could ask what to do. "He will be very displeased if he returns to find me standing on his doorstep," Kate added. The maid thought one moment more and then said,

"Go around to the back of the house, there is a small room by the servant's entrance, you can wait there."

"But..."

"That's the best you'll get," the maid said decisively. Kate nodded, it would have to do.

As she waited in small, warm room, Kate ran through her encounter with the Alderman that morning. She had gone to the prison once more to try to speak to her husband and once again she had failed. However, today as she was outside Alderman James came out. She approached him as he got into his carriage.

"Sir, can you please tell me something about my husband." He looked down at her and seeing who it was he stopped getting in and stood to face her.

"He maintains his innocence Mrs. Mullins, but the evidence is against him."

"All of the witnesses are in the employment of Mr. Edwards!" James looked piteously at her as she said this.

"This again?" he asked in a tired voice.

"He has told me plainly that if I leave my husband, he will see to it that all the witnesses disappear."

"He said this to you? Outright?"

"As clear as I say it now to you." Anger flashed on his face momentarily, and then he looked to her with almost apologetic eyes.

"If you believe he is telling the truth in this matter you would do well to do whatever he asks of you. It may be the only way to save your husband." Kate had been stunned by this, and she realised for the first time the actual power Mr. Edwards must wield. She knew that he was very rich and did pretty much as he pleased, but she never thought anyone could be beyond the reproach of the law.

"What will happen to Tim if I don't?"

"Most likely he will be hanged."

It was those words that sent her straight on her way to this house now and had her sit here waiting for Edwards to come home. She cried now as she thought of Tim and how what she had to do would pain him. She knew that he had grown very accustomed to the life of a married man and he was unlikely to ever find another woman again; there was nothing wrong with him it was just his way. Had it not been for the awful events of two years before he and she would never have gotten together in the first place. It was as much as a surprise to her as anyone else that she fell in love with him.

A door rattled open, and the same maid as before popped her head around the corner.

"The master is home. He says that he will see you soon, that you are to wait here until he calls for you." Kate knew that Edwards was punishing her, this is what she got for not agreeing that afternoon in the carriage when he had proposed this arrangement. He would be aware she had tried to see how it would pan out without his help but that had been worth nothing

She was in that room an hour longer before the maid came in and led her to another. It was a small study and at the desk sat Edwards, a grin on his face.

"Can you bring Kate something to eat please May, anything at all will do," he said politely to the maid who nodded and left the room. When they were alone, he looked over her body in a greedy way. "I know this is hard for you," he said finally, the grin dropping for once.

"You'll never understand how hard this is for me," Kate said, barely managing to squeeze the words out before a lump came to her throat.

"It's not like you haven't done it before," Edwards said, not happy with her defiance it seemed. She wasn't quite sure what he meant by this, but she was sure it was some slur on her past.

"Why do you want me here?" she asked.

"It's simple, I love you, Kate."

"You don't love anyone."

"I found it hard to believe myself, it's true. I was fine when you worked in the brothel as I could visit you any time, I didn't know who else you were with, and I didn't care. But when you got married and I had no access to you anymore, and I knew exactly who was with you at night it started to eat away at me."

"Jealousy!" was that what this was about.

"Maybe a little, but I knew soon after it was more than that. There are any number of prostitutes with looks like yours or even superior, but there is something else about you that gets deep inside of me." She blushed. She didn't like this line of conversation.

"Call off your witnesses," she said, this was what she was doing this for after all.

"First things first," he said, and he stood up. She what was coming next and without a word, he took her by the hand and began to lead her out of the room. May, the maid was just about to come in with a tray of sandwiches and some tea. "Put them in the dining room please," Edwards said to her, and then he continued on with Kate. She felt the full weight of her betrayal and her predicament at the first footstep on the bottom thickly carpeted stair. Tears began to fall down her cheeks, and they were hot, and she felt sick. He walked ahead, looking on up the stairs and she followed with her hand outstretched in front of her in his grasp, being led like some reluctant animal on a farm. How had it come to this? She closed her eyes and thought of Tim in that rat infested gaol and then forced herself to think of the moment he would get out, the moment of freedom and happiness, and that moment alone. She couldn't go beyond that and see what would come for him soon after when he realised that he was alone in the world again. They reached the top of the stairs, and he led her into a room and shut the door behind them.

# Chapter 34

Alderman James looked out over the Liffey watching the water shift and muddle on its way out to sea. It was hard for him to feel anything other than revulsion and dread at the thoughts of another wave of murders here, by someone pretending to be something supernatural or animal. Tensions were rising in this city all the time, and it wouldn't take much to incite a riot. These new United Irishmen were going be a nuisance now; on top of everything else nationalist rhetoric was on the rise once more in the fair city.

He was thinking of Cleaves, the man this place still insisted on calling the Dolocher, giving him a spirit and reputation that was indefatigable and refused to dissipate. Cleaves was simply a man just like any other. He was a delivery man, and he unloaded boats at the docks. James recalled talking to him, seeing him sitting at a table. He was polite and cordial and answering James' questions as though he were talking about going for a walk on a nice sunny day.

Cleaves hadn't denied a single thing, he told James everything that he asked of him, he even jested with him about the night the Alderman chased him up onto the roof, the closest that James had come to catching him himself. He said that he was sorry that all those people had to die and he seemed sincere in this, his pale eyes glistening as he spoke of them collectively. When James asked him why he had done it, he said that James would not understand but that he would tell him anyway. He said that he saw that Dublin was dying, that soon it would lose its heart and become nothing more than a middling town in the British Empire. He said that the Dolocher was an attempt to hold on to the dazzling Dublin that existed now, well two years ago when he was active. He thought that the deeds of a man were not something that could carry the weight of the future, but that something truly terrifying, something that had grown men fear to tread the night streets alone would live on, no matter what might befall the city. He said that if something of the city could survive then the city itself would survive, would be passed on in the fears of men and women on dark nights when all they wanted was to be at home in bed, safe from this terrible world. They would fear the Dolocher, even those who lived well after its demise would fear meeting it in the alleys and quiet streets. That was all that could be saved from Dublin and all he wanted when he donned the razored arms and furry pelt that so scared the Liberties and Dublin beyond.

James remembered the eloquent way that Cleaves had said all this and he still heard those words at night sometimes as he tried to make sense of them. Some nights he thought he could see what the murderer had meant and what he wanted to achieve, but on others he would condemn them as the words of a madman bent on killing for its own end, using words and pleasant smiles to cover up the Devil that was at work within him.

The thought of the Devil had him look up the hill towards Hell and that alcove with the wooden statue. This, in turn, led his mind to wander to Mr. Edwards. He thought about what Kate Mullins had told him. He wished that he could have overheard any one of the conversations Edwards had with her, to hear the insinuations that she was talking about. So far James had not gotten a sense that

Edwards could be in any way involved in these new killings. During the Dolocher ones, Edwards had been a suspect, if only in James mind. This time he didn't seem as interested as he had, there was no passion at the discovery of a new body or new clue as there had been before. He was almost listless now and apathetic in the face of slaughter. Where James had seen a kind of childish glee in Edwards during the Dolocher investigation, something that led him to believe at one point that Edwards was the killer, this time he only saw boredom and scarce interest.

Could this be a way for him to cover up his crimes? Was Edwards clever enough to hide behind this ennui? It was a stark change in attitude from before, and he was innocent last time. This rubbish went back and forth in his head all the time now, the paranoia of the situation drilling deep inside. He knew that at one point in the Dolocher case, he found good reason for the very people he was trying to protect to see reason to believe that he himself was the Dolocher. This is what not knowing did to a person. Many times James had wished he was dead and none more forcefully than when killers ran free in his city, and there was nothing he could do about it.

He ran through his suspects in his head once more. There were only three, and he decided on the spot that he was going to follow all of them individually. He would start with the most likely of the three, and he was surprised to be able to say this, and follow Mr. Edwards for a few days. He was probably wrong, but he had to rule him out all the same. There was something beyond the reckless playing of his membership of the Hellfire Club, James could see something beyond compassion in Edwards, a lack of empathy that was far more than the general disdain most of the upper classes showed for the poor.

He looked back to that night on Montpelier Hill and felt that same inner fear and sickness he had felt that night when the horse looked in the door at him. He'd seen something more than a horse, something evil and residing in that place where these rich and powerful men went to while away their nights in debauchery and dedication to the supreme evil. He started to walk, the river was somehow making him feel ill, as though the bridge was swaying with the water instead of standing still over it.

He walked towards Hell. It was time to start walking the streets once more in the hope of coming across this killer in the act.

# Chapter 35

Colonel Spencer stepped out of the Chocolate House and took a deep breath of the air on Fownes Court. It had been his first time in the establishment, and he thought that it would be his last. It was not that he did not like the chocolate on offer, but more that the whole room being overpowered by the aroma made the taste seem less exquisite. He would leave his chocolate consumption for at home from now on where he knew he would enjoy it much more. He cast one more look back inside and thought what it a pity it was that it was not a coffee house; the decor was very elegant and the atmosphere lively.

As he looked inside Spencer caught sight of himself in the glass and saw his collar had become bent. Using the window as a mirror, he set about righting it. Out of the corner of his eye, he saw something that made him freeze. His eyes went to the place and showed only a reflection of the gathered people walking about in the street behind him. But he was sure he had seen it. In the crowd, there had been for one moment and bright smiling red face, one that he had intimate knowledge of from all those hours spent painting it. He blinked and turned to look at the people wondering if it were possible that his vision might be among them? Spencer could feel his hand trembling still at his collar, and he put it to his side in an effort to control it. Even in battle, he had ever been so uneasy and ready to be scared.

Then the real fear came; he was sure that someone was looking at him, someone unseen to him at that moment. H scanned the crowd again, searching out the faces of those whose heads were cast down but still he saw no one. Just then, his eye set on a hooded man who was about to pass out of sight around the side of a building. At the last second, the hood turned from profile and showed that grinning, malevolent face he thought he'd seen. Spencer gasped and unintentionally took a step backwards.

The man disappeared, and a rush of his military courage came to Spencer, and he set off through the crowd in measured pursuit. Anger was growing in Spencer now, surging over his fear. If this man or creature or whatever it was wanted to haunt him he could do it to his face!

Spencer reached the corner and looked into what turned out to a very narrow street with a few people buying from street traders. No one in sight was his quarry. The street was long, and Spencer had to assume the fact that he could not see the man meant that he had entered one of the buildings. He walked slowly along looking for some public house, whiskey cabin or coffee house but nothing like this seemed to be present on the street. Spencer stopped walking and looked about at the people he could see once more, this time scrutinising them. None was in a hooded garment, and more importantly, he could see all of their faces, and there was no sign of any redness in any one of them. Casting a long look in both directions along the street he was about to admit his defeat when he felt those eyes on him once more. Spencer cocked his head and looked all about at once, his whole body moving in a wild circle like something was on his back. Infuriatingly, there was still no source for his feeling, no one seemed to be paying him any attention at all.

"Where are you?" Spencer muttered under his breath. He felt the handle of his blade and tilted his sword a little, enjoying the weight of it. How dearly he would love to use it right now on this tormentor. For many weeks now he had seen signs of this red faced menace, and it was grating on his nerves now, affecting his sleep and making him second guess everything he was doing.

Movement at a window just above him caught his eye and Spence turned and looked to see a curtain flapping and a dark shape moving away.

"I've got you now!" Spencer shouted running to the door of the house in question. He banged on it but didn't give anyone the chance to answer. He barged in shoulder first and almost fell to the floor. A woman at the rear of the house screamed in fright, but Spencer ignored her and proceeded up the stairs. He drew his sword and heard the scrape of it against the wall as he reached the top stair. Rushing in a frenzy from room to room he pulled at beds and wardrobe doors until he came to a stop on the landing once more. He stood there out of breath, there was no sign of anyone at all. How could that be, he wondered.

The woman downstairs had been calling out for help since he came in and now a large group of people were gathered at the doorway looking up at him. Spencer looked at the windows of the house and saw that one was open. He walked to it and looked out. It was a short drop to the ground below, and if the man got out there, he was long gone. It was even less of a drop to the neighbour's chicken coop, and Spencer looked around idly for a possible escape route. To his horror, there many rooftops over was his man. Standing tall against the skyline and though Spencer could not see him properly, he got the very distinct impression that this Devil was laughing heartily at him. Spencer looked away, not knowing if it were possible for a man to get so far away in the time since he saw him at the window.

Spencer sheathed his sword and started to walk back down the stairs. The people went silent and made a path for him to leave the house. Spencer looked at nobody, and when he was outside, he started walking down the narrow street, not sure where it led but not caring either. He felt a heavy burden and a feeling that this was the last chance he would get to stop this evil presence.

# Chapter 36

It was very cold on November 7th, 1791, and single thin snowflakes fluttered from the grey above from time to time threatening to flurry at any moment. Alderman James stood outside the newly opened Custom House taking some air from the throng inside. It was a magnificent building, and he marvelled at the sight of it when he came to it. He could remember not long ago when this very land was nothing but swamp ground. He gazed upon the stonework and knew why it had been so hard to acquire a mason over the last year, truly great work. When he'd heard about this building being built, he didn't like the idea. He was amongst many who thought that it would move the axis of the city for the worse. Thousands had protested its construction, but he had not gone so far as to join them. Now that he saw the magnificent structure he couldn't imagine the city ever being without it. He wondered would it drag any of the problems that plagued Templebar down to this part of the city as the shipping moored first here now.

A carriage pulled up, and James recognised it immediately. Mr. Edwards climbed out, and he was followed by Colonel Spencer. They were laughing in a way that convinced James that they were drunk.

"Alderman!" Edwards called out when he saw him.

"Hello," Spencer said in more subdues tone, though there was a bright smile on his face.

"How are you, Gentlemen?" James replied.

"Very good," Edwards said.

"Fantastic building isn't it?" Spencer said to James.

"Astounding really," James agreed.

"What's the crowd like inside?" Edwards asked peering into the building.

"The same as ever for this sort of thing," James said with a jaded air.

"People have been asking you about the murders?" Edwards guessed and before James could answer he went on to Spencer, "The Alderman is cursed when it comes to murders. The locals blame him personally for each one and the rich plague him for gossip and salacious details whenever they meet him."

"It's not quite as bad as all that," James said to Spencer with a weak smile.

"Must be a very interesting work all the same?" Spencer asked politely

"It has its ups and downs."

"What are the paintings like inside?" Edwards asked.

"Some fine works," James said, "But I wasn't really looking at them."

"Spencer here is quite the artist himself," Edwards said slapping the Colonel on the back.

"Really?" James said, and he saw a worried look on Spencer's face if only for the briefest moment.

"You might have heard about his latest one?" Edwards suggested.

"I'm afraid not, but don't be offended, I'm not a follower of the art world," James addressed Spencer.

"Few are," Spencer chuckled, his composure back and flawless.

"What do you paint?"

"Oh, it could be anything."

"Tell him what you're working on at the moment," Edwards said in a goading tone. Again there was that brief moment of worry on Spencer's face, but once more he hid it as quickly.

"I'm painting the portrait of a woman who has a badly scarred face." James thought this quiet an odd thing to be painting but he didn't want to betray his artistic ignorance, and he nodded interestedly.

"Not just any woman," Edwards said in a sing song voice, and this time there was no hiding the annoyance in Spencer's face as he flushed red. James looked at him inquisitively, was it one of the victims? "Mary Sommers!" Edwards went on with a knowing look to James.

"Is this what you bought me here for?" Spencer said angrily to Edwards who looked back as though he were shocked at the thought.

"I didn't know the Alderman was going to be here," he said laughing. Spencer looked at James.

"He's been trying to insinuate that I've had something to do with the recent murders," Spencer explained.in a vexed tone.

"Have you anything to do with them?" James asked humourlessly; he wasn't in the mood for these two drunks right now.

"Of course not," Spencer said offended. He looked around as though impatient to get going.

"Do you draw as well as paint?" James asked, realising that he had been rude and hoping showing some interest would erase it all.

"I sketch before I paint."

"I think I'd like to see some of these sketches," James said.

"I was only joking Alderman," Edwards butted in again laughing, "I've seen his sketches, and they are not what we are looking for."

"All the same I'd like to see some for myself," James said, "Nothing to do with the case."

"You don't actually suspect me do you?" Spencer asked incredulously.

"No, but I like to rule people out instead of ruling them in. The killer is an artist, so are you. The killer is fixated with the Dolocher murders, you are painting one of the surviving Dolocher victims."

"This is all coincidence," Spencer said, "Come right now, this instance and see my sketches," he said earnestly, and he looked at Edwards again with a dark look to which Edwards just laughed. He was extremely drunk, James had not seen him in a state like this for a long time.

"He's also in the Hellfire Club," Edwards said in a loud whisper.

"Come now, I'll show you the sketches," Spencer repeated addressing James alone.

James wondered if he should go. If Spencer was the killer, he could be walking into a trap and Edwards would be of no use in this state. But then Edwards was always doing this sort of thing, embarrassing people and putting them on the spot. If he thought for a moment, Spencer was the killer he wouldn't be putting on this show. It would be a waste of time to go and look at these sketches, James decided.

"Don't worry," James said dropping his formal tone and adopting a large smile. "I know you didn't have anything to do with it. There has been a new development. I won't say more. Come on inside and have some drinks and mingle." Edwards looked at James though dimming eyes at the mention of a new development. James mouthed

'Later' to him, and they all went inside to see the grand opulence of this new building at the gateway to Dublin.

When they were inside, they were immediately flooded with greeting from all sides. Edwards ignored these and went straight to a waiter with a tray of drinks. Spencer was engaged with another officer who was there, and James stood back against the wall and looked at him, watched him interact and laugh with his colleague. Though he didn't think Spencer was guilty he was a sound suspect, more so perhaps than any other, who had come to the fore so far. He was part of that same club as Edwards, however, and this one had the resources of the army behind him as well. It could be quite difficult to stop a man from that type of background, with a myriad number of people who might give him an alibi for any given night. It was even worse than when he suspected Edwards might have been the killer. An artist, and painting a picture of one of the Dolocher's victims. These things added up to suspicion in his book.

# Chapter 37

The low scratchings of the mouse came through the cold stone walls of Newgate Prison. Mullins listened to this noise and his heart warmed by the slightest degree; this was, after all, the only visitor he received. Cabinteely would pop by and talk to him from time to time, but the joviality of the man was unnerving and irritating, especially give Mullins' own dire predicament. Where did the mouse go each day at this time, what food source led it by the nose, or female by the loins? What Mullins wouldn't give for that same freedom. He leaned his head against the damp wall and sighed.

Kate came to mind, as she did so frequently, and he ached in sorrow. Though he wanted nothing more than to see her, to feel the gentle touch of her small white hand on his own, it pained him deeply to feel the absence of her. Though he tried not to think it, the idea that he may have already seen her for the last time haunted his mind night and day. HE owed her so much, owed her indeed all the happiness that he'd had in his life. Before he met her Mullins had gone through his life without love, and though he'd been fine at that time with not knowing what he was missing, Kate had changed everything. To have her there when he came home in the evening, to feel her warmth against him at night as they slept. In his mind's eye he saw her smile and this, in turn, brought a smile to his own face. Images of her laughing at his gruff ways and simple outlook on life shored up in him;

"How beautiful she is," he whispered to the darkness. Of all the things of the earth, what he wanted most was one single moment of silence alone with his wife. With aqueous eyes he pounded the wall with his fist, feeling the moist mossiness come away with his skin.

Who had done this to him? Who had machinated to put him back in this dank hellhole, and more puzzling still, why had they done this to him? What could he have ever done in his life that he would deserve this? Mullins couldn't even imagine that someone he might have doled out a beating to in the past would be so vindictive that they would go to the trouble of having him hanged for murders he had no part in.

There was no power in Mullins to stop his mind from going now to the gallows, to imagining himself atop the frame like he was on a stage; all the people of the city out to shout curses on his soul and condemn him for the evil they believed him to have committed. Would anyone believe that he was innocent, even hear it in the sincerity of his voice as he decried all that had happened to him? 'You will be recalled in the same way that Cleaves is remembered now!' he thought. If only Mullins had seen through his friend, from the start, none of these things would ever have happened. But this thought displeased him too- if Cleaves had never donned the guise of the Dolocher, Mullins, and Kate would never have become man and wife. How odd an idea this was,; that it took murder and mayhem to bring the love of his life into being and this same murder and mayhem were the things that would take it all away.

A cheerful whistle down the corridor announced Cabinteely's presence. Mullins listened and hoped the gaoler would not come in his direction. Gentle footsteps on the smooth stones told Mullins his wish had not been granted. He sighed and stood off to the back of the cell where the lamplight would not hurt his eyes when the hatch in the door was opened.

Three loud raps came on the wood,

"Mr. Mullins, how are you today?" the happy voice called out and then his gormless face peered in through the flap.

"Same as before," Mullins sighed. Cabinteely made a face of understanding sympathy,

"I am afraid I have no news to tell you," he shrugged. Mullins nodded at this; he hadn't been expecting any good news so was not disappointed.

"Is there no way I can see my wife?" he asked the gaoler.

"Were it up to me Mr. Mullins, you would see her every day, but I am afraid that this decision has regrettably been taken out of my hands." To his credit, Cabinteely looked genuine, and Mullins believed him.

"Can I not be moved to a different cell hen, one that overlooks the outside?" Cabinteely shook his head slowly,

"That is also something I have been forbidden to do," he said.

"Please sir, I'm begging you. I feel that I shall die soon and the only regret I would die with was not seeing my wife for one last time," Mullins said in desperation. He really did feel the icy hand of the end approaching rapidly. Cabinteely squirmed uncomfortably, and Mullins knew that he was moved and wanted to acquiesce to his request.

"There is just no way," Cabinteely said finally in vexation, "There are men working here who report on everything, there is no way anything associated with you could go unnoticed, and then God only knows what the Alderman or the army would do with me!".

Mullins nodded in understanding, "I'm sorry' the gaoler whispered," and after a slight pause, "If there is some other way I can make things easier for you, please let me know." With that, the flap closed down and locked, and Mullins was let alone once more.

Though he knew in his heart and soul that it was no doing of the gaoler's if Mullins had been able to get his hands on him at that moment, he felt he would have killed him, dashed his head against the stones of the floor until he was no more than a ragdoll in his hands. Perhaps violence was the only way Mullins was ever going to get out of here. He thought on this a moment, and then the reality of it dawned too. If he were somehow able to battle his way through the guards and get out the gate, that would only be the beginning of it. He would then have to go on the run and live the rest of his life looking over his shoulder. That was no life for Kate to have to live, assuming he could get them both out of the city before he was caught. He leaned against the door and slumped down in sadness. Everything seemed more hopeless than ever at that moment, and nothing came to mind save the darkness that lay ahead.

# Chapter 38

Spencer came into his dining room, a smile beaming from his face until he saw it was Edwards who awaited him.

"Sorry to use a false name to get you down here Colonel," Edwards said cheerily.

"Had you said it was you I still would have come down," Spencer said taking Edwards' outstretched hand and shaking it.

"Oh, I don't know about that. I've had a distinct feeling that you've been avoiding me lately."

"Not at all, I've just been at home a lot finishing off some paintings." Edwards looked at him, saw his nervous face. Spencer's hands were shaking.

"I've seen one of your latest works," Edwards said, and he looked Spencer dead in the eye with a very serious look on his face.

"Which do you mean?"

"The one of the boy whittling at a stick." Spencer looked confused, but Edwards thought he was putting it on. "Don't touch that boy, I know who he is," Edwards went on in a menacing voice.

"I don't know what you're talking about." Spencer looked rattled, he had lost weight lately, and in his artist's thin shirt he looked particularly emaciated.

"Look at what this is doing to you," Edwards barked waving a hand at him, "You need to put an end to it."

To Edward's surprise, Spencer burst into tears and leaned against the wall. This was not at all a reaction that he had counted on, and it left him both perplexed and lost for words. He looked pityingly at the army man but stayed silent. He thought it best that Spencer get this outburst out of his system.

"I'm not who you think I am," Spencer said though a hiccough as he regained his composure.

"I'm not here for confessions, Spencer."

"No, I'm not what you think, I'm not a killer."

"Please!" Edwards said incredulously. How could he be like this in the face of what Edwards knew? "Those sketches are your work, I know it and so do you."

"I swear to you that they are not by me, I can see the resemblance in style though," Spencer's voice was shaky, and his hands trembled as he spoke and Edwards found to his surprise that he believed him.

"Then why are you painting Mary Sommers?"

"Her face," he said sobbing. Edwards was confused. He thought he had known what was going on, thought the Spencer had been the killer and that he was so inept at hiding it that he would be caught soon enough. It was only when he saw that picture of Thomas Olocher's son, and he thought that Spencer's plans would impinge on his own that he came to confront him about it. He felt out of control, and his mind raced for an alternate face to pin the killings on. None was showing.

"What is the matter with you then?" he asked grabbing Spencer by the front of his shirt and standing him up properly.

"The painting in the lodge," Spencer replied weeping again.

"What about it?" Spencer was talking about the portrait of the Devil that he had painted for the lodge on Montpelier Hill.

"It did something to me, I see it everywhere, I see him

everywhere."

"Who? What are you talking about? Make some sense will you man!" Edwards looked into his eyes, and he could see fear there, and terrible tiredness; he looked like he hadn't slept in weeks. Edwards let go of his shirt, trying to calm things down. "It's alright," he said, "Calm down now, have a seat, and we'll get you a drink."

Spencer let himself be led to the table and sat down like a child and Edwards went to the drinks cabinet and poured him a large brandy. He sat down across the table with a drink for himself and waited while Spencer calmed down and took a big gulp of the drink. His breathing returned to normal, and he smiled sheepishly at Edwards when he was more relaxed; his face alight with embarrassment now.

"What's going on?" Edwards asked in a concerned way. Spencer looked at him like he was weighing up his soul, testing to see if he could be trusted with what he had to say.

"You'll think I'm mad," Spencer laughed nervously.

"I already think that," Edwards said smiling back at him. "Come on, you can tell me."

"Ever since I painted that picture I keep seeing it everywhere."

"What do you mean?"

"When I am in a room, and there is a painting on the wall, I see in the corner of my eye that it is my painting, but then when I look at it, another painting is there in the frame."

"That's just tiredness and drinking too much," Edwards said, scoffing at the idea that it could be anything else.

"It's not just that. When I am in the street, walking somewhere or in my carriage, I might feel these eyes on me. I look up, and I know that I see that same face each time, but it disappears before I can settle on it in the crowd."

"You think that you are seeing the Devil in the streets of Dublin?" Edwards asked to be clear that this was what the Colonel was saying. Spencer nodded, and then he laughed again, but his face broke just as quickly, and Edwards saw the fear in him once more. "There's no such thing as the Devil," he said dryly.

"I thought so too," Spencer nodded looking around the room as if something might appear at these words.

"And you were right," Edwards assured him, and then in a business-like manner, her said, "What do we need to do to cure you? You need sleep that is the foremost thing but what else, women? Do you need to go to war again?" Spencer smiled at this.

"War would probably be the best as it is the most distracting."

"So let's go start a war then!" Edwards cried. Spencer laughed, and he put a hand on Edwards' sleeve.

"I'll be fine once I get some sleep," he nodded at this idea like it made perfect sense to him. They were silent for a short time.

"I need you to think about something for me," Edwards broke the silence.

"What is it?"

"I need you to think who has had access to your sketches and would be able to copy your style." Spencer nodded,

"I'd like to know that myself. I don't generally show the sketches to most people, just the finished painting."

"That should narrow the search down then."

"I'm sorry I've been so odd lately, I can't believe I led you to think I was a murderer."

"Don't worry, I think that about most people." They both smiled, and Edwards wondered how true his flippant remark might be. He thought again of Scally, his real reason for coming here tonight. He would have to go to him and get him hidden, tell him that he was in danger. From who, though?

They drank some more as the dusk set in, and they lit no candles in the room.

"We can destroy the painting in the club if you want the next time we are up there?" Edwards said, almost as an afterthought.

# Chapter 39

The lustrous green expanse of the Phoenix Park glittered in the sunshine. Alderman James was uneasy in his hunting clothes, and he feared to show himself up with a bow as it was not his preferred hunting tool. He had been cajoled into this social outing with Edwards, the doctor Adams, and Colonel Spencer. He was sure that all three men would best him in skill with the archaic bow and arrow. This was just the type of jaunt that Edwards probably got up to all the time, but James wasn't sure how often the other two men would partake of such a pastime.

"Great day for it!" Edwards said jovially, looking out over the park lands.

"What are we here for?" Adam's asked, nodding to Edwards' comment.

"Pheasant, or any bird saving that."

"How are you with a bow Alderman?" Adams asked him with a big smile, he evidently liked this outdoor life away from corpses and dying soldiers.

"I think I could hit the ground if I aimed carefully," James joked. The group as a whole laughed at this.

They set off further into the wooded area of the park, away from the open plains where they had met.

"These men have been busy with this new killer," Edwards said to Spencer, loudly enough that the other two could hear.

"Really?" Spencer said looking from Adams to James.

"The Alderman more so than me," Adams said, "I just see the results of the killer's handiwork."

"We'll apprehend him soon," James said disinterestedly; he did not want to talk about this topic right now.

Edwards stopped walking and pointed ahead. They all looked, and no one spoke. There was a fine chested pheasant on a low branch preening itself not far from them. It hadn't seemed to notice them, or else it was so used to humans that it took no notice.

"Would you like the first shot Alderman?" Edwards whispered, a childish excitement in his eyes. James shook his head,

"I don't think we should start the day with a sure miss," he said and motioned for one of the others to go ahead of him. Edwards looked to Adams, and he stepped forward and unsheathed an arrow from the quiver and placed it delicately in his fingers against the bow. Edwards watched his fingers and technique with interest as he pulled back the drawstring, quietly and slowly, holding it there for a long time. Adam's had one eye closed, and he pressed his back hand against his upper cheek bone. The whole park seemed in complete silence at that moment.

There was a loud thwack, and the arrow pierced the neck of the pheasant who only had enough time to look up at them before the arrow struck him. All around other birds fluttered out of their nests, and resting places at the sound and feathers fell from the air like snow.

"What a shot!" Edwards said laughing and walking towards the dead bird. Adams looked immensely pleased with himself, and James felt further embarrassed now that he was yet to fire and a shot like this had been made.

"Well done," Spencer congratulated Adams.

As the men looked down at the bird and Adams lifted his trophy to remove his arrow, James noticed that Spencer seemed quite nervous at times. His eyes constantly darted around in all directions, looking beyond the group and the tree lines as if he expected some attack would come at any moment. He wondered was this leftover from his campaigns in India with the army, had some great trauma befallen him over there?

"It will be hard to beat that, but perhaps Spencer here can equal it?" Edwards said with a smile and patting the Colonel on the shoulder.

"I don't think I will," Spencer said as they carried on into the woods.

The next shot was Spencer's and this time the target was a smaller bird but a pheasant again.

"Not much neck to aim at there," Adams said in a whisper to Spencer as he got ready. James wondered if this was some sportsman's tactic, to put off the shot of the army man.

"I'll have to aim for one of the eyes then," Spencer said with a smile to show that he was not put off in the least by Adams' attempt. Edwards smiled and looked at James and then back to the bird. Was there some meaning in that look, James wondered, but he couldn't be sure. He looked on himself and waited for the shot. All was quiet once more. Then the arrow let fly with the familiar noise.

This time the bird was quicker, and it rose slightly before the arrow pierced its neck down near the chest, and it fell to the ground with a thump. It was not dead yet, and they watched for a moment as it squirmed around and then it stopped and lay motionless.

"I'd say that's an equal shot," Adams' said cordially.

"Not at all!" said Edwards with a look of shock on his face, "He missed the eye by miles!" They all laughed.

"The dinner tables are filling up for tonight," James said as Spencer collected up his bird.

They continued on for a time but saw nothing, not so much as a seagull. It was beginning to look like James and Edwards were not going to get a shot off at all, but then Edwards raised a hand, and they all stopped. James looked about the trees, looking for whatever it was Edwards had seen, but he could see nothing. He looked to Edwards as if to ask 'where/' but Edwards was not looking up at any tree, he was looking down a short slope to a clearing where a small deer stood. It was alert and must have already heard them, but had not yet perhaps seen them. No one moved. James looked again to Edwards, who he saw was taking an arrow from his quiver and loosening his bow from his shoulder. James was almost sure that these deer were not for hunting, that they were the property of the city or the Earl of Westmorland. He cast a look at Edwards to indicate this, but Edwards just smiled and looked back at the deer as he placed his arrow and drew the bow.

The crack rang out, and the deer bolted, but the arrow still hit the creature as it fled, catching it at the top of one of the hind legs. It was not enough to fell it, however, and it continued off into the undergrowth and disappeared.

"She won't last too long with that wound," Edwards said in a matter of fact tone.

"Should we go after it?" James wondered aloud.

"Perhaps I should have brought the dogs after all," Adam's said.

"No, leave it. Some fox or birds will have a field day with her when she finally lies down to die," Edwards said. He then looked to the sky, which had darkened, and said, "We'll get your shot done Alderman, and then I think we can be on our way." They all looked up and nodded in agreement. James would have liked to say that they could skip his shot and go home now but he felt he couldn't do this without losing face. They went on a little further until finally, Adams pointed out a crow cawing on a thick branch,

"Will that do?" he said, and Edwards nodded. James drew his bow and aimed. "Are you going for the eye, the neck or the rump?" Adams asked mischievously. Though James knew he was doing this to put him off, it still managed to have that effect. He held the bow for a long time and finally, just as his arm had started to quiver, he let go. The arrow flew through the air in what initially looked like a perfect shot but just before the bird it dipped, and there was a loud clatter of the stem against the wood of the branch. The crow rose up in fright squawking all the way as if reprimanding them.

"He's told you!" Edwards said with a laugh.

"Sorry men, there'll be no crow at the dinner tonight," James said.

"Don't worry Alderman, it was an educational day out all in all," Edwards winked at James so that he was the only one who could see this, but James didn't know what was meant by this. He would have to ask him later when they were alone.

The first drops of rain began to fall as they made their way back out of the woods.

# Chapter 40

Mary Sommers waited on Essex Bridge, and she watched the carriages of the better off people pass by on their way home, or to the theatre or some other places she could only dream of going. She kept an eye out for Colonel Spencer in case he passed, but there had been no sign of his carriage. John arrived behind her and poked her at the sides, scaring her and making her jump and then laugh as she hit him on the arm.

"Don't do that," she scolded him with a smile.

"I'm sorry," he said holding his hands up in the air "Truce?"

"Fine." She started to walk, but he didn't move.

"Do you mind if we walk somewhere else?" he asked.

"How come?"

"I was unloading from ships today, helping out a cousin of the tavern keeper who is in the dock here. I'd rather not see him again if I can avoid it."

"Yes, we can go somewhere else then. Have you anywhere in mind?"

"Well, I like the idea of walking by the water, do you want to go as far as the canal?" Mary didn't like the sound of this, it was too far away, and it would be getting dark before they would be back.

"It's very far," she said.

"Not to worry, we can walk there some other time."

"We could walk west along the river here?" she suggested.

"Of course we could," he smiled. He put his arm out for her to take and they began to walk.

Mary was nervous with him, she always made sure to be

on the side of him where her scars were hidden, even though he didn't seem bothered by them. He had been mannerly enough not to even mention them thus far. John seemed to her to be quiet tonight. She felt that he wanted to say something, that he wasn't his normal ebullient self. They walked Essex and Wood quays in relative silence, pointing out a boat or something else on the river from time to time. He asked about things at the market as they crossed Ormonde Bridge onto Merchants Quay.

"I've heard something, and I wanted to ask you if it was true Mary," John said suddenly, his voice was serious; his look equally so.

"What is it?" she asked, worried about what it might be, but at the same time knowing that it couldn't be anything she had done.

"I've heard that you are..." he seemed not to be able to finish the sentence or was searching in vain for the right words.

"I'm what?" she was worried even more know that she knew it was about her. Had she done something? No, she was sure of it. Someone must have been making up some lies about her, and her face reddened as she tried to figure what those lies could be and who could have been spreading them around.

"I've heard that you are letting a man paint you for money," John said this fast, as though if he didn't, he wouldn't be able to get it out at all. Mary let out a short burst of a laugh at the relief that this was all it was, but he looked at her in shock at this reaction, and she quickly controlled herself.

"That is true," Mary said seeing no reason to lie. She could tell by his face, however, that he was unhappy that the rumour turned out to be based on fact.

"How can you do this?" he asked her, and there was something prudish in her tone that made her think he had the wrong end of the stick.

"It's nothing..." now it was she who was searching for the right word. "Immoral," she settled on, but it didn't sound correct.

"Well that's a relief," he said clearly easing, "What is it then?" Mary didn't know where to start, now she was going to have to draw attention to her face and in particular her scars.

"He's an artist, he thinks that I have a unique face and that is what he is painting." She blushed, and her face felt boiling with it. John looked at her sympathetically, and they stopped walking and faced one another. He took her face in his hands and looked into her eyes. His hands were cold and felt good on her hot cheeks.

"You do have a unique face," he smiled at her. His left hand moved a little, and his eyes shifted to her scars as he caressed them tenderly, the first person since the doctor to have ever touched them. She recoiled a little but he stopped her and looked into her eyes again, and then he kissed her on the lips. His eyes were closed, and she was taken by surprise, but she quickly joined the kiss and shut her own eyes. He squeezed her in tight to him, and she felt her hand go up and through his hair.

It was all over in a few moments, and they stood awkwardly looking at one another. Mary glanced around to see if anyone had seen them but though there were people around no one seemed to be paying any attention to them.

"I'm sorry," he said, "I should have asked."

"No, don't be. It was nice," she replied, a smile coming to her lips. This had been her first ever kiss, and she had quite liked it. They began to walk again, and she leaned her head on his shoulder this time. Everything seemed different all of a sudden, as though she knew him better somehow for that one kiss.

"Just so you are aware, I wear as much as I am now for the sittings for the paintings," Mary said, still feeling that this may be an issue that needed to be resolved.

"I'm sorry, it just sounded worse when I heard it. Of course, I should have known you wouldn't do anything immoral," he smiled at her as he used her word and she smiled back.

"Where did you hear about this?" she asked.

"I have a friend who works in the Eagle and the painter and his friends drink there sometimes."

"Is the painter saying bad things about me?" she was mortified suddenly in anticipation of his answer.

"I wouldn't imagine so; if I had to guess, I'd say that my friend has taken something he heard part of, up wrong."

"Because I promise you that not so much as the bottom of my neck is on view for the painting sessions!" Mary felt hot again like some invisible hand was pointing in judgement on her.

"Mary, calm down, you're getting very excited about nothing," John said squeezing her hand gently.

"It's not nothing, I can't have people saying things about me that aren't true." The very idea of this was enough to make her want to go scurrying home and get off the streets to where no one could see her.

"No one is, I'll talk to my friend and set him straight. He won't have said anything to anyone else. He only told me because he knows that I am trying to court you," John's raised eyebrows and joking manner as he said this soothed her, and she smiled back at him. "I promise no one is talking about you Mary," he affirmed when she had calmed some more.

"I'll stop going if you want me to?" Mary said; she would certainly miss the money, but it would not be worth losing a relationship over, not know that she felt the way she did this evening.

"No, no, not at all," he said waving the idea away with his free hand.

They walked some more along the quays and then up Bridge Foot Street before turning back and sauntering slowly towards home again. Mary could not remember a time in her life when she had felt so carefree. It was a pleasant feeling, and one she hoped to come to know well.

# Chapter 41

It was dark, and rain promised as Scally left the blacksmith for home. The young boy was watched from across the street, as he walked the short distance, by Edwards who matched his pace and studied him as he walked. He looked on as Scally entered his building and then looked up at the lit window that was his home. His mother would be there waiting for him with his dinner made no doubt. Edwards still couldn't believe that he had found the son of Thomas Olocher, that he had been under his nose for so long unrecognised. A shadow appeared in the window, and Edwards knew it was Scally, and he looked at the silhouette and imagined that it could be the father back to life somehow. The shape moved, and Edwards imagined that he was at the table now eating. He waited for a time, not wanting to interrupt this meal, one of the few remaining ones he would be having with his mother for a long time.

As Edward's waited, he saw images of Olocher's trial play over in his mind. He was so defiant there, claiming that he hadn't done any of the things that he had been accused of, and looking for all the world as though he believed that. Edwards recalled Olocher's snarling face however when Mary Sommers came to give her evidence and all who doubted up to that point, knew by his demeanour that he was the man who had killed those women, and no doubt Mary Sommers' aunt. But Edwards could recall a different Olocher, from long before that... Enough time had passed to go up and see the boy.

Edwards climbed the same rickety stairs and heard the same noises and smelled the same smells as his last visit here. He knocked on the door and waited. He expected the mother to open the door in the same defensive way she had the last time and he was pleasantly surprised when the door was thrown open, and Scally stood there.

"Can I help you?" he asked, he seemed to recognise Edwards and was clearly confused as to why this gentleman would call to his home and that he knew where he lived.

"Ah, Hello!" Edwards said jovially. The mother appeared behind Scally, and a look of fear came over her face. She looked at Edwards but didn't say anything, probably afraid that she would spark his anger somehow and have him reveal everything in a fury. "I wanted to have a little chat with young Stephen here if that's alright?" Edwards went on addressing the mother. Scally looked behind at her not aware that she had been there.

"What for?" she eyed him suspiciously.

"I want to talk to him about his future," Edwards said with a smile that seemed to relax her.

"Come in, you can talk in the kitchen," she said.

"I thought we might go for a little stroll," Edwards countered, "How does this sound Stephen?" Scally looked again at his mother, and she nodded.

"Go on son, and listen to what Mr. Edwards has to say to you." She handed him a coat and helped him on with it. Scally was looking at her as if for some explanation but she was avoiding his eyes.

"I won't keep you long young man, just a few minutes' walk and a talk and that will be all. You'll be back having tea with your mother before you know it."

"Is this about the drawings?" Scally asked a look of guilty fear coming over his face suddenly.

"No, not at all!" Edwards laughed. The mother looked at him with a questioning eyebrow. "His current boss was being investigated for something, and some drawings were at the centre of it," Edwards said by way of explanation. She nodded as though this made sense to her but didn't say anything.

When they were out on the street and had walked a little Edwards finally spoke again.

"How do you like it at the blacksmiths?"

"I like it."

"I've noticed you've still been going over there, even though your employer is in the 'Black Dog.'" Edwards said.

"Just checking on the place, making sure nothing has gone missing," Scally told him.

"Very commendable, Stephen, very commendable," Edwards said, and then he stopped and faced the young man, "I'm not going to beat around the bush on this with you Stephen, I have something to tell you that at first, you are not going to like." Scally nodded, but his face betrayed his worry.

"What is it?" he asked nervously. They had reached the place in their walk that allowed them to see the tower of the 'Black Dog.' Edwards pointed up to it.

"Do you know what that is up there?" he asked. Scally looked up and then back to Edwards.

"The prison tower."

"That's right," Edwards said, and he looked Scally deep in the eyes, he could see fear in them. "That is the place your father was killed." Scally's eyes widened with shock, and he looked instinctively at the tower once more. His mouth opened but no sound emitted. Scally had obviously never heard anything about his father, the mother must not have even told him any lies about the man. "You don't know anything about your father do you?"

"No," Scally admitted still looking upward.

"His name is known to you, is known to every person in Dublin." There were tears starting to form in Scally's eyes, and it showed up so bright in the nearby lamplight. "Do you know his name?" Edwards asked.

"No!" There was a hint in his voice that Edwards felt was a pleading tone not to tell him the name, that it was something that was best left unsaid.

"Your father was Thomas Olocher," Edwards said, and now the tears did start to fall. Scally remained with his eyes fixed on the tower as though he might be able to see into the past and the see the man he had no doubt heard so much about.

"No, I don't believe that," he said flatly and purely as a denial for the sake of denial.

"Your father was known to me many years ago before he killed anyone."

"He can't be my father."

"He is Stephen, you have to face up to that. I have spoken to you mother already on this point, but even if she had not confirmed it to me, I would know for sure by the look of you. You couldn't look any more like him if you were him."

"Why are you telling me this?" Scally shouted, tears streaming down his face now and he grabbed Edwards by the lapels of his coat, but he was weak with sorrow.

"You have a right to know," Edwards said, and he took Scally by the wrists and held his hands away from his coat, looking into his eyes until the boy looked back at him.

"I'm going to make sure you and your mother are looked after. I liked your father, he was a friend to me, a good friend."

"Do you think he killed those people?"

"I think so yes." The boy let his head fall into Edwards' chest as he sobbed uncontrollably. Edwards smiled and put his arms around him and patted his back. "Don't worry. No one else knows, and one else needs to know. I will get you a new job, something that pays much better than the blacksmith and I will make sure that you and your mother have a good life from now on." Scally went on sobbing, and he nodded to what Edwards was saying until seeming to compose himself he asked,

"What about Mr. Mullins?"

"From what I hear it looks as though they have plenty of evidence that he is the killer, but even if that turns out not to be the case, I don't think it is a place you should be working. It is too unpredictable, and trouble seems to follow that blacksmith everywhere he goes. Try put that out of your mind, I am going to give you the kind of life you could only have ever dreamed of before now," Edwards answered.

Edwards looked up at the tower and smiled. If only James knew of his past association with Olocher, he wouldn't be so quick to have let him tag along on the Dolocher murders. It started to rain, and without speaking, Edwards began to lead Scally for home.

# Chapter 42

The carriage bobbed over the uneven stones on the way to Lord Muc's house. Edwards looked at Scally, sitting there sullen faced and serious.

"What is it?" he asked. Scally didn't answer or even look at him for that matter. Edwards sighed. "This is for you, it will be good for you." Still, the boy said nothing. "I know you liked the blacksmith, but you would never have been able to become anything if you stayed there."

"I could have become a blacksmith," Scally said sharply.

"You can be so much more than that," Edwards said and then in correction of himself, "You will be so much more than that."

Edwards could see that Muc was waiting at the gates for them. He leaned against the post of the gate, and there was a wide smile on this face. He was clearly relishing being part of what was going on here.

"I hate him," Scally said when he saw what Edwards was looking at.

"Who, Muc?"

"Yeah."

"He didn't get on with the blacksmith, but that doesn't mean you can't like him. They often drink together in the taverns at night." Scally looked at him, doubtful of this.

"Why do I have to come here?"

"He is going to train you how to fight."

"I already know how to fight."

"Not like Muc, no one knows how to fight like him."

"Why do I need to know how to fight like him?"

"It is part of making you someone special. There will

be other parts to this as well. You will be with Lord Muc for a while and learn from him, then you will come and learn some of the finer things in life from me."

"Like what?"

"You'll have to wait and see, but I promise you it will be worth the wait." Scally didn't say anything until they pulled up outside the gates of the house.

"I'm only doing this because you're looking after my mother," Scally said getting out without looking again at Edwards. Edwards smiled and climbed down too; he was enjoying the petulant spirit of the boy, it would come in handy in the future.

Lord Muc was bleary eyed having probably been out most of the night. He was looking the boy over, something that clearly made Scally uncomfortable.

"This his him eh?" Muc asked.

"It is," Edwards nodded.

"Show me your arms," Muc said grabbing him by the biceps at which Scally recoiled from and tried to free himself. Muc laughed and let him go, "Not bad, not bad, the blacksmith had you doing more than delivering messages and whittling on sticks I see."

"What do you think?" Edwards asked, and Muc looked pensive for a moment and then looked Scally over from head to toe.

"I can make him worthy of the Liberty Boys, I can't tell anything about his brain until I get to know him better."

"He has a brain, don't worry about that."

"Does he have a temper?" Muc asked.

"He can be very sullen and grumpy, but I haven't seen a temper yet."

"I'm standing here," Scally snapped.

"Well if that's the extent of his temper he should be a good student," Muc said, "Good fighters don't tend to lose their tempers too easily," Muc said to Scally in a fatherly way.

"Have you got a place ready yet for him to sleep and put his stuff?" Edwards asked. Muc nodded.

"Go in by the first shed and take the door on the right. You'll see a bed set up in there in the corner near the stove." Scally looked at Edwards.

"Go on and have a look, make yourself comfortable," Edwards said, and Scally sloped off past Lord Muc and into the yard.

The two men watched him go, and when he was gone far enough to be out of earshot Muc said,

"Is he much like his father?" Edwards wasn't expecting this, he didn't think Muc would have known who Olocher was or that this was his son. "I fought him once, down by the docks, drank with him a few times too," Muc said by way of explanation, "This was years before he started on those women."

"I see, I trust I can trust you to keep this quiet?"

"I can. Does he know?"

"Yes, I told him only a few nights ago," and then a thought struck Edwards. "How long have you known?"

"Only a while, he's grown up very fast that lad, only two years ago you wouldn't know it, but know it's nearly like looking at the man himself."

"I wonder has anyone else ever noticed it?"

"Maybe, but no one cares. Anyone who might say anything about it would have to admit that they knew Olocher better than from the gossip that did the rounds, and people don't want that type of association." Edwards nodded in agreement.

"How long will you take to train him?"

"A few months is all. He's strong but probably has no skills. He'll have to unlearn body movements that he's been using for years."

"How will you treat him?"

"Depends."

"On what?"

"What type of fighter are you looking for? His father was a frenzied attacker, hurting himself as much as his opponent but I prefer the mind game type of fight myself."

"I want him to be a clever fighter and for him to be able to control his temper if he turns out to have one."

"I'll treat him like an animal to begin with, and then it will get better for him as he learns."

"How do you want to be paid for this?"

"I don't, this will be a pleasure for me, not work."

"I'll come by from once a week or so to check in..."

"You won't come near him again until he's leaving here," Muc interrupted. "I'll see you around, and I'll let you know how he's getting on."

"I don't want a pure fighting dog when he comes out, can you try to get him to use his brain as much as possible."

"That's the way I fight, and he'll fight like me."

"That should be good enough, I suppose," Edwards said and he smiled at the look of disdain Muc gave him.

"When are we going to the place on the hill?"

"Soon."

"How soon."

"Very soon, I'll let you know when I see you next." Edwards climbed into the carriage, and Muc looked at the horses.

"Don't push him too far on his father, he never knew him, and he only has vague ideas of what he actually did."

"I'll do the training fancy man," Lord Muc sneered, and then he walked off into his holdings and didn't look back as the carriage pulled off and rolled nosily away.

# Chapter 43

The next murder, when it came, was heinous in the extreme. The body was badly mutilated and laid out on Limerick Alley. It was the body of a man, and his thighs and biceps had been removed from his body as if bitten off by some giant mouthed creature. The edges of the wounds were gnarled and shredded, and there was blood all over the scene and splashed on the walls of the alley. There was a frenzy in the area when the body was found by a woman going to the fetch a doctor for a woman who was giving birth and was in difficulty nearby. She had screamed hysterically when she saw the man and then had been most unfortunate in that she slipped on the blood soaked stones and fell to her knees to come face to face with the body. Her screams had brought others to the scene, and more had fallen and slipped as they tried to help her up. As this had happened the blood was on all sorts of people's clothes and the ground was muddied red and caked all over the area.

Alderman James arrived and looked over the scene and tutted at the state it was in. If there had been anything of use here in the way of clues, it was probably trampled away underfoot or taken away on someone's sole. There was a doctor here, a man called Steven's who had come to assist in the birth and having missed it, had come to examine the body afterwards without being asked. Steven's stood to one side when the soldiers arrived and waited for the Alderman to give him his findings.

"Was the place in this state when you got here?" James asked the doctor.

"Yes, it is a mess," Steven's replied looking about the

alley.

"And what of the body?" James did not know this man, and as such he did not know if he was any good at his profession or not, he assumed not as he was helping poor women give birth in places such as this.

"Looks like an animal did it only it is very specific."

"In what way?"

"It is only the muscled areas that have been removed really, an animal would not have been so precise."

"Did you see anything unusual on the body?"

"Apart from the wounds, no."

"There was nothing inside the wounds?" The doctor looked at him as though he didn't understand and James took that for a no. "Don't mention this to anybody, not a word," James ordered.

"Of course," Stevens said with a slight bow of his head.

"You can go now; if we need you, someone will come to talk to you."

"Yes, fine. Good day to you," the doctor said and then left.

There was a loud carriage rattling up the nearby Francis Street and without having to turn around James knew that it was going to be Edwards to add his level of mystique and jesting to the proceedings. While waiting to be proved right, James went over closer to the body and looked at the wounds, looking inside for the markings that he came to expect now. This time, however, he was not so sure that he could see them, this looked to be a different type of wound to the rest of them and was maybe not done in the same way at all.

"Good morning Alderman!" came the cheerful voice of Edwards, always so inappropriate at scenes of murder. He was like a young man out for a stroll on a beautiful morning, and he wanted everyone to know how good he felt. James stood and turned to return the greeting and shake his hand. Edwards looked down at the body and scrunched his eyes up,

"What is it?" James asked.

"I know this man," Edwards said, and he tutted.

"Who is he?"

"I'm not sure," Edwards looked to be trying to place his face. "He works in a tavern or whiskey cabin," he said. "Or maybe a coffee house or casino?" he added after a half second pause.

"Somewhere you frequent from time to time then?"

"Yes, I'll remember where soon. I don't tend to take too much notice of the staff except at the brothels," Edwards smiled, and James did his best not to react to this.

"There was a local doctor here, but I'm going to wait to get him to the morgue before I go on."

"This is different this time," Edwards said, and he looked at the body and then around at the surrounding areas. "This is not a Dolocher site, and there is something different about this man's wounds, also look around you, before this was all walked into the ground, there was fresh blood here, and see on the walls there?" Edwards pointed with his cane. James had seen this already, but he nodded. "The murder still wasn't committed here, though," Edwards opined.

"No?"

"I don't think so Alderman, do you?"

"No, there is not enough blood for those wounds."

"That's what I was thinking," Edwards looked at him then with a serious face, like he had some bad news to impart.

"What is it?"

"Those wounds do look like those of an animal this time."

"They do don't they?" James nodded.

"I don't have to tell you what people will make of that," Edwards said. James didn't say anything. The hysteria about these killings to date had not been as bad as he had feared and he felt he would be able to disassociate this one from the others by virtue of the fact that it had not happened in one of the same places as a Dolocher one.

"I guess this gets Mr. Mullins out of Newgate," James said.

"You don't think that may be a bit hasty?" Edwards asked quickly.

"No, why do you?"

"Well, you can see yourself that this is a different kind of thing and the wounds are different. This could be a completely different killer."

"I don't think either of us believes that Mr. Edwards," James said, "If there is some other compelling reason that you know of to keep Mr. Mullins locked up, please let me know." Now James smiled to himself as he got his own back for all the taunts and immoral acts and blasphemies he had to put up with from Edwards.

"Not at all," Edwards said in defence, "If you think he is innocent by all means let him go, but don't say I didn't warn you if he turns out to be our man."

"This is the same man, I'm sure of it Mr. Edwards, I can feel it."

"And if your 'feeling' is wrong?"

"If I am wrong Mr. Mullins won't be going anywhere

soon."

A soldier came over to the Alderman and let him know that the cart had arrived to bring the body to the morgue.

"Look over this entire alley and bring me everything you find on the ground, I don't care how small of how trivial it may seem to you," James ordered and then as an afterthought, "Make sure to go through the sludge too, there could be something hidden in there."

When the soldier was away a bit, Edwards asked,

"What do you think is the significance of the wounds this time?"

"I have no idea, but I hope it will become clear at some point."

# Chapter 44

Footsteps tramped along the stone floor of the corridor, and Mullins stood up to await whoever it was. He heard the keys rattle, and the door creaked opened. A dim light came in to the dank cell, and Mullins peered in this new light to see who had come.

"Time for you to get out of here," a cheery voice said. It was Cabinteely, the gaoler.

"Where am I going?" Mullins asked perplexed.

"Home for a wash would be my advice."

"I'm free?"

"Yes, just got a letter from the Alderman."

"Oh thank God," Mullins said, clasping his hands together and shaking them to the air in thanks and then blessing himself. The relief sent a shiver through him and for a moment he felt light headed, his thighs wavering feeling like his legs were going to give out.

"I thought you'd be happy with this news," Cabinteely said smiling.

"I thought I was going to be hanged!" Mullins said, and a nervous laugh escaped from him.

"Well, there's been another murder, so they know it wasn't you this time."

"It was never me."

"I know, I know," Cabinteely waved off his defensiveness.

"So I can just walk out?"

"Yes, the Alderman asked that you be at home today, though, he wants to call in to you."

"But the shop will need looking after, I'll have no money after being in here."

"I'd go home and stay there if I were you, Mr. Mullins, the shop can wait one more day, but you don't want to get on the wrong side of the people that can put you back in here."

"I supposed you have a point." Mullins was worried about the business; if this new stay in prison would erode any more of his customers. At the very least he thought it might be like the time when people thought he'd known what Cleaves was up to and that he was guilty by association. He wondered how Kate had fared while in he was locked up; he knew she had come to see him but had never been allowed to come in. He longed to see her, and he smiled at Cabinteely. "Anyway, I have a wife I need to see."

"Off you go then," Cabinteely said, standing aside and putting his hands out to indicate his freedom to pass.

It was cold outside as the gates of the prison closed behind him. Mullins looked to see if Kate might be anywhere about, but he didn't see her. He hurried off then in the hope that a few people as possible would see him. He knew that this was a silly thing to do as no doubt word of his incarceration would have spread rapidly as soon as he was arrested. He glanced at the shop in the distance, and he hoped that Scally had put out all the fires and had locked up properly when he was taken away. He spared a thought for Scally and his mother going without the meagre pay he gave the boy for the last three weeks.

When he got to his home he could feel the eyes of all the playing children on him, their cries went quiet when he appeared. He jostled at the door but it was locked, his own keys had been in the shop and Scally would probably have them now. He cursed at his luck as he traipsed back the way he had come.  As he walked, he again tried not to make eye contact with anyone.  He changed his mind about going to Scally's and stiffly changed direction and headed for the market at Templebar where he hoped to find Kate or at least one of her friends who might know where she was.

The market was heaving with people and boats lined the docks.  Merchants watched as their men unloaded crates, and prostitutes and street hawkers of all kinds flitted about trying to sell their wares. Sarah was at the vegetable stall, and Mullins saw that is was very busy with customers.  He went over, but he didn't want to ask her in front of all these people where his wife was.  She saw him and nodded at him with a smile.  He mouthed 'Have you seen Kate?' and used elaborate hand gestures to amplify what he was trying to say.  For a moment she looked at him oddly and then she seemed to catch on to what he was trying to convey.  She shook her head vigorously and tried to mouth something back, but then she gave and called over to him,

"Haven't seen her for a few days."

"Alright, thanks," he called back in an embarrassed tone.  He set off for Scally's home then in search of his keys.

Scally's mother was clearly surprised to see him, and she started back as she opened the door to him.

"Mr. Mullins?" she said.

"Is Scally here?" he asked, offended by the way she had reacted to seeing him.

"No."

"Did he leave keys for the shop here by any chance?"

"He might have, wait here," she said, and she closed the door. He could hear he moving things around, and another door opened and then closed inside and finally the door opened to him again. "Are these them?" she asked holing out the familiar bunch to him.

"That's them alright," he said and took them from her with a nod of thanks.

"You're out of the gaol then?" she said as he was about to leave.

"I was in there a long time for someone who didn't do anything don't you think?" She nodded in a non-committed fashion. "I'm hoping to open the shop up again tomorrow, can you let Scally know when he comes in?"

"Scally doesn't live here anymore, and he won't working at the blacksmith anymore either." Mullins eyed her in surprise at this- both what she had said and the way she had said it.

"Where is he gone?"

"A gentleman has taken him under his wing and is going to give him a better life."

"What gentleman?"

"That's none of your concern." Mullins realised this was true, and then he thought about Scally becoming a young man. As much as it might pain him to lose the lad, he could see that this was obviously better for him and more than Mullins would ever be able to offer him or his mother.

"He's a good lad, I'll miss him, but I wish him all the best, can you tell him for me?"

"I don't know when I'll see him again myself." His words had softened her towards him, and they shared the loss of the vibrant boy, as though he were dead, for a moment.

"No boy can stay away from his mother's table for too

long," Mullins said to her with a reassuring smile. He threw the keys up into the air caught them as he backed away.

As he walked home, he thought more about Scally leaving in this way. It was very odd, definitely not something that happened every day. He wondered why someone would have chosen Scally for such a thing. He was a nice lad and hardworking, but he wasn't all that clever that Mullins had ever noticed.

He was tempted, with the keys in his hand, to look in at the shop but he knew that he should get home. The fear of the Alderman calling on him and finding him out worried him. The last thing he wanted was another stint in the 'Black Dog.' He rushed along the street and tried to think of Kate and not the things that had gone wrong so these last few weeks. He hoped that she would be home this time and imagined grabbing her by the small waist and lifting her, laughing, into the air.

# Chapter 45

Adams was not in the mortuary when James and Edwards arrived with the body, so they waited in the cold building for him to arrive. James looked as Edwards poked around the room looking at the different medical and surgical instruments on the various counter tops.

"You shouldn't touch anything here," James said.

"If someone is here, there is no more harm a dirty piece of equipment is going to do them." Edwards wore that smirk on his face that James loathed.

"Have you remembered yet where this young lad is from?" James asked looking down on the body. Edwards walked over to the table and lifted the sheet from the victim so as to peer at the face again.

"I can't place him, maybe he's only a bar boy or something, and he blends in well, I recognise him, I'm sure of that, however."

James leaned in as well and had a look in the hope that in this new light he too might have seen him before. The blank dead face offered up nothing to his memory. "It won't be too hard to find out who he is, a quick trip around a few places and we'll have him placed," Edwards assured him.

"Good morning gentlemen," Adams said as he came into the room. They returned his greeting as he came over and pulled the sheet completely off the body, getting straight down to business.

"This one looks different," James offered, and Adams looked at him and followed his eyes to the wounds on the legs. Adams prodded inside with a wooden pointer and moved from the thighs to the arms and then looked again at James.

"This is indeed different," he said as he looked at Edwards and then to James.

"You can speak in front of him," James said.

"The other killings had parts cut off after the murder to make it look like the victims were killed by an animal," Adams began as though he were giving a discourse to some medical students. "This man's wounds, however, were inflicted by an animal."

James was stunned, he had not expected this at all, he'd assumed that this was the same as the others and that the doctor was going to confirm this as soon as he looked at the body.

"Are you sure Doctor?" he asked.

"Very, it's not what killed him, that would have been the blood loss, but the wounds were made by something with jaws and teeth designed for that purpose." Straight away the metal teeth used by Cleaves came to mind.

"Could it have been done by something like the metal jaws Cleaves had made?" James asked.

"Or something like the metal tusks Lord Muc was looking to have made?" Edwards suggested. James looked at him and tried to recall if he had told Edwards about this or not. The doctor didn't know what he was talking about, but he answered James' question.

"Anything is possible, but in my opinion, these wounds were the work of a hungry animal, I see nothing of design or craft here." James' mind whirled about as he tried to place this is in the canon of the other murders.

"Why would the animal choose these places to eat?" Edwards said, coming close to the body and looking at the wounds again. James looked again too.

"The thighs I suppose would be normal enough, what with all the meat, but the biceps might be a little odd," Adams answered, and he looked closer at the body again as though his interest had been piqued.

"What are these lines?" James asked pointing; he'd seen some light lines on the skin below and above the wounds that looked almost like tan lines, but the difference was much lighter than that effect would have shown. Adams bent to the thighs and examined this, and then he lifted one of the legs and looked at the back of it.

"I think we have your answer," he said to Edwards. "These were the only parts of the body that were exposed to the animal."

A sense of revulsion ran through James at the thought of this poor boy shackled and covered in some protective shell save for his biceps and thighs as a hungry dog or something like that was let loose on him. He could imagine how horrific this death would have been and it seemed so much worse to him for this than any of the others thus far.

"Our man fed these parts to the animal," Edwards said as though it had to be said aloud for anyone to be able to comprehend it.

"It certainly seems that way to me," Adams agreed.

"Is there any chance this boy would have died quickly?" James asked. He knew the answer already, but he still had to hope he was wrong. Adam's perhaps sensing this replied,

"It's possible he passed out quickly and felt nothing until there was enough blood gone that he never woke up."

"What an awful way to die," James said, and he blessed himself which was quickly copied by Adams. Edwards,

James could see in the corner of his sight, didn't even bother to affect the religious movement. James didn't know why he was surprised by this. "Can you keep this to yourself for now?" James asked Adams.

"Of course."

"Any idea of the type of animal?"

"I wouldn't like to guess, but something with a large mouth, a big dog maybe but I couldn't be sure," Adams said, his shoulders shrugging in apology.

"Thank you, doctor, for your assistance this morning, "James said, "Goodbye."

When they were in the carriage and alone once more, James looked at Edwards who he knew was waiting to say something.

"Out with it," he said in a gruff tone.

"What do you think?"

"About what?"

"A different killer or our man again?"

"Still the same man."

"How so sure?"

"I can't believe that there are two people that sick in the city at the same time, doing the same thing."

"There are a lot of sick people doing sick things in Dublin!" Edwards laughed as though at James' innocence.

"Not like this, not in this way," James said and then after a thoughtful pause added, "Think of it as a hunch, a feeling I have."

"So what do we do now, listen out for barking dogs who might be hungry?" Edwards asked.

"I know you are being facetious, but yes, that will be one of the things I will be doing from now."

"If it has to do with animals I think we should talk to

Lord Muc again," Edwards suggested.

"Does he keep animals?" James had not known of this.

"Not any more but I'm sure he is still involved somewhere in the business."

"It's a place to start I suppose," James said. He looked out the window, and he could see the face of the boy that lay dead in the morgue, and he saw that same face cry in fear as he was circled by some unseen beast and the horror as he knew that this was the last thing that he was ever going to see. James shook his head to be free of the image, and when he looked up, Edwards was looking at him.

"You know that people are going to think Dolocher when they hear about an animal?" he said.

"I know, I know," James replied.

# Chapter 46

The Alderman called not long after Mullins got home on the day he was released from prison, and the blacksmith was relieved that he hadn't gone to the shop on his way home. Mullins let him inside, noting with thanks that he didn't have any soldiers with him this time. They sat in the chairs by the fire.

"Would you like something to drink?" Mullins offered.

"No, no. I won't trouble you for long," the Alderman replied.

"What can I do for you," Mullins asked, wondering if he should be calling him sir in this context.

"Do you know the man who was with me when we came to your business and your boy did a drawing for us?"

"I've seen him before, but I don't know exactly who he is."

"Not even his name?"

"No, I'm afraid not."

"He told me once that he met you in the street one night when you were looking for the Dolocher."

"I followed him one night, thinking that he might have been the killer," Mullins admitted.

"And what happened?"

"I came around a corner, and he had a blade to my throat, and he asked me why I was following him."

"You told him your suspicions?"

"Yes."

"What did he say to that?"

"Well, he laughed at me and told me I was looking in the wrong place."

"Did he tell you where you should have been looking?"

"No, he said that he if he met the Dolocher he would tell him I was looking for him, but he was laughing when he said this."

The Alderman mused on this and Mullins didn't know if he should say anything more when suddenly he remembered something, "His name is Edwards," he said.

"So you do know him?" the Alderman said with a curious glance.

"No, I just remembered that he told me his name that night, he introduced himself." The Alderman seemed to be deep in thought again, but finally he said,

"I'm going to assume that you are not idiotic enough to roam the streets at night for the time being, but if you see Edwards around without me can you let me know about it?"

"I can do that," Mullins said, and he wondered now if the man he had followed that night, whilst not being Dolocher, could he the killer this time. Was this what the Alderman was getting at? "He drinks around here the odd time," Mullins offered, and the Alderman nodded. He stood up, and Mullins did the same.

"I'll be going, thank you for your assistance." They shook hands and Mullins saw him to the door. As he was leaving the Alderman looked back and said, "Don't let on to anyone, even your wife, about this eh?"

"Of course, sir. I'll keep it to myself," Mullins said, and he felt his eyes widen like a child trying to convince an adult of their sincerity.

When the Alderman was gone, Mullins sat down again and thought about times he'd seen this Edwards fellow. He didn't recall ever seeing him before the night when Mullins was arrested for one of the Dolocher killings, but since then he had seen him many times. He'd avoided eye contact with him, or any association at all for that matter, as he saw Edwards somehow as a bad luck omen for him.

He boiled water for tea, and his mind drifted back to the Alderman and his possible fears that the very person who was helping him with his investigations might be one who was doing all the killing. The Alderman seemed a different man than the friendly one Mullins had first encountered two years previously. Back then he seemed warmer and more aware of the people around him, more just than was the case now. Before that Mullins had only known him by reputation, by the moniker of 'Level Low' that was given him. Mullins had seen the weavers strike and riots and he could understand why force was called for, but violence was in him, and he knew that not everyone agreed with this view of things.

Something wavered in the back of his mind, and he pushed it away, but it came back a few times until it pushed to the fore of his thoughts. The Alderman was harder than he had been before the killings, he was in better shape physically than he had been at the time of the Dolocher killings. He had been very quick to lock Mullins up for the murders, and now he was pushing suspicion towards another of the night's travellers in Edwards. Could it possible that Alderman James was, in fact, the killer this time around? Could he have given up on his trying to win over the people, appalled at their lack of interest in his attempts to catch the Dolocher? So much so that he had turned inward and back to the same man who had a soldier killed without blinking, who killed those weavers without a second thought?

It would make sense, wouldn't it? The Alderman was

probably the only person save the army and parish watch who could roam the streets at night without raising any eyebrows. He had access to places where the killing could take place and the means to travel and dispose of the bodies on the streets. It was suddenly making too much sense to Mullins, and he had to temper himself, realising that he had gotten carried away.

This was all fantasy, he told himself. The Alderman couldn't do this. Or could he? What if he did, what then were the chances of him being caught if he was the one doing the investigation? Mullins thought about this scenario and thought it best to be on his guard and to go along with anything the Alderman asked him.

As far as Mullins knew there were no leads on who the killer was. It had been going on for months, and nothing had come of it, there didn't seem to be any witnesses to anything. There was not the same frenzy as when Cleaves was killing everyone under the rumours of Olocher's ghost but this time there was no real public outcry, which he thought was odd.

He went to the front door and looked out into the street to see if there was any sign of Kate coming. Some children looked at him, and a few women spoke in a huddle ground near the square, but they ignored him or didn't even notice him. He sighed as he looked out knowing that this used to be a nice place to live, where people had trusted him and asked for his help. Now he was lucky if they even came to the shop for something done for them. All because of murders he had nothing to do with.

# Chapter 47

The morning stayed dark, the black of night seeming to refuse to lift. Alderman James sifted through his correspondence. The letters had piled up half read, and very few replied to since this new wave or murders had begun. He recalled his weeks or apologies and entreaties after Cleaves had been caught and he started to go through his amassed mail. This time he was determined that it not get so bad and he focused twenty minutes on this task alone every morning before he left the house. This was the task he was seeing to when there was a knock on the door, and his butler came in. He had a concerned look on his face

"What is it?" James asked brusquely.

"There's a boy here with a letter for you."

"Well give it to me."

"He said that he has been ordered to only place it in the hand of the Alderman." James stood up.

"What is this nonsense!" he barked, "Send the little brute in then."

A minute later a young boy of about ten years old came in. He was dirty and wore the clothes of the extreme poor, but then James noticed that his hands alone were immaculately clean. James saw the envelope and recognised it as the same as the one he had received from the killer.

"Who gave you this letter?" he shouted at the boy, snatching the letter from his hand. The boy shrank back and looked terrified. "Answer me!" James shouted at him.

"A man," the boy said, he was trembling, and he looked to the Butler as though he might be able to save him from this tirade.

"What man?" James grabbed him by the clothes and pulled him in close to his face. The boy started to cry.

"A man with paint on him," he wailed.

"Paint?" James said, but it was not really a question for the boy. He let go of his clothes and stood up straight again. "He made you wash your hands before he gave it to you?" James asked in a tone much less angry, he felt bad now for being so hard on the boy. The sight of this letter, a mocking jeer to him, had set his passion alight but now he simmered, and he knew that this boy was going to be able to be of very little help to him. The killer had chosen him because he was a nobody who wouldn't know how to describe the man he met.

"Yes, sir."

"Did he say anything to you?" The boy shook his head. "Did he give you a message for me?"

"No sir."

"This paint, was it on his clothes?"

"No sir, he had it on his face."

"His face?" James wasn't expecting this answer.

"It was all red."

"Red?" What was this supposed to say to him James thought? Was it something to do with the blood of the victims, or perhaps a reference to the Devil? "Where did he give it to you?"

"On the Quays."

"And he told you where to go?"

"He brought me to this street and pointed at the house."

"When was this?" the Alderman was shocked that the killer could have been right outside his door only moments before.

"Last night, he told me not to come until this morning." What relief there was left a sour taste in his mouth as he pictured this boy and the killer standing across the road and maybe even watching him as he came home. He went to the window and looked out now in the hope that this man would be watching them now, waiting for a reaction to his letter. Though there were a few people about none of them seemed to look towards the house in any significant way.

"How tall was the man?"

"About the same as you sir."

"Did you see his eye colour?"

"No, it was dark."

"What was his voice like?" When no answer came, James turned and looked at the boy, and he seemed not to understand the question. "Was he Irish?"

"I think so, sir."

"What was he wearing?"

"He was in a big cloak that covered all of his other clothes, and there was a hood on it. When he had the hood up, you couldn't even see his face."

"Do you think he was a rich man?"

"Oh yes, sir. He gave me this." The boy held out a large coin, and James looked at it. It was a large sum for a small job but not something a poor man couldn't rustle up if he wanted to impress someone or throw the Alderman off his scent.

"Give my man here your name and address young man," and then to the Butler, "See that he gets something to eat and maybe something to bring home to his family."

When he was alone, James sat down at his desk and looked over the envelope. He held it in different positions for different light to see if he could see anything on the paper but to no avail. He used a letter opened to carefully open the side, and then he eased out the paper with thumb and forefinger slowly. He looked inside the envelope, but there was nothing there this time, no object and no drawing.

He moved his attention to the paper now. There were two sheets this time, folded one inside the other and in three bends. He could see one of them was a sketch by the shading in the corner visible to him so he decided that he would look at this one second and see what the other had on it. As suspected it was a letter.

*Dear Alderman, greetings once more. I can assume by now that you know that the wounds on the last body were made by an animal and not by human endeavour. I have enclosed with this a sketch of my new pet. I think he may escape soon as sometimes I forget to lock his cage.*

*Don't be too concerned that I know where you live or that I have been outside of your house if I wanted you dead Alderman there have been any number of opportunities I could have taken.*

*The next murder could happen anywhere. It will depend on the wind, the smell of human flesh as it wafts to the nose of the beast. It will be in the next few nights.*

*Yours,*

*The Dolocher*

James put the letter down and with trembling hands he opened up the other sheet. On it was drawn a large shouldered grey wolf from the side profile, its face to the viewer and meat hanging from its jagged teeth. It had the effect of blood dripping to the ground. The eyes were malevolent and seemed to study James own eyes as he looked upon it.

Before the cursed soul of Thomas Olocher was blamed for the murders there had been a theory that a wolf may have been responsible for the attacks and James wondered if this killer knew this? Or was this just another twist of the game he was playing to cause the havoc he so craved, havoc James was glad to say had not fully materialised as of yet. He put it down to the murders being carried out away from where the bodies were found and the long gaps between them. People quickly forgot, letting their own little lives dominate. Though the Dolocher killings were a terrible shock to the people here, it made it easier for people to resort to murder; it was no longer something so reviled and feared in the way that it once was when it didn't happen so much.

James couldn't dwell on this, he had to think of what was happening now. What should he do? Sending out a general alert about a wolf in the city could cause panic, but if he let the army and the parish watch know so they could keep an eye out for it, it would only be a matter of time before one of them let it spill, and everyone knew. That would surely spread panic, and the secrecy would be another reason for the panic. He looked over the sketch of the wolf one more time and sighed. The way to go this time was to let everyone know, let people have a chance to defend themselves until the army had tracked it down and killed it. But then, he thought, what if that is what he wants me to do, and there is no wolf? This was, of course, possible, this was all a game to this killer. James decided he couldn't afford to take the chance. This killer had some kind of animal under his command, something that could kill a man and tear off his flesh.

He put the killer's words and drawing aside and crafted a letter to be sent to the barracks and he prepared to go around to the parish watch in the various areas and get them to spread the word officially.

# Chapter 48

The news of the wolf spread faster than even the jaded Alderman could have ever imagined. The general response, however, was one of excitement and not of dread. Everywhere people talked in excited tones about the wolf who stalked the streets at night and had killed a man. Reports of sightings and near misses and daring escapes from the creature spread all over every shop and tavern and parlour room. No one seemed to be particularly afraid of running into the beast, and people came out at night without giving it a second thought. Children ran to parents with stories of the wolf walking past the top of the lane or chasing them home.

The parish watch and the soldiers who were keeping an eye out for it seemed to be the only ones who never saw it. A pig was killed one night, and the squeal could be heard for miles around. Closer to the scene people spoke of the sound of the wolf as it growled and bellowed at the pig. No one was brave enough to go see the scene until morning when the pig was found with a large chunk from its flank missing and claw and bite marks on its hind legs and rump. The stories of this spread and for whatever reason this was what started to let fear seep into the collective consciousness of the people.

This fear gripped fast and refused to let go. People began to question the efficiency of the army and the parish watch. They demanded that the streets be made safe. The taverns filled with talk of hunting the wolf down, like they had with the pigs a few years before. And this was where the route of the fear lay; it had been the slaying of the pig and the blood and gore that this produced that was seared into the thought processes of all the people of the Liberties as being associated with the time of the Dolocher. The change was sudden, as sudden as the change in weather that brought the winter crashing down with a force that November of 1791.

Snow blanketed the earth, and this was yet another omen, a reminder of the night of the slaying of the pigs, when the blood splashed all over the city and yet not a drop remained the following morning when all was white and covered and pristine. To many, it suddenly felt as if history was repeating itself and this was more than most could bear.

# Chapter 49

Edwards sat in Thomas Tavern on Ward Hill and looked over the collected clientele of the place. He had been here only a few times in his life and had never liked it much. The customers were local and boorish and drank themselves into oblivion on slops most nights of the week. He saw the boy who carried drinks to and fro and beckoned him over.

"Yes sir?" the boy asked.

"Get me the finest brandy you have, from the tavern keepers own cabinet," he said.

"Yes sir, I'll ask,"

"Before you go, did you tell your colleague what I said?"

"Yes sir, he didn't like it one bit, just like you said," the boy smiled at him as a child who has been up to mischief.

"Is he here tonight?"

"No sir, but he will be."

"Soon?"

"Yes."

"Get my drink," Edwards ended the conversation, and the boy went off to fetch his brandy.

It wasn't long after that Edwards saw Mary Sommers' boyfriend walk in through the side door and go in behind the bar before disappearing down into the cellar. Edwards got up and went to the bar.

"You don't mind if I go down and talk to your boy do you?" he said to the barman.

"John?"

"Yes, thank you," Edwards said, and he came behind the bar without getting permission. The barman didn't know what to do so he just let the gentleman pass, and he looked on as Edwards went down the stairs to the cellar.

When he got down, he could hear the grunting of the lad and the wooden shuffling of a barrel being tilted and rolled on its rim. The boy stopped when he saw Edwards.

"Hello John," Edwards said in a friendly way.

"Hello," John said, wary and trying to place Edwards.

"You're seeing Mary Sommers," Edwards stated, and John nodded, eyeing Edwards more suspiciously now.

"Are you the painter?" John asked.

"No, but I've come here to warn you about him."

"Warn me?"

"If I were you I wouldn't let Mary go to his house for these painting sessions," Edwards said with an affected concerned tone.

"And why is that?" John's tone was defiant, and Edwards smiled, happy to put this little runt in his place.

"He boasts of sleeping with every woman who has ever sat for him," he smirked.

"Mary wouldn't do that!"

"What choice would she have if he really desired it?" This shut him up, and Edwards was filled with glee at the anger he could see he was rousing in the boy. "I want you to come with me."

"Where?"

"I want to show you something, something I think you will want to see."

"I can't go anywhere, I'm working now."

"I'll sort that out with the barman," Edwards waved his protestations away. "Besides, you'll only be gone a very short time. It's only a few streets away."

"What is it you want me to see?" he seemed very wary,

and his eyes flicked to the stairs back up to the bar.

"I think it will be better if you see first and then I tell you what you are seeing," Edwards smiled and then before John could say anything more, "Come on, it won't take long," and Edwards turned and went back up the stairs. "John will be coming with me for a short time," Edward said throwing down a note on the bar, "This will no doubt cover his absence." And then he walked outside.

A few moments later John came sheepishly out, and without a word, Edwards began to walk waving for John to follow him. John hurried after and soon caught up.

"Did you know that Mary used to work in the same place you do now?" Edwards asked.

"Yes, she told me that when I told her I worked there." They walked on across New Market and down Fordam Alley and then on to Ash Street.

Edwards stopped abruptly at a junction on this road, and he looked at John who also stopped.

"Do you know where Mary was attacked?"

"No, I've never asked her about that, and she hasn't said anything." Edwards walked a little into the road and said,

"This is the exact spot!" John looked around, and he seemed to go pale, he walked out to where Edwards was, and he looked up the alleyway on either side and saw how quiet a place this was.

"Are you sure?" he asked.

"Of course, I was investigating the case with the Alderman, I have been to all the sites of the Dolocher attacks and this new killer too," Edwards boasted. "Anyway, enough with this, this is not what I wanted to show you, I just thought I'd point it out seeing as we were here." Edwards went on and walked down Garden Lane towards Francis Street. John followed, but he kept looking back to where Mary had been attacked as though he expected to see it happening any second.

Edwards cut through a back yard and into the back of the Hellfire Club house on Francis Street, and John followed without question. Edwards knew he had the boy on edge now; that he would be afraid of his own shadow and wouldn't want to be left alone.

They came into the house, and Edwards lit some candles.

"Wait here," he said, and he went into the room he had set up earlier and lit all the candles in this room. By the time he was finished, it looked like the middle of a bright summer's day in the square furniture-less room. He went to the door and beckoned John to come in.

John came into the room, and immediately his jaw dropped, and he looked out over the many paintings that adorned the walls, all lit up and garish. Naked flesh and hands roving over it covered the walls, men kissed women's bare necks and in other women lay draped over couches or beds, everything in the vivid colours of life. Edwards watched John face redden in embarrassment and waited for the moment when it would change to anger. He knew that all of this would have a terrific effect on a young man and would almost blind him to anything else at that first moment of seeing.

John's eyes dropped to the floor when he finally came back to himself, his Christian shame rising to the fore.

"Why did you bring me here?" he asked angrily, and Edwards laughed at this reaction.

"You know why, young man, what do you think you are looking at?"

"All of them?" John asked, an incredulous look on his face.

"Every last one, and every last one a real woman who if I had the time I could show you all," Edwards peered greedily at John's face as the shock wore away and the anger began to seethe. "There will be one of Mary in this very room soon if you don't put a stop to it."

John ran from the room without saying a word, and Edwards laughed loudly as he did, hoping that John would hear it and the echo of the laugh would follow him out into the night and all the way back to work. He wondered what route the boy would take to stop Mary. It was unlikely that he'd go to Spencer and have it out with him, it was much more probable that he would go and order Mary to stop. He would have to wait and see, and this was often Edwards's favourite part of any endeavour he undertook. It was at these moments of devilish wickedness that he felt most alive. Now all he had to do was wait and watch the pieces fall from this latest move. Then all that wold soon be left would be for him to go to the killer and let him know he was found out. Edwards could already see his surprised face, and he laughed at the image it brought to mind.

# Chapter 50

Kate and Sarah chatted and warmed their hands with cups of tea; their bodies wrapped in blankets as they huddled close to the fire. Mary came in unexpectedly.

"What has you home so early?" Sarah said, a look of concern on her face.

"He didn't come," Mary said, her voice was sad to the point of breaking, but she held off from crying.

"Oh dear!" Kate said standing up and going over to her to take her into a hug. This is what put Mary over the edge, and she began to sob.

"Come over to the fire, Mary, you must be chilled to the bone," Sarah said getting up and offering her warm place. Kate guided Mary over, and she slumped down.

"He must have been held up somewhere." Kate offered as a reason for John's not showing up.

"He's gone off me, I know it!" Mary said, her voice higher than normal in her sorrow.

"No, no," Sarah said. "Did you have a fight the last time you saw him?" Sarah said. Mary nodded.

"You did?" Kate said, her tone of surprise unmasked. Mary would always tell them what was going on with her; if she had a fight with John, it was unusual that she wouldn't have at least told Sarah about it when it happened. Kate exchanged a glance with Sarah and knew by her face that she didn't know about this either.

"What was it about dear?" Sarah asked, handing Mary a hot cup. She took it with trembling hands and sipped at the hot liquid.

"He didn't want me to go to the Colonel's house for the painting anymore."

"Did you tell him that it was a proper painting, nothing scandalous?" Kate asked

"I told him it was nothing," Mary said. "The first time he brought it up he seemed fine when I told him. But I think someone where he works has been putting ideas in his head, and he got upset and said that if continued going there, he would have nothing more to do with me." She spoke in stuttered sentences between sobs and the two women waited patiently for her to finish,

"And how did he leave you last time?" Sarah asked.

"I told him that I'd stop going and we left on good terms."

"Maybe he found out that you haven't stopped going?" Kate surmised.

"Who would tell him?" Mary asked.

"Probably the same person who's filling his head with ideas about the painting in the first place," Sarah said.

"Do you know who it is?" Kate asked.

"I think he said it was another young lad who worked with him."

They were all quiet for a moment. Kate wondered if there was any way they could find out who was talking to John and to get them to shut up. Her thoughts went to Tim and perhaps asking him to pay a visit to the tavern, but she knew she couldn't do this, perhaps earlier in their relationship but not now, after he had spent time in the prison and this would seem so frivolous to him. The shame of what she had done with Edwards to secure Tim's release swarmed her senses, and she felt nauseous for a moment.

"I'm sure it will be fine Mary, he'll come to you at the market tomorrow, or on the street and tell you why he hadn't been able to make it," Kate said with forced joviality as she hugged Mary in tight to her. Mary looked at her and nodded bravely, holding back the last tears that were trying to fall from her fire reflecting eyes.

"Yeah, these things always happen near the start of relationships," Sarah said.

"I shouldn't have lied to him," Mary said after a brief silence.

"It was only a little white lie," Sarah said. "You will be finished at the Colonel's at some stage, and you need all the money you can get at the moment from it before it ends."

"I agree, did John offer to give you the money you'd be losing out on if you stopped going?" Kate said bitchily. Mary looked at her in surprise but answered,

"No, he wouldn't be able to do that."

"I'm sorry Mary, I didn't mean to sound cruel there," Kate apologised. She had been angry at herself and what she had done in her own life, and she knew there was no need to push any of this onto John's shoulders. From what Mary had said about him, he was a very nice boy, and there was no reason for any of them to have a bad word to say against him up to now. Kate sat down where she had been before Mary came in and took up her own cup once more. She longed to be able to tell the girls what she had done, to be told by them that she had done the right thing: that she had no other choice, but she was so ashamed.

She still didn't really understand what had happened with Edwards, he was so insistent on getting her to go with him and then only days later he had thrown her out and sent her back home before Tim had gotten out. She was lucky that she had not thrown out her key or else she would not have been able to get into the house before Tim got home. She recalled sitting in the house, Tim's house that she had moved back into, and feeling terrible shame at being there, for having the gall to come back at all. She had steeled herself to Tim's sense of betrayal, to his fomenting hatred of her when he found out what she had done, but she had done it to save his life. She hoped that someday he would be able to see that and in the distant future there might be the possibility of their getting back together. She loved him deeply, and she would do anything for him, she had proved that in her own mind but now it seemed all for nothing. There had been a murder while Tim was in prison and she doubted that Edwards had anything to with his release at all. Had he ever any intention of helping or was it all part of some sick joke he had perpetrated on her? He was such a confusing man, you never knew really where you were with him. Now he had this information on her, and she felt sure that he would use it against her in the future, she was realist enough to know that it was unlikely that she had shared his bed for the last time.

"Are you alight?" Sarah asked looking at her. Kate looked up and saw the two pairs of eyes gazing at her in concern.

"Yes, sorry, I was miles away there," she answered with a smile, one that she had learned to throw at customers at Melanie's.

# Chapter 51

Kate watched from the corner as Thomas looked over a delivery that had arrived for his eponymous tavern. He was arguing about something, as she knew he would be. Finally, some arrangement was come to, and the delivery cart started off slowly to its next boozy destination. Thomas barked instructions at two young men who were to bring the barrels in to the store room in the cellar. As they began to work, Kate crossed the road,

"Hello Thomas," she said, sickly sweet in tone. He turned to see who had spoken and when he saw her he blushed red and his face dropped in surprise.

"Hello," he mumbled, darting quick looks at the boys to see if they were looking.

"Can you talk for a moment?"

"I'm quite busy," he tried to walk away, to go inside the tavern. He was so befuddled by her visit that he didn't know what he was doing. She knew that no one knew of his visits to the brothel, that he was married and passed himself off as a good decent Christian.

"It's about John," Kate said rushing after him. He stopped at the door and turned to look at her once more.

"If you know where he is you can tell him not to bother showing up here again!" Thomas said gruffly.

"I don't know where he is, I wanted to ask you if you knew?"

"I don't."

"Have you noticed anything different with him lately?"

"I don't have time for this..." he started to say,

"Maybe your wife might have time to talk about it?" Kate threatened. He looked about once more and then beckoned her to follow him inside.

"He was in work a few nights ago, a man came in and pushed past me and went down to him in the cellar and they left together," he said in one breath once they were inside.

"What man, who was he?"

"I don't know, he's been here a couple of times before, always wants something from my own drinks cabinet."

"Is he about your own height, dark hair, well dressed?"

"Yes."

"Blue eyes and an abrupt manner, like he was laughing at you without actually smiling," she described Edwards as best she could. He stopped at this last description as though she didn't know what she was talking about but she saw it dawn on him as he remembered who she was sure was Edwards and he smiled,

"That's a perfect account of him," he laughed a short, loud snort.

"When was this?"

"Oh, it must have been," he put a hand to his chin and looked to the ceiling in a display of memory. "Five nights ago, I think."

"And no one here has seen him since?"

"Not that I know of. Andy, outside of doing the delivery, is a friend of his I think, but he tells me he knows nothing."

"I'll go talk to him then."

"Kate," he said after her. She turned to look at him. "It was nice to see you but please don't ever come here again."

"I only came this time for some answers, I doubt you'd ever have another one again," she smiled and left.

She walked around by the side of the tavern, and she

could hear the men working, heaving and grunting and the sound of wood cracking against other wood. She walked down the slope that ran to the cellar and peered into the darkness.

"Andy?" A face popped out of the gloom and looked at her with curiosity.

"I'm Andy," he said, wiping his hands with a cloth tucked into his trousers.

"You're a friend of John's?"

"That's right," she felt him go on the defensive.

"Have you seen him?"

"Not since the night he left here with some man."

"Do you know who the man is?"

"No, he was only here a few times."

"Do you know what he wanted with John?"

"No, but I think it had something to do with his girlfriend."

"Mary?" Kate was not expecting this.

"Yeah, he paid me to tell John that some fella from the army was painting her." So that was how he found out about that.

"Did he get you to do anything else?"

"No, just to say that she was still doing it the next time he came in." What was Edwards playing at she wondered? Was this some new way that he had decided to get back at her? By using her friends and making them miserable?

"Do you know where they went?"

"No, just that they headed towards New Market, but beyond that, you wouldn't be able to see from here."

"Do you know John well?"

"Sort of, we share a room with a few other lads."

"Have any of them seen him, has he been home?"

"Not since that night and I don't think any of his stuff has been touched since then either."

"Did you report this?"

"Report what?"

"That he was missing!" At this, he laughed,

"Who cares if one of us goes missing, he's probably gone back home to Galway, maybe there's something up with his family, or they finally have enough to leave, and he is going with them." It did sound plausible, but she felt that anyone who knew Mary would not have been able to go without at the very least saying goodbye. She had a terrible feeling about this, and her suspicions of Edwards deepened. She couldn't help but picture John turning up dead in some alley somewhere soon, his body cut and savaged. Mary would be devastated if she ever had to deal with that.

"Thanks," she said absently as she began to walk away. She could feel him watching her, but he didn't say anything else. Kate decided in the time that it took her to walk up the slope back to the street that she would have to go to Edwards herself, it was the only way she was she was going to find out the truth.

# Chapter 52

The shadow of the house fell in a slant across the road as Alderman James hid in the darkness it provided. He could see Edwards' coachman getting ready to leave. James looked behind to Bessie, his own horse waiting obediently a few yards back in the alley. Her breath lit the air around her nostrils, and the black of her eyes shone in the light they caught. Looking back to the house James saw Edwards trot down the steps and climb energetically into the carriage. James was not used to seeing him move in this way and he wondered was he drunk already, and would he only lead him to one of his drinking haunts this evening. James mounted Bessie and set out slowly after the carriage as it trundled down towards the Liffey.

James didn't like being back in this position; of not knowing what was going on and not being able to trust anyone. Was he too quick to listen to bad things said about Edwards just because of his affiliations and the immoral life that James abhorred so much? He'd thought on numerous occasions of following Edwards but had so far never acted on them, but now as he found himself with so little to go on and numerous things pointing in Edwards' direction he had decided to act. He did so with some trepidation, however, as he feared another incident like that at the Hellfire Club. He knew that Edwards was very clever and could be completely unpredictable. He probably expected James to follow him at some point, but he was also the type who wouldn't care that he was being followed.

As expected Edwards crossed the river and went into the Liberties area. James trotted along at a distance and as close to the buildings as he could get away with. James was muffled against the cold, and he cursed his choice of night to do this and even more so when the carriage pulled up outside the Hellfire Club house on Francis Street. James came as close as he could, and he wondered why Edwards had not alighted as of yet, but no sooner had he thought this than the door opened and Edwards popped jauntily to the ground.

"Wait here, I'll be back in a minute," Edwards called to his coachman, and then he disappeared inside the building. This at least warmed James, the fact that he was not going into the house for the evening. James found the most concealed spot he could and waited, and soon Edwards came back out, his head wrapped against the cold, he saw Edwards' shoes and sword to be sure it was him, and he jumped into the carriage, and they set off again. James followed.

After about fifteen minutes they came to a house with some stables attached, a place the Alderman did not know well. Edwards got out and dipped into the one of the sheds and the coach went off and left him there. A few moments later a horse and rider came out of the barn and James looked to see that this was still his man and once more he saw the giveaway shoes and weapon. James followed again, he was more careful know that there was no carriage to block Edwards' view should he look behind and there was also the trouble with the sound of the horse walking that hadn't been an issue when he was in a carriage.

James had never known Edwards to ride on horseback, and this was intriguing to him. He followed Edwards along some streets and through alleyways and none of the time did he turn so much as to look to the side or behind him.  Soon it was clear that he was leaving the city and almost as soon as they had done so, it was too dark to be able to see much of anything.  James hesitated in the blackness and wondered if Edwards was taking a longer route out to Montpelier Hill and if he should bother following at all.

Suddenly a light flickered, and James could see up ahead that Edwards had lit a lantern and that he was now starting to head east.  This was not the way to the remote club house, and James nudged Bessie forwards and followed at a distance.  James let the distance between them lessen a little, knowing the there was no way that Edwards was going to be able to see him in this light and also that the wind in the trees that lined the road would make it impossible to hear him either.

This walk went on for over an hour, Edwards stopping every now and then at crossroads as though he was unsure of the way to get to where he wanted to be.  At last the light came to a halt and James was sure that he would see the sea in the moonlight, and he wondered where on the coast they were right now and what Edwards was up to.  Was he waiting on a furtive boat to come in?  Presently the light went out, and James couldn't be sure that he could see either horse or man any longer.  The world felt dark and sinister now to James, the black and shadows almost alive in his mind, something evil in all directions closing in on him.  It was freezing, and the wind moaned and surged all about, and the squalling noise of the sea sounded like something breathing heavily and moving hugely on the landscape.

The sound of galloping hooves took him by surprise,

and the horse and rider were upon him as if from nowhere, and the shrill scream of the rider and whinnying of the beast shocked and scared James to his very soul, and he put his hands up to protect himself from some attack he felt coming. He lost his balance and feel heavily from the horse, who also frightened by the sudden noise, and nearby movement cantered in agitation in elliptical circles.

James was then aware of a man laughing, and he heard something flint, and a light sparked, and then a torch came alight.

"Best not to always believe what you see Alderman," the man said with a grin.

"Who are you?" James demanded, getting up from the damp earth.

"I'll tell you who I'm not," he laughed, "Edwards!" he laughed more heartily now.

"So he sent you to lead me out here?"

"He's hurt that you don't trust him."

"Hurt my eye!" James said and grabbed Bessie's reins angrily and remounted. "You better lead the way back."

"I'll take you some of the way, my home is on the way, so I won't be going all the way into the city."

"Brilliant!" James grumbled.

Their walk back was silent, and James was furious in his embarrassment. He was ashamed that Edwards knew he was following him and he was annoyed that Edwards had purposefully sent him on this hour's long walk on such a cold night. He imagined Edwards drunk as a lord now and laughing in a well-lit and warmed room, thinking about James' suffering. He wondered too during some long moments of the walk home if this was going to affect his relationship with Edwards regarding information.

Edwards was a source of knowledge through avenues that the Alderman would never be able to gain access.

The thing that most occupied his mind, especially when the rider reeled off and pointed him in the direction of the city and he was left alone, was that he still didn't know if Edwards was his man or not. Was no closer to still knowing if he could trust him or if he was just along for the laugh of seeing James trying to catch the very man he was using for information.

# Chapter 53

Mullins was itching to get out of the house. He'd only very recently come in from working and had washed, and stoked the fire that Kate had left for him. She was down with Mary and Sarah and probably wouldn't be back for a good while yet. In his mind, he could see the cabin and a jug of whiskey in front of him, and it pained him to sit with rapidly cooling tea in his hand instead. It had been many nights now since he had been out and it was not good for him, he had felt himself growing cranky and snappy with Kate, though he knew she was doing no different than usual. He needed some freedom, to be able to blow off some steam, being cooped up like this would be the end of his marriage. He emptied his cup into the fire and stood up as it hissed to nothing in the grate. Pulling on his cloak, he went out into the dark, icy night.

It was still early in the evening, and many people milled about; there were even some retailers still open for business and lights came from many places of trade as people finished off the day's work behind closed doors. The cabin was not a long walk from his home, only about eight minutes at an amble and he could see it for a long time before he would get to it. It always looked so welcoming to him.

It was going to be another icy night, and his breath steamed the air in front of his face. Mullins felt snow was likely as he looked at thick blanket of clouds that covered the sky. He stepped out of the road as a fancy carriage came by, the noise of the wheels and the clopping of the horses the only noise he could hear for a time. As this subsided, he thought he heard something else, something unwanted and unpleasant, but then it was gone before he could hear properly. The carriage was still in earshot but only as background noise now.

Another sound in the night.

This time there was no mistaking it. It was a woman screaming. Mullins looked around; it was coming from a laneway just to his right, though it was one of the narrow winding ones, and he couldn't see beyond a few feet into it. The scream came again; it was one of terror. Mullins was torn, his body tried to lead him to the scene so as to offer his assistance but his head was telling him that it was none of his business, that he should walk away like he'd never heard a thing. If there was a murder and he walked in on the scene, he was sure to be taken to gaol again, and this time there would be no getting back out.

The cry came out again, but it was a voice this time, someone shouting, "Get away!" and then he heard a growl and he thought there is no murder happening, but some woman is cornered by a hungry dog. He went into the alley and around the corner. It was hard to see as sheets and blankets hung from a rope across the width, people trying to get whatever drying they could do in this cold. Then he heard something that turned his blood cold- there was a shuffling of feet, and then a baby's cry rang out, and the woman shouted again at the dog.

Mullins rushed on towards the noise and when finally he came to a clearing he could see that it was indeed a woman cornered, clutching the wailing baby to her chest. It was no dog, however, that cornered her but a great stalking wolf, the wolf that the whole area lived in fear of, who was seen everywhere and who had killed people too.

The woman's eye went to him, and he could see her fear

and her pleading. Mullins looked at the animal, and he made a loud noise to draw its attention. It turned to look at him, arching its back and crouching into a defensive position, baring teeth and growling at him. The woman was too afraid to try to move, and Mullins said,

"Don't move fast when you do move, I'll distract it as much as I can." The woman gave a slight nod back to him. Mullins looked around to see if there was anything he could use as a weapon should he have to. He felt very vulnerable in front of the animal. Implements he used in work or saw at the shop every day came to mind, and he wished he had even the least of them with him just then. Some slats of broken wood lay on the ground but nothing that could be of any defence against the wolf.

"Get away now!" he shouted waving his arms a making himself as big looking as he could. The wolf backed away slightly but remained in the same position and only growled some more. A door opened, and all eyes shifted to that noise, and the wolf manoeuvred so as to be able to see Mullins, the woman and the door all at once. A man leaned out and grabbed the woman by the arm and pulled her in, slamming the door shut as the wolf made a lunge for the fast moving shapes of the people. Mullins went to leave but no sooner had the door closed than the wolf reeled to face him, and there they stood once more, the same as before.

Mullins edged backwards, but this seemed to rankle the beast all the more, and he made a move as if to pounce on Mullins but stayed on the ground and flashed another deep angry and guttural growl. Mullins could feel the weight of a draped blanket on his back, and he knew that if he tried to run for it, he would get entangled and fell and be done for.

He cast about the ground once more, looking for anything that might be of use to him but all the time trying to keep a firm eye on the wolf for any movement it might make at him. If only someone would open a door for him to escape. He had no idea what to do; as strong as he knew he was there was no way he thought he'd be able to cope with the speed and strength of this animal and even if he were to come out on top somehow, he was sure it would be at some high cost to his own body. His mind was blank of ideas, and he just stood there dumbfounded.

"Have a bath you dirty dog!" a cry suddenly went up and from behind Mullins a flood of water, the steam of its heat whipping everywhere, came past his shoulder and boiling hot water landed on the wolf and splashed all around it. It wailed and ran in circles for a moment, crashing into doors and walls and then slipping on the wet it turned and scurried away yelping and whining in pain.

Mullins turned to see Lord Muc standing there laughing so hard there were tears in his eyes.

"Thanks," he said and Lord Muc looked at him and nodded in reply. "Where did you come from?"

"I saw you coming into the lane, and I thought you might be up to your old murderous tricks," Muc said with a smile. Mullins soured at this.

"What is that supposed to mean?" he asked.

"Come into the cabin and get me a drink, and I'll tell you all about it," Muc said. Mullins looked once more in the direction the wolf had fled and then back to Muc.

"Come on then," he said, and they left the lane.

# Chapter 54

The cabin was as busy as ever when Mullins and Muc walked in. There was a momentary quietening as they entered, such was the impression these two men made together, and everyone looked them over for a moment before going on with their own business. There were some wry smiles, no doubt people thinking that there was bound to be another bout of fisticuffs if these two men were drinking at the same time.

"Two jugs!" Mullins called to the barman. There was nowhere for them to sit, so Mullins leaned against the bar. Muc wasn't so diplomatic, he looked at some men at a table under the window and gave them a menacing look. They tried not to return his gaze but then he went over, and Mullins was prepared for a brawl to erupt.

"Can I ask you nice gents to vacate this table please, my friend here," he gestured to Mullins, "Has just had an encounter with the wolf and I'm sure his legs could do with resting." His voice was sweet, and Mullins had to laugh at this pretended politeness. The men looked relieved of the chance to get up and be helpful, they all nodded to Mullins as they went to the far end of the room and gathered in a group to continue their conversation. Muc sat down and waited for Mullins to come over with the drinks.

"That was very civilised for you?" he said putting the jugs and glasses on the table. Muc shrugged.

"I don't know why they always wait for me to ask before they get up," he made a show as if he just didn't understand people.

"Thanks for helping out in the lane there," Mullins said.

"He'll be up and able to kill again before the night is out," Muc said of the wolf. Mullins nodded in agreement.

"So what is it you have to tell me?" he then asked, recalling what Muc had said just before they came in.

"Someone's been wanting an eye kept on you," Muc said, his eyebrow raised towards Mullins in mock suspicion.

"Who?"

"I can't tell you that, but I have been paid a nice sum to follow you and report back on what I have seen."

"And what have you seen?"

"Nothing until tonight,"

"I haven't been out until tonight."

"I know and then what do you do the first night you do leave the house?"

"What?"

"You skulk about an alleyway, and then there is a woman screaming."

"She was already screaming, that's why I went down there," Mullins protested.

"I didn't hear a scream until you were in the alley."

"Is this what you're going to report?" Mullins felt all of a sudden that it was the Alderman who was having him followed and that if Lord Muc wanted to, he could make quite a lot of trouble for him.

"That depends on you," Muc said, his smile of menace coming over his face. Mullins regretted ever leaving the house now, but at the same time, he felt comfortable being in the cabin with a jug in his hand and people all about him.

"I saved that woman's life," Mullins said, "And her baby."

"I don't care about that, or that I saved your life," Muc said. With the distance from the wolf now Mullins didn't think he had been in all that much danger before as he looked back on it.

"I was doing fine," he said, and Muc laughed out loud of this.

"You were only short of wetting your trousers when I came along!" Mullins didn't other rising to this, he was indebted to Muc, he was not so vain that he couldn't see that at least a little, and now he knew also that Muc had him over a barrel in terms of lies he could make up about him for the Alderman.

"I've thanked you for helping me," Mullins couldn't bring himself to say the word 'saved.'

"You have," Muc nodded and he took a deep draft of his jug and sat back satisfied. Mullins could see he was going to make him ask.

"What do you want from me?" he said after a short pause.

"I want you to make those tusks like I asked you before," Muc said. Mullins remembered this refused request from many months before, and he sighed. He saw no point in denying him this time.

"I'll start on them tomorrow," he said looking into his jug and seeing part of his reflection in the liquid.

"I'll drop them to the shop at the start of the day. I'll want the real ones' back too, and in the same shape I give them to you."

"They'll be looked after," Mullins said.

They didn't speak for a long time after this, each man drinking his whiskey and suffering through his own thoughts. Mullins wanted to know for sure that it was the

Alderman who was paying Muc to follow him but he knew that it would be pointless asking; Muc loved hoarding secrets and having information over people, and there was nothing he would find more amusing than Mullins' pitiful attempts to get it out of him.

"So how much am I worth to you?" Mullins asked

"Depends on how much I find out,"

"What if you find nothing?"

"I'll always find something," Muc smiled wickedly, and Mullins didn't know if was bragging about his tenaciousness or joking about his lack of regard for the truth.

"It must be a lot to take you away from your other activities," Mullins said. He wanted to put Muc ill at ease for a moment; though he had no idea what Muc got up to, he was sure that a lot of it would be illegal. He wanted Muc to think he might know something about this, something that he could hang over Muc. Muc looked at him and laughed; Mullins flushed with embarrassment.

"I've nothing to hide from anyone," Muc said with a grin. "I'll tell you one thing blacksmith," he went on, "The person who wants me to keep an eye on you has no love for you."

"Why so?"

"I can't say as he's never told me, but I can feel it from him," Muc replied. That didn't sound like the Alderman, Mullins thought, but it also didn't sound like anyone else he could think of. The only person Mullins would even come close to considering an enemy would be the man who sat across this very table from him. Was it possible that Muc was just engineering a scenario whereby he could make Mullins feel that his freedom was in jeopardy? It would be just like him and his sly ways to do such a thing. The real question was not this, however; it was if there was a possibility that he was telling the truth. If he were, Mullins would be silly, stupid even, to not go along with his wishes. He thought of Kate, hopefully at home and safe by now, and he knew that he couldn't risk going back to gaol. He finished his jug in a long swill and put it down on the table.

"I better get going," he said standing up, "I'll want a clear head if I'm to start work on a fine piece tomorrow."

Out on the street now the snow had begun to fall. He glanced quickly at the alley were he had his encounter earlier with the wolf but moved on briskly towards home. He looked all about, feeling almost sure that he was going to see the beast again. It was late enough that the streets had cleared now, only a few people here and there, moving fast just like him and avoiding eye contact. It was a terrible relief when he got to his front door, and he could see the candle inside, and he knew that Kate was inside waiting for him.

# Chapter 55

When Mullins opened his front door after a heavy battering from outside, he was surprised to see the smiling face of Lord Muc standing there, clad in furs and animal hides that looked as though he'd made them himself.

"I'm going to the cabin," Muc said. Mullins looked at him, was this an invitation to go drinking? "I think it would be best for you to come too."

"Why is that?" It was still early enough, Mullins had not been home long at all. He could hear Kate moving around behind him, most likely craning to try to see who was at the door.

"Your 'benefactor' is going to be there," Muc said with a wink.

"The man who is paying you?" Mullins asked with sudden interest.

"The same."

Mullins turned and took up his coat,

"I'm going out for a bit," he said to Kate.

"What about your dinner?" she protested throwing a poisonous look at Muc for good measure.

"I'll be back in a little bit," Mullins said, and he went out closing the door behind him. Muc had already started to walk, and Mullins caught up and fell into step with him.

"He's going to make some announcement," Muc said.

"The man who's paying you to follow me?"

"Yes."

"About what?" Mullins was nervous suddenly that he might be walking into some kind of trap; perhaps this man aimed to humiliate him somehow in public. He stopped, and Muc stopped after a few paces and looked back at him questioningly.

"I don't know," Muc assured him.

"Has it something to do with me?"

"I don't think you're at the top of the bill," Muc seemed to laugh at this opinion of himself, as though people didn't have anything better to talk about than the blacksmith. They trudged the rest of the way through the thick snow.

Inside the cabin the atmosphere was electric and red merry faces smiled out from all corners. It reminded Mullins eerily of the night that everyone had gone out to slaughter all the pigs during the time of the Dolocher. It was that same type of bravado infused drunken frenzy feeling. Mullins looked around the room, but there was no sign of the Alderman. He looked at Muc, but he was too busy getting to the bar and ordering drinks. Mullins did feel a pair of eyes on him, however, and he looked about the room until he met them. It was Edwards, the man who worked with the Alderman. He nodded to Mullins with a thin, false smile and Mullins nodded back. Was he the one paying Muc, perhaps on behalf of the Alderman?

"Here, blacksmith!" called Muc and Mullins turned to catch a jug that was all but thrown at him. He nodded thanks to Muc and stood away from the heavy throng at the bar where he was soon joined by Muc. Mullins was looking at Edwards still, and Muc followed his gaze.

"Is that him?" Mullins asked.

"It is," Muc replied, looking around at the drunken scene in front of him and smiling fondly at it. It was possible that he too was thinking of that night of orgiastic and unbridled violence when the pigs were killed. It had been a night filled with snow just as this one.

"What is he going to say?" Mullins asked. Edwards was

not looking back at him any longer, he was talking to a man who looked like he may be of military bearing but who looked quite ill, Mullins didn't recognise this man.

"I have no idea, but the rumour is a reward,"

"Reward for what?"

"For the capture of the wolf," Muc said like it was the most obvious thing in the world.

"Capture!" Mullins looked at Muc who looked back at him with mild irony.

"Or kill, I suppose," he said with a shrug.

The door opened, and Mullins looked to it and felt the gust of the cold coming in with the Alderman. The Alderman didn't seem to see him, he was just another man in this mob. Edwards waved, and the Alderman nodded in return and went off in that direction.

"What do you suppose the Alderman is doing here?" Mullins asked Muc.

"Who knows; maybe he's hard up for cash," Muc smirked and then drank some whiskey. There was a general stir then, and the focus of the entire room turned to centre on Edwards who called out in a loud ringing voice,

"Listen up men, I have a proposition!" His face beamed with delight and there was something almost child-like in his manner. Everyone was silent and looked on, waiting to see if the rumours had been correct. Alderman James was sitting beside the standing Edwards, and he looked out over the crowd of men with a suspicious gaze. The room fell silent as Edwards lowered his arms from where he had tried to quiet the mob. He looked over them all in a half moon around him before he spoke. James looked unimpressed with the proceedings.

"We all know of the wolf on our doorstep," Edwards

began. "We all know how elusive a creature it has been. It turns up out of nowhere and disappears without a trace as soon as it does." There were nods and murmurs of assent from the men. "There is enough crime and villainy in this city for the parish watch and the army to deal with without also having to be animal trackers." There were some hisses and booing at the mention of the parish watch and army, and the sick looking man whom Mullins thought was an army man looked about indignantly at this. "I will put up the sum of twenty guineas for any man or group of men who bring this animal in." There was a whoop of joy as everyone looked at his neighbour for his reaction to this news. This is what they had come to hear, and they were delighted for it. Some men rushed to the bar as if to spend the twenty guineas like it was already in their possession. Edwards went on, "I would like to see it alive, but I know that will be beyond most men, so dead will have to do." He sat down now having said his piece and the revelry of earlier started up again. A few men finished their drinks and then left with determined faces as though they were going out that minute and expected to be back within half an hour with the dead creature over their shoulders. More men huddled in groups as if to make a plan.

Mullins looked over the group that contained Edwards, the Alderman, and the army man.

"You going to say anything?" Muc asked him. The truth was that he didn't know what to do. He wanted to go over and confront Edwards as to why he was having him followed, but now that the Alderman was here and probably an officer of the army he didn't feel that he could. He was also ashamed to say that he had been cowed somewhat by the flippancy with which Edwards had offered the massive sum of money for the wolf, which was more money than Mullins made in a good month.

"This is not the place to do it," he answered after a long pause. He finished his drink and ordered another for Muc. He handed to him as he was on his way to the door.

"They're looking over at you now," Muc said, but Mullins didn't turn to see if they were or not.

"I'm going home, but I'll catch up with him soon and find out what his game is."

# Chapter 56

Mullins was dealing with a customer when he saw Edwards coming across the road, seemingly with the intent of coming to the shop. He hovered outside for a while, and Mullins wondered what he wanted and was hardly listening to the man who was talking to him. When the customer was finally gone Mullins stayed inside; if Edwards wanted him, he could come in and talk to him. About a minute passed when the smiling face of the gentleman poked through the door and looked about until it saw Mullins who had pretended to be working on straightening out some soft metal with his hands.

"Mr. Mullins, isn't it?" Edwards said, he was standing in the doorway now, but he was still not inside the building.

"What can I do for you?" Mullins said when he had nodded to Edwards.

"I'm afraid that I have come to do you some service," Edwards said, his manner suddenly grave.

"Concerning what?" Mullins was unsure as to what he might be alluding to, but he remembered Lord Muc's words that this man was no friend to him.

"Oh, a few things," Edwards said. He poked at some tools hanging by the door and looked back at Mullins. "It seems you were attacked by the wolf?"

"Not attacked no?"

"I didn't think so, there's not a scratch on you," Edwards said looking him over.

"I went to the aid of a woman who had a baby; I heard her scream."

"I'll be frank with you Mr. Mullins, there is a rumour going around that the wolf is yours, that you have trained it to kill and that was why you were able to escape from it without harm." Mullins was astonished by this claim, and for a moment he didn't know how to answer to it.

"That's completely incredible!" he said at last. "The reason I got out of there unharmed was that someone came to my aid, they threw a pot of scalding water over the wolf," he said hurriedly as he recalled he had an alibi in Muc.

"I heard that it was Lord Muc who saved you."

"He helped me," Mullins said, he still couldn't reconcile with that word. Edwards smiled seeming to know that it rankled him. "Why are you paying him to follow me?" Mullins asked suddenly; he was annoyed at Edwards now.

"He told you did he?" Edwards laughed and looked like he was thinking for a moment.

"He didn't say why?"

"I wanted to be sure that you were not this killer who is going around."

"Are you satisfied now?"

"Not entirely, but I'm beginning to rule you out." They looked at one another, but neither spoke for a few moments.

"You said there was something else, I think?" Mullins said.

"That is much worse news for you I am afraid," Edwards had a look of mock sorrow on his face, and Mullins felt his stomach lurch with worry as to what he might be alluding to. There was something in Edwards' demeanour that told him that this was not going to be some trifle or rumour that he could bat away.

"Out with it," he almost growled it, his teeth clenched against the pain he felt was coming.

"It concerns your wife Mr. Mullins," Edwards said, and Mullins' stomach dropped another level.

"What about her?"

"It seems that she did something rash while you were in the gaol over there," Edwards nodded across to the visible 'Black Dog.'

"What do you mean?"

"She was terrified for your safety, she had not been able to gain access to see you and all the rumour out here was that you were going to hang for your alleged crimes."

"What about it!" Mullins was desperate for Edwards to get to the point, he was fighting off all sorts of things in his mind that wanted to leap forward as possibilities.

"It appears that she gave herself up to a man to secure your release," Edwards looked quite grave, as though he was terribly sorry to be the one relaying this news to him.

"What?" Mullins was stunned, this was not at all what he had thought was coming, and for a moment he was dumbfounded by it.

"She didn't know that there had been another murder committed, one that would free you as it was the work of the killer of the others." Mullins got hold of his thought, and he rushed and grabbed Edwards by the collars,

"You liar!" Mullins shouted. Edwards made no motion to defend himself, and he took his time before speaking again.

"I know that you must be upset Mr. Mullins, but I think you should go and talk to you wife, you will know by speaking to her, I'm sure, if this awful rumour is baseless or not." His calmness exuded and Mullins felt it affect his own body, and he lessened his grip on Edwards and then released him completely and took a step back.

"Who told you this rubbish?" Mullins asked looking him in the eye.

"I'm afraid I can't tell you that," Edwards said as calmly as before. "Speak to her tonight, hear her part," Edwards said, and then he nodded goodbye and waked out of the shop.

Mullins was dizzy and leaned against the door frame. He felt ill, but he didn't know what might make him feel better. Could it possibly be true? He grew angry at this, and his dizziness got worse. No, he thought, she wouldn't so something like that. Her past was drifting by his reason and letting itself be known, a tantalising doubt that this was indeed something she might have been capable of. He wondered then who could have told Edwards about it and why they would tell him in the first place. He could think of nothing. He heard a carriage outside, and he stepped out, he needed some air.

The carriage stopped in front of the shop, and Edwards leaned out of the window.

"I'm sorry Mr. Mullins, but the reason I couldn't tell you who had told me this information was because no one had told me," he called out. Mullins didn't understand for a moment what he was talking about. Edwards was smiling mechanically, an evil bent to his face but before Mullins could piece his thoughts together, the carriage moved off. "There was a nasty bruise on her hip a few weeks ago wasn't there?" Edwards' mocking voice rang out from the fast disappearing carriage.

Mullins charged after it, but they already had a good head start and a decent head of steam going before he even set off and it was clear to him after only a few seconds that he was not going to be able to catch up with them.

"Come back here!" he shouted after it, "Coward!"   He stopped running and looked after the carriage until he could see it no more.  His head throbbed with his pulsating blood flow at the temples, and he bent over to catch his breath.

# Chapter 57

James stepped into the whiskey cabin on Cook Street, and it seemed to him that this was becoming a regular meeting place for them. Edwards had suggested the place in a note sent to James late the previous evening. It was nearing Five O'clock now and dark outside; the first of the evening snow was falling. As expected, Edwards was there already, sitting in that same corner at the same table as the previous times- James thought that he must pay men to vacate it when he came in, that was the only way he could get it in a place that was always busy like this. Their eyes met, but neither waved or nodded acknowledgement of the other. Edwards' eyes were alive with mocking menace as James made his way to the table. This is what James had feared most; the mocking was the worst of it all and Edwards had some talent for it to be sure. James sat across from Edwards but still neither had said a word. James looked to the bar and called for a jug and then turned back to Edwards.

"It was very cold out a couple of nights ago wasn't it?" Edwards said with a grin.

"You'll want to know what I was doing?" James said, not wanting to get into semantics with him.

"I know what you were doing Alderman, you were following me," Edwards said leaning back in his chair, "What I don't know is why?"

"First off I must apologise," James said. The barman dropped the jug and tumbler to the table and left without a word.

"Accepted," Edwards said.

"Someone has come to me and named you as a possible

suspect for the murders."

"Did she now?" Edwards smiled, and James didn't bother pretending that it was not Kate who had said it. "What else did she have to say?"

"She said that you are trying to ruin her marriage," James looked at him indignantly at the recall of this. Edwards laughed at this, seeming to find it very amusing.

"What type of a marriage do you suppose a whore can have?" he laughed. James didn't respond to this. He didn't approve of her former life, but he knew that Kate had been a changed woman since she got married to Mullins.

"Anyway," James said wanting to get back onto the subject at hand, "You could have just asked me why I was following you the other night, and it didn't have to end up in that ridiculous charade!"

"You could have come to me with your concerns Alderman, you could have spoken to me instead of skulking around on that silly horse of yours." James nodded in defeated agreement with this.

"I can only apologise for not taking that course of action, but..." James didn't go on, and his eyes fell to the table. He'd been about to say how much this case was getting to him but he didn't want Edwards to know this.

"I will continue to assist you if that is what you wish Alderman," Edwards said, "But if not I do not expect to followed again. I may be many things, but a murderer is not one of them." James looked at him again.

"I'm sorry, I would like you to continue to help if you can."

They were both silent for a time and drank a little. James looked about at the clientele of the place, and he felt that these people's faces were becoming more and more familiar. These were the people that he was trying to protect and here each one of them sat or stood drunk and messy and a possible next victim. No one returned his gaze.

"It just so happens Alderman," Edwards started, getting James' attention once more, "I have another clue for you and one that this time I'm sure you'll be delighted with."

"What is it?"

"Something that I believe points to our man directly," Edwards was almost sneering in his smile.

"Don't do this, tell me what it is?"

"That amulet you gave me?" Edwards said.

"Yes?"

"Did anyone else see it apart from you or I?" James tried to think, had he shown it to anyone, he couldn't remember if he had.

"I don't think so?"

"So if it were to show up in say, a painting, would that seem strange to you?"

"It would indeed," James said. He was already seeing Colonel Spencer and his nervousness at the opening of the new Custom House a while back.

"I was in Spencer's house yesterday, and I got him to show me where he did the painting of the Devil that adorns the club house in the countryside. As I was looking over the attic, that is where he does some of his darker paintings, I saw one against the wall that had a woman wearing the very same amulet as you found. The painting was dated to last year. I didn't recognise the woman, but I feel sure that it would be of one of the early victims, whose face was not recognisable."

"Did you confront Spencer about this?"

"No, he doesn't know that I've seen it."

"So you think he is our man?"

"I do now, he has spoken to me of seeing the devil everywhere he goes, and he has been unhinged for a long time. I think doing that painting of the Devil, being up close to it, eye to eye with Lucifer as it were, has done something to him."

"He sees the Devil everywhere?" James asked surprised

"Yes, a face in a crowd, out on the street if he happens to look out a window."

"Really," James wondered if any of this might be the cause of being part of the Hellfire Club, a divine punishment perhaps.

"I think he's definitely worth investigating more, perhaps we could go to his house, and I could show you the painting I mean?"

"I think that should be our next step," James agreed.

"We can go over there tonight if you want?"

"I think we should go now, this instant. If he is the killer, he could have something terrible planned for tonight for all we know."

"He won't be home until later," Edwards said, "I arranged to call in this evening in anticipation of out meeting." James looked at him and wondered if he ever stopped scheming.

"What time?"

"Eight."

"Gives us some time to eat then," James said noticing that his drink was falling on an empty stomach.

"Not here, however, I've seen the food, and it could have been the cause of more deaths than the Dolocher and Spencer put together!" Edwards smiled at his joke, but

James was once again put off by his casual manner in relation to murders and the feelings of people in general. James looked around to see if there had been any reaction to the mention of both sets of murders but if there had been one he had missed it.

James threw down some money on the table for the whiskey, and they left to eat somewhere decent before going on to Colonel Spencer's house.

# Chapter 58

Mary waited once more for Spencer in the downstairs room. She had been nervous about coming, had almost not come having promised John that she would stop soon. The money lured her here, there was no way she could turn it down, herself and Sarah needed it. She just hoped that he did not want to go up to the attic again for this session.

Spencer came in, his movements frantic and he looked as though he were in a great hurry. Mary was startled by his appearance -so much so that she did not say hello when he came in. His face was white and wax-like with tiredness, and he looked as though he had lost weight, his clothes hung instead of clung to him.

"Today will be the last session, Ms. Sommers," he said, and he looked at her with a thin smile, "Thank you so much for your time and willingness." Mary had not expected this, and she nodded back,

"Your welcome." He must have seen something in her face, some facet of disappointment.

"I will be paying you more than usual, this is a last payment to say thank you, and who knows, and I may ask you to pose again for me some day." She was embarrassed now that he had known she was concerned about the money, but he seemed to take no notice. He glanced out the window and then uncovered the painting and looked at it and then to Mary as though comparing the two.

"How would you feel if you did not like the painting?" he asked her.

"I'm sure I'll love it," she said.

"What if it was a painting by someone else, and you

didn't like it, how would you feel?" Mary thought about this for a moment. She had never known from the start if she was ever going to actually see the finished painting and she hadn't given it much thought.

"I don't know anything about art so I don't know what I could think," she offered weakly.

"Would you be upset if it didn't show you as how you feel you are?"

"If it made me look much worse than I am, I think I might be annoyed, but I don't think I would be angry." He nodded at this answer like it was the wisest she could have given, that she had given him something to think about.

"Would you like to see it?" he asked.

"Yes, please," she replied. She was nervous now that it was hideous, that she would hate it and would not be able to get it out of her head. He beckoned for her to come over and she walked across the room slowly and stopped beside the canvas. He moved out of the way,

"Come around and see," he said. He seemed very nervous, and she was afraid of her reaction, of hurting his feelings unintentionally. She stepped around and looked upon the painting, something she had wanted to do since the first day.

What she saw took her breath away, and her mouth fell open. It was her, unmistakably so, but not as she had ever seen or imagined herself. She looked beautiful, even with the scars shown clearly and not hidden in the least. There was a light coming from her image, and she suddenly felt a knot in her throat, and she felt tears coming to her eyes.

"Do you like it?" Spencer asked looking apprehensively at her.

"It's wonderful!" she said, and the effort of speaking set

forth a gush of tears, and she looked at Spencer. "Thank you for making me look like this," she said.

"This is how you look Mary, this is what people see every time they meet you," he said in reply. He looked relieved, and there was a smile on his face, and even his eyeballs looked lacquered.

"I never thought it could be like this," she said.

"I'm sorry it's come to an end," he said, and he rummaged in his pockets for something. He produced a coin purse and handed it to her.

"I can't take anything else from you, Mr. Spencer," she said withdrawing from him a little.

"This is less than you deserve for what you have enabled me to create," he said and taking hold of her hand he pressed the purse into it, closing her fingers around it. He let go of her then as though he felt he had been improper touching her in this way. He looked to the window again and once more he looked nervous and agitated. Mary's own gaze wandered to the window, and she saw a man pass by in a large hooded cape that completely covered him and hid his features. She looked back at Spencer, and he looked terrified.

"You better get going," he said to her, almost pushing her, "I have a lot of work to do." Still his eyes were on the window.

"Thank you again, so much," Mary said, and she picked up her coat and made for the door. She looked back at him once more, but he was not looking back at her. He studied the painting seriously, and she left without another word.

On her way home in the carriage, Mary wondered what had made him so fearful, but she couldn't know anything that was going on in his life. She felt the mass of the purse in her pocket and tried to guess at its weight and hence value. Though she was amazed and still emotionally charged by the painting, she wasn't all sad to be leaving this place for the last time. Ever since her encounter in the attic, she had been nervous there, and now with the added pressure of John asking her to stop doing it, she was relieved that it was all over. She wouldn't have to feel that fear any more, and she wouldn't have to lie to John any more either.

The main focus on her journey, something that wouldn't leave her mind, however, was the look of fear on Spencer's face. She had never seen anything like it before. It was so bad that she doubted her own fear of being attacked by the Dolocher had been so great.

# Chapter 59

Colonel Spencer arrived home on foot one evening to a very peculiar state of affairs at home. He knocked on the door of his house- he rarely had a key with him- and after waiting for a time, no one answered. He knocked more forcefully wondering what the hold up inside could be. Still, nobody came to answer him. This was very odd indeed, and not something he had ever come up against before. He looked up at the house and saw that there were candles burning lots of rooms, but he didn't see the silhouette of anyone passing by them. Spencer called out those servants whose names came immediately to mind but still there was nothing stirring within. He was getting annoyed now, and thoughts of punishment started to come into his head. Giving up on gaining entry by the front door he walked on down the street with the aim of coming around and entering through the servants and workers entrance at the rear of the house.

When he got there, however, he was surprised to find no one out the back either. He entered the house and called out from the kitchen. No one answered. This was very odd indeed. Spence didn't know what to make of this, but it did not feel good. He found that his heart was beating a little faster as his mind raced for some rational reason everyone could have disappeared like this. Nothing was coming to mind as he walked from room to room still calling his servants. Spencer realised that he had never known the house to be empty before. It roused a very odd and sinister feeling in his heart. Was the Devil here, and if so what had he done to everyone in the house. Spencer's head wanted him to leave the house at once, but his anger at the red faced tormentor was stronger, and he started to pace the house and ball his fists in fury.

"Who's here!" he shouted loudly, "Come and show yourself!"

This was it, Spencer was not going to run anymore. If now was his time to face what he had let loose on the world and face the same fate as his staff then so be it.

"Come on!" he shouted again, "Do you plan to hide in the shadows forever!" At this Spencer heard a noise come from above. It was like a couple of heavy footsteps on the landing. Spencer swallowed and took a step towards the door. His hand went to his sword, and he drew it. It felt good in his hand like he had been missing it for a long time. He looked along the blade and felt it gently. This could be the last time they would be in combat together, and he felt a great fondness for it at that moment. He should have made it part of his will to have it buried with him; perhaps someone would think of it after he was gone. With this last thought, he smiled and went out to the bottom of the stairs.

He stood there a moment looking up into the darkness at the top. He could imagine that red face coming from the dark and peering at him through the light, ready to whisk him away with that manic grin of his to his seat in Pandemonium. Spencer steeled himself and put one foot on the bottom step of the stairs. This was a battle, he thought, no different to the countless others he'd fought over the years. He thought of his men around him, all waiting for his lead and he started to walk up the stairs to meet his enemy head on.

About half way up he heard the noise of the heavy footsteps again, but this time there was a new noise, a sound that he had not expected to hear. It started as a low rumbling that he could not make out, but very quickly it became something much more familiar and terrifying. It was a low deep growl! Spencer knew now that this was no man he was up against, this truly was a beast, and there was little chance of coming out on top against the Devil himself. Spencer let out a roar of anger and plunged into the darkness with his sword thrust out before him. The growl became a sudden howl of an animal, and something very heavy and hairy barged against Spencer. He felt his blade tear flesh, and he twisted the sword for maximum damage. The creature let out a screech of pain as Spencer fell to the ground. His sword fell from his hands and disappeared into the darkness of the landing. Terrible thundering sounds rang out on the thickly carpeted floorboards of the stairs, and Spencer looked after the beast to see that it ran on four legs. It did not negotiate the steps well and fell as much as ran down to the bottom. With astonishment, he saw that it was no Devil, but was, in fact, the wolf. It had been hurt and was looking to escape. Spencer could not believe either his eyes or his luck. He leaned on an elbow and realised that his ribs had been badly bruised. The wolf was gone from sight now, and he heard it crash from room to room as he followed its progress with his ears, When a woman shrieked outside somewhere he knew that the wolf has finally found the back door and was running wild once more in the city. Colonel Spencer lay on his back and took some deep breaths. That had almost been the end of him. He could not believe his luck.

He had been a long time lying there in numbing pain before he began to wonder how the wolf had gotten into the house in the first place. It seemed obvious now that someone had duped the staff out of the house and brought the wolf in, leaving it upstairs to feed on him when he got home. There was only one person in the world who would want to do that to him, and that was the red faced man, the man he had upset so much by capturing his likeness in paints. He didn't know how much more of this nonsense he could take before it drove him completely around the bend.

## Chapter 60

The latest body hung from a spike hammered into a door. Blood had drained to the steps of the building, a disused shed on the land of a small livestock trader, and soaked into the scraps of strewn hay and the sodden earth. The woman was cut along all of her limbs, and the skin was splayed outward slightly so that the exposed bone could be seen inside. She was young, probably only about twenty years old and her face was scarred and bruised.

"Does anyone know her?" Alderman asked the soldier who stood guard over her body.

"No sir, not so far, sir."

James looked over the body, the only parts exposed were the limbs and head, but the clothes were slick and thick with dried blood, and he wondered if there were more wounds inside apart from the obvious impalement through her chest that she hung on.

"Someone must have heard this happen?" he said in vexation; incredulous already at the idea that maybe no one had.

"The men are asking around sir," the soldier assured him. At least they had the sense to do that, James thought. "This poor girl," he went on looking at her. It was moments like this that he was glad he had no children of his own, he didn't know how he could deal with something like this ever happening if he had.

Taking a thin quill from his pocket and wiping it with his handkerchief he peered into the crevasses made by the slicing of the limbs for some foreign object that might be in there. He didn't see anything, but he still had to examine the wound when the stake was removed, and that would be a more likely hiding place for this sadistic killer.

When the first soldiers came back with their reports from the surrounding houses no one had heard the noise of the hammer being smacked into the door. The reason for this was not that people were afraid and that they were keeping things to themselves but that there had been a terrible commotion on the street to the front to the houses whose backs looked onto the traders' yard.

When the Alderman enquired, he was told that apparently there some boys who had tied strings to some tin and had run up and down the streets causing an awful din and the resulting echoed noises brought all and sundry to their front doors to see what was going on. As a result of this, the body was able to be mounted without anyone seeing or hearing.

"We need to find out who those children were!" James said, they must have been paid by the killer. James then noticed that one of the soldiers was talking to his Sergeant in a furtive way that for some reason hooked James in. He knew it was something important, something that had been missed up to now, he didn't know how he knew, but he was sure he knew. He raced over to them, "What is it?" he demanded.

"This man says that there were reports of a similar disturbance at the site of the murder in the alley a few weeks ago."

"Why did you not report this then?" James asked of the man.

"I'm sorry sir, at the time it was not part of our investigation, it's only now that it seems to me to be relevant." The man was squirming, and his face had driven a deep red in embarrassment.

"Idiot!" James said but quickly went on to the Sergeant, "Find out if any of your men who were on duty at the other sites heard similar complaints, have a report to my house by this afternoon!"

James left the Sergeant to go about this business, and he waited again by the body. He looked around and was surprised that the rattling noise of Edwards' carriage had not been heard on the street yet. Was he not going to show for this one? This was one he would particularly enjoy. As much as he still hated to admit it, it was good to have eyes like Edwards' on these scenes, you never knew what he was going to spot or point out.

Soon after the cart came to take the woman away and James watched as two soldiers held her up and a third pulled the stake from her chest. When he finally loosened it, it came out with a sickening sludging sound, and some more viscera slopped to the ground as it did so. The men took her down, rearranged themselves and carried her to the cart a few feet away. James saw something flutter to the ground, and he looked at the stooping soldier who leaned to pick it up, blocking his view of what it was.

"What is that there?" he called, and the soldier turned and held up an envelope. James came over and took it and looked at it. He knew what it would say before seeing and when he did he saw his own name on the same paper that he'd seen twice before. It had been held up by the victims back against the door, but above the wound and as such it held only the smallest bit of dirt from falling to the ground.

There were no other markings on the envelope, and he pocketed it without a word to anyone.

"I'll ride in my own carriage to the morgue," he said and walked back over to it as the cart was slowly led away.

When they were away from the scene, James took the envelope from his pocket and looked it over again to be sure that there was nothing on the outside before he opened it.

There were two sheets inside again this time. This time he decided to look at what he knew was going to be a sketch. He opened the page, and he saw something he was not expecting. Instead of a charcoal coloured sketch of a gruesome body or some such scene his eyes were greeted with a street scene, buildings on either side and crowded street in the centre, many featureless heads and faces going about their business. What really stood out though was colour, one piece was coloured red, and it was one of the faces near the back of the crowd. It was a hooded figure who looked out unnoticed by all others in the scene, a devilish face, smiling in a sinister way as though it knew something that only he and the viewer were aware of. James thought for a moment of what Edwards had described of Spencer's hallucinations before putting the sketch on the seat beside him as he looked at the letter.

*Dear Alderman,*

    *I would have thought by now that you would have been closer to catching me, but it looks again like it will come down to the blind drunken luck of a blacksmith or some other tradesman to take me to task. I was very sorry to hear you are now also having trouble with a wolf. They are very beautiful creatures if treated and looked after well.*

    *I shall continue with my work, though I may now take a break, in the way that I did during my first round of killings. That way the people are all the more worried when they hear of my return.  You'll know soon enough which way I have decided.*

*Yours,*

*The Dolocher*

# Chapter 61

When Mullins got into the house, Kate was not there, and he cursed her for always being out and about, constantly visiting people or going to the market. He paced back and forth in the small room, and his temper grew as he began to feel constrained, like and animal in a cage. If he hadn't believed at first what Edwards had said to him he certainly believed it now, there was no way anyone other than he could have known about the bruise on her hip unless she had done what he had said she had. His anger mixed with terse emotion and the idea of losing her and the life he had built for himself in these last couple of years. How could she have done this to him?

He sat down at the table and images of his time in 'The Black Dog' roiled in his head. It was a terrible experience, and he believed for a time himself that he was destined for the gallows. He recalled his despair, and that the saving grace to him in there was that he had Kate in his life. And all the time she was doing this behind his back! It didn't matter to him at all that she might think she was doing it for his benefit; as far as he was concerned, it would have been better if he had died than for her to do this in his name.

A long time had passed before he heard her at the door. In this time he had calmed significantly and sat resigned and patiently at the table for her to come in. She was surprised to see him at this time of the day.

"What are you doing home?" she asked him, setting her basket on the table. He didn't answer her, and he saw the look of concern come over her face. She looked at him and waited for a response. "What is it Tim, you're scaring me?"

"I want to ask you one question, and I want to you to answer me only one word, either yes or no," he said slowly. She nodded that she understood, but he could see the fear in her face, the fear that he already knew what she had done. He faltered for a moment now that he could see her in front of him, and tried to convince himself that maybe things could be alright if he never knew for sure. But he couldn't go with that idea, however blissful he might imagine it could be. "Did you sleep with a man to get me out of gaol?" Kate burst into tears and collapsed on to the table. Her sobs were heavy and seemed to be choking the air out of her. His hand went out automatically to console her, but he stopped it, knowing what this display meant.

"I'm so sorry Tim, I just wanted you to be free!" she wailed in one fast gasp. She looked up at him imploringly, "I thought they were going to kill you!" she cried. He didn't know what to say. Up to now, he had been angry and hurt but angry at the idea of it. Now that he knew that it was true, was something that had actually taken place, he felt dead as if he was no longer there but just an ethereal watcher of this scene. It was like he too was waiting for Timothy Mullins, the blacksmith, to speak.

"How could you do that to me?" he said slowly, his eyes cast down on the table now.

"I didn't want you to die!" she wailed.

"This is worse," he said after a long pause, and he heard her sobbing start up once more.

He let her cry for a long time while he sat there. He would look at her head, the hair falling about and her shoulder bobbing every now and then, but he could feel no compassion for her, no need to comfort her. She sat up much later still and wiped her eyes, her face was puffed up, and she looked terrible and pale.

"Did he tell you himself?" she asked finally.

"He told me what you had done, but not that it was with him until he was dashing away in his carriage and I couldn't catch up with him."

"He's an evil man," Kate said.

"I'm not married to him," Mullins said, and even to himself, it had the tome of finality.

"What are you going to do?" she asked him. It was growing dark out now, and there were no candles lit in the room.

"I'm going to do something the next time I see him, I won't know what exactly until I'm already doing it." He knew he own rage and anger and what it would lead him too and also that he was in no control of it. Right now he welcomed that loss of control.

"Tim you can't, you'll end up in gaol again, or worse. He knows people everywhere, and he has the money to do what he wants!" she pleaded with him.

"That's of no regard to me." There was another long silence, and Kate fidgeted in her chair.

"What about me?" she asked.

"You will do what you want, but you will no longer be living here with me. I won't throw you out tonight but I will go to work tomorrow, and you will be gone when I get home," his coldness was hard to maintain, but he thought this would be the only way he could get through this.

"No, please Tim, don't do this!" she dropped to her knees and grabbed at him, but he pushed her hands away.

"I haven't done anything Kate, you did this," he told her

in a low voice. He stood up and moved away from the table. Kate stayed where she was on the floor.

"I'm so sorry Tim," she said crying again. "I did it for you." He didn't look at her nor answer her. He pulled on his coat and walked to the door.

"I expect you'll be asleep when I get home," and he went out into the cold evening.

Once outside he felt the full tilt of the heartache slap him, and he walked quickly towards the river so that no one he knew might see his teary face and hear the bellow he would have to release from the depths of his soul soon. He rushed on slipping and sliding at times on the icy surface until he was crossing the Liffey and in a place where he was alone and not himself and he cried and roared and shook with anger. His life as he knew it draining from him in once last great gasp.

# Chapter 62

Kate cried solidly for an hour after Mullins left that night. She was so ashamed of herself and how things had worked out. At moments she grew into a rage, and sometimes they were aimed at Edwards and other they were squared at the ungratefulness of her husband. She had done this awful thing for him, to see that he was not hanged for murders she knew he had not committed. Did he think that she had enjoyed what she was doing? It had broken her heart to do it, and she felt cheap and disgusting all through the act and ever since. Edwards had done this for his own amusement, and she had since found out that he had played no part in Tim's release, that there had been another murder and that was why he had been let out. Her mind raced from one hurt to another, and she grew very tired of it all.

When she finally stopped crying she chewed on a crust of bread and drank some water. She was cold now, and she set herself the task of lighting a fire. This took her mind off things for a while but as soon as she was done the world came back in on her. She shivered as the heat hit her and she wrapped a shawl around her shoulders. What was she going to do? She could tell by Mullins that he was devastated and she knew he was not the type of man to let these things drop easily. She probably shouldn't be here when he came home tonight. Where could she go? The obvious place was to Mary and Sarah, to the place that she herself had once called home, but she was so ashamed of what she had done that she didn't think she could face them. If she lied to them, it would be worse when they found out the truth. She hated Edwards, so there was no way she was going to go there. There was no one else she could think of who might take her in, she had no family and only two real friends.

The future was trying to come to her, but she resisted it. She saw herself going to Madam Melanie and asking if she could stay for one night but beds and room were at a premium there, and she knew that the only way this could happen was if she agreed to work once more for the house. She couldn't go back to that life, not now that she had seen a life without it. She had been so happy these last two years, it had really been the happiest time of her life. She longed to hope that Tim would see that what she did she did for him alone and he would be able to forgive her. She couldn't see it happening, but she knew above all else that what she wanted was a life with him. He was a stubborn and proud man, and this would be an almost mortal wound to him, she could understand that but surely his love for her, which she knew was as real as her own, would bring him round in the end.

"Don't be a foolish woman!" she said out loud, she would have to stop this silly day dreaming. None of it was going to happen. Tim was going to come home later with whiskey in his belly, drunk and these thoughts of what she had done in his mind swirling around and getting worse and worse and worse. The truth of the matter was that he had a temper on him when drunk and though he had never raised a hand to her before she was probably in danger being hit tonight.

Kate got up and packed a bundle in a blanket and wrapped herself against the cold of the night outside. She looked over the home she had enjoyed so much one last time, and the tears welled in her eyes, and she thought that this was the last time she would see it. She left and closed the door with a bang, leaving her key inside on the table, a visual clue for when Tim came home that she was already gone.

It was bitterly cold out as she walked the streets. She had no destination in mind, but she found that she walked in the direction of Christ Church. The ground was icy, and a few times she almost lost her footing. Businesses were closed, and the taverns were the only real sources of noise on the streets. She passed Tim's preferred cabin, but she could not see inside to see if he was in there. She hoped that he was not looking out and able to see her. It would be too hard to see him now that she had to leave. She walked on and soon found that she was outside the blacksmith. She looked at the building and thought of the times she'd been inside, she thought of Tim working and his muscles, and he did so. She wished for the warmth of that place now and the protection of those muscles.

As she stood there, she wondered again if she knew of anyone who would take her in to save her from going to Melanie's. She was desperate, and in her desperation, she even thought briefly of going to the Alderman to see if he could do anything to help her, but she quickly dismissed this as ridiculous. She looked around, and she saw the basement barred window of 'The Black Dog, ' and she recalled the time she had spent in there. She tried to convince herself that had been worse than now but she didn't feel it. When she was in there, she had been a single woman, unmarried and being punished for her job. Now her whole life was gone, she may be free to walk where she pleased, but she had nothing. It was so cold, and the wind whipped up and made it seem even more so. She was sure that this was the most miserable moment of her entire life.

# Chapter 63

There were ten children in all, each one of them terrified looking as they stood in a line as if about to be shot by firing squad. Alderman James arrived and looked them over, they were suitably scared for his needs. He walked up and down before them and then suddenly rounded on one boy in the middle of the group.

"Who paid you to make all the noise the other night?" The boy stood upright but failed to speak, even though he seemed to be trying to. "What about you?" James said turning to a little girl next to this boy.

"A man," she said. She was trembling, and it softened James a little. He took a step back from them and sighed.

"What man?" They all looked at one another. "What did he look like?"

"He was in a black cloak with a hood," a boy, a little older than the others said. James looked at him. "His face was red," the boy added. James instantly recognised this as the man who had given the letter to the boy to bring to his house. This moment of elation was sort lived, however, as he knew that their children would know or remember no more about this man than the boy with the letter had when questioned.

"Can you describe him better?" James asked this boy.

"He was a gentleman, I could tell by his voice."

"What did he sound like?" This seemed to perplex and embarrass the boy.

"Well," he fidgeted and looked to the other children for help, "He sounded like a gentleman."

"What did he say to you?" James asked, knowing he was not going to get anything of use in relation to the voice from them.

"Only that he would give us money for making noises at a certain time."

"Did say what would happen if you didn't make the noise?"

"He said he was the Devil and he would take us to Hell if we didn't do it!" the little girl suddenly piped up and she started crying, as though being in that same moment again. James could see the image of the Devil looking at him through the crowd in the picture he'd received at the site where the most recent body had been displayed.

"He wasn't the real devil, dear," he said wanting to reassure the girl and the others. He didn't want them to believe that such a thing might be possible. It didn't seem to make any difference to them.

"He said it we did it we would never see him again," the boy said.

"Where did he talk to you?" James asked.

"In the lane around the back of the houses," the boy said, angling his head as though he was using it to point.

James turned to the soldiers and said,

"Go around these houses here again, ask them all this time did they see a man in a black hooded cloak or anyone who may have been painted red in the weeks before the murders." He then turned back to the children, "I promise you that this was not the Devil you were speaking to, he is a very bad person, to be sure, but he is a man." He wondered would they recognise this man if he were in front of them, without the cloak and hood or the make-up? He knew that if he asked them he was only going to give them nightmares about coming face to face with Beelzebub once more. He dismissed the children, feeling that they were going to be of no use and if he thought of anything he could be able to find them again easy enough.

When he was left alone, James wondered about Spencer. If Edwards was right, he was the man behind all of this. Was he a mad man, seeing the Devil all about him because he was going about dressed himself as the Devil? Was the last sketch how he saw the world, a sea of faceless bodies and a laughing Devil in the near distance, egging him on or mocking him to action? James had seen men committed to asylums before and in all those cases it was not a pretty sight. Spencer hadn't seemed wild or manic the few times that he had met him, but when James looked back, he seemed to recall Spencer looking around and being fidgety quite a lot. Perhaps he was at the early stage of his madness then. Then there was the sketch! This had simply popped into his mind at that instant. Had this been the work of Spencer too? Was it almost an admission of guilt, a man wanting to be caught? It was looking more and more likely that it had been Spencer all along.

There was no way around it, Spencer would have to be questioned. It would be an awkward scene, and there could be divisions within some of the circles these army men moved in. Spencer was also a member of the Hellfire Club, and that was another obstacle that would have to be overcome. If Spencer was the man they were looking for it would also come as quite a shock to the general populace, they weren't too surprised when the identity of the Dolocher was revealed to be one of their own, but for a killer to be a gentleman, an officer in the Kings Army? That was quite a different matter, and there was no way of telling how they might react to it.

James went outside and got into his carriage, asking the

driver to take him home. It seemed so often he was in this confined box going from place to place and contemplating everything and living with the frustration that he knew nothing, that he was ways behind these killers and never got a break on them. He often thought that if Cleaves had not mistaken Mullins for a woman that night and been subdued by the blacksmith he would still be going about killing in Thomas Olocher's name and James would be no closer to catching him that he had been at the time.

It didn't feel to him that Spencer was the man but the evidence did seem to be pointing that way and he couldn't ignore it any more. He wondered if he should bring Edwards with him when he questioned the Colonel. Edwards had turned him in, so there was obviously no love lost but did that mean that the Hellfire Club was going to let one of its members go down like this? He could already feel the pressure that would come with his even talking to Spencer about the killings let alone arresting him as the perpetrator.

# Chapter 64

It was Kate's second night on the streets. She had spent the first night hiding in a place that she thought she would be completely safe, once, that was, she was not discovered. Late on the first night, she came on the idea that she could go to Lord Muc's land. He had sheds and outhouses there, and she felt sure she would be able to conceal herself in one of them and go unnoticed. She knew Muc by reputation, and he would most likely stumble home near dawn and sleep in the main house, she could be gone long before he got up. If this was not the way things went, she still felt sure that she would be able to hide herself in one of his barns so that even if he did come in there, he would not see her. She also felt safe in the knowledge that no one in their right mind would come there to steal from him.

Kate arrived there at a very late hour. It was almost bright out such was the force of the moon, but also shadows clung like draped cloth over everything. She watched Lord Muc's gates for a time, searching with her eyes for any movement beyond. All was still for a long time before she decided to go over and duck inside. Her heart was pounding as she hunkered down and again looked over the shed and house for anything living. When she was again satisfied she ran another short distance to one of the sheds.

In here she felt some of the chill of the night lift. The wind no longer rattled her body. She looked about and saw that there were no animals in here but that there was some hay where she could lie, and there was enough to cover herself and her bundle as well. Soon she was comfortable and warm, and with her nervous energy exhausted as well as her mental and hence physical fatigue, she soon started to drift in that state between sleep and wakefulness. She wasn't expecting a decent night's sleep, but she thought a rest would do her a world of good.

It wasn't long before she began to regret her decision to come to this place. She woke to an odd sound, and she cleared some hay from her head so as to hear better. It was animals, they were moving around in the other sheds in the compound. They sounded agitated, and she wondered what could be the matter with them. Then she heard a pig, and it brought her immediately back to that night in 'The Black Dog' when Thomas Olocher was brought in, and all the pigs squealed in the night and tried to force their way into the yard of the gaol. Some more pigs sounded out now in Muc's sheds, and she jumped to her feet and looked about terrified and slow with sleep. The animals were clearly moving around in the corrals now, and she could hear the wood of the fences crack and bend in the otherwise silent night.

They were trying to evade something or someone. This thought came to her, and she thought straight away of the killer who now prowled the streets, who killed somewhere and dropped bodies off in spots where the Dolocher had killed. Was this the place where it happened? Was it possible that the noises she was hearing were not animals but of people, trapped and about to be killed by some frenzied maniac? She stopped herself, she was getting way out of hand, and the panic had made her think like this- coupled with only waking up. Of course, it was animals, she could hear clearly that they were pigs, a noise that she had heard many times before.

Kate managed to calm somewhat, but then she heard a new noise. It was a person this time, there was no mistaking it, and they were breathing heavily. It must be Lord Muc she thought, he had in come home without her hearing or had he been at home all the time? She gathered up her belongings, she wasn't safe here now and would have to get away. She didn't know what he was doing or what he was going to do. The animals were squealing now worse than ever, and she could feel the fear in those noises, a fear that she shared with the pigs.

Kate crept out of the shed and looked around. She could tell that the pigs were in the shed closest to the house. The whole place was rocking, and the noise was getting to new heights. She heard something metal, like knives or cleavers, sharpening and she couldn't take it anymore, and she threw caution to the wind and set off towards the gate. As she began to run, she heard the roar of a man like he was entering combat and she heard the implement pierce and tear flesh and one of the animals screamed out in pain, a new sound that went right through her and caused her to run ever faster away.

Though she hadn't seen anything and wasn't sure what had actually happened, Kate was sure that there was no way she was going back to that place. She would have rather stayed in the 'Nunnery' in the gaol than in one Muc's sheds again. Now she walked as the night wore on with no more ideas as to where to go. She was terrified of everything but had no clue what to do with herself. Every second was spent fighting her urges to go to Melanie's or even worse still to Edwards' house.

As she walked from Nicolas Street into Bride's Alley she heard something fall and roll along the ground, it was a metallic sound, like something tin perhaps. Kate looked about and saw nothing that could have been the source of the noise and no person who might have dropped something. She crossed quickly to Chancery Lane, and then she rounded the bend where she could see Golden Lane. As she walked towards this, she heard something behind her, and she turned just in time to realise that they were footsteps and someone was coming behind her at speed. She didn't see a face, but she felt the massive weight of man careen into her and send her flying to the ground. She was completely winded, and she could make no noise.

A heavy punch thundered into her ribs, and this made it even harder for her to breath, and still, she could make no noise, or cry out for help.

"Get away!" a voice she knew called out and the weight on her lifted, and the man was gone, running away and out of sight as quickly as he had returned. She lay there as the face of Edwards, concerned and almost in tears, came into view.

"Are you alright?" he asked, helping her to a sitting position. She nodded, but she still couldn't talk yet. "Did you see who he was?" he asked. She shook her head, she hadn't seen anything really except his shape. She started to get up, and he helped her. Her breath was back now, and she looked at Edwards properly for the first time.

"Why did you tell him!" she shouted suddenly and she pounded on his chest and began to sob. Her energy quickly dissipated and after the attack, her adrenalin was sapping now too, and she slumped down until he had to take her weight, "Bastard!" she managed to say weakly before she closed her eyes and fell unconscious.

# Chapter 65

The wolf was not caught on that drunken evening that the reward was offered. Some dogs paid the price for their resemblance through alcohol eyes, and one pig was killed perhaps in memory of that night when that breed was the hunted animal. Not one man even saw the beast that night that anyone can be sure of.

Mullins had known this would be the case. In all of Dublin, he knew of only one man who he thought would be capable of bringing in the wolf, and that man was Lord Muc. Each morning he woke, Mullins expected to hear that the reward had been claimed and that it would be the former gang leader who had claimed it. He took some comfort in knowing that Muc probably thought the same about him, but he'd had enough contact with that creature without looking for more. It was true that Mullins was the one who had brought down the Dolocher, but despite all the rumour and fear that had been about, the Dolocher was only a man in the end. Mullins was also drunk that night and had he seen him coming he might have fled. But he didn't see it coming, and he had fought only to protect himself. What a shock that night turned out to be, an instant sobriety when he saw that it was his friend who had tried to kill him, who had been killing all those people for so long, whom Mullins thought had been a victim of this same killer.

Any time Cleaves came to mind of late, he could think only of the empty grave and wonder where his body was now. Who was this new killer and why had he dug up the grave? He could see that it was part of the whole linking of these crimes with those of the Dolocher, but none of it made any sense to him.  Mullins looked out and decided that he could do with some of the cold fresh air that was on offer outside and that he was going to go for a walk.

He walked out towards the river and looked into the murky water.  Floats of ice moved here and there on the surface.  He crossed over at Queens Bridge and walked on the other side of the river along Arran Quay and then onto King's Inn Quay.  Though it was only a matter of a couple of hundred yards from where he conducted most of his life, it felt like a new place altogether to be on the north side of the city.

This was where the rich people lived, the Alderman, this man Edwards who had a contract on his whereabouts, the politicians of the parliament.  They were the people who could do what they wanted and never have to give the consequences a second thought.  As he walked over here, however, Mullins began to feel out of place and somehow in danger.  He had a feeling that he shouldn't be seen outside the regular neighbourhood, memories of this same feeling as he fled Cleaves' grave boiled in him.  He felt he was somehow implicating himself in something being on this side of the river, a place he didn't belong.  He crossed back at Exeter Bridge, and he could almost physically feel a weight being lifted as he stepped back on the south side.

He felt the chill of the wind hit him head on as he walked up the incline of Parliament Street.  He continued around onto Cork Hill and then to Copper Alley.  He decided he should start for home as the bruised sky looked threatening.  He walked more briskly along John's Lane, looking up at the Cathedral as he passed, a building that caught the eye of everyone who ever passed by this way.

As he came on to Winetavern Street, he heard a call.  It

was a young voice, and for a moment he thought that it could be Scally, who he had not seen for some time now. He stopped so his heavy steps would not impede the sound and listened. The cry came out again. It was a boy's voice, someone who was scared and the second call had the rounded echo of tears in it. Mullins followed the sound and came to a thin alley between buildings. Again he was in a nervous situation as to what it might look like if he was to come upon a murder. But he knew that he had no choice, this was the type of man he was, and he went headlong into the alley.

Rounding the corner, he came upon the sight of a boy of about twelve years old brandishing a bit of stick out in front of himself that he was clearly using to try to fend off a man. Mullins had never seen the boy before, that he knew of, but he did recognise the man. He didn't know his name, but he had often seen the man in the streets, and sometimes in the cabin. He regarded Mullins with a guilty face, but that quickly turned into a scowling one. Mullins looked at the boy and nodded towards the exit,

"Get going lad," he said. The man looked to Mullins again warily as the boy used the full width of the alley to come around to Mullins' side and then he ran off without a word. Mullins didn't know what had been going on and he didn't want to know; all he desired now was to leave this lane without having to do any harm to this fella.

"The blacksmith, skulking the alleys as ever," the man said. His voice was a little slurred, and Mullins thought he was drunk. He turned without saying anything and walked away. "If there's another body found I'll be sure to remember this!" the man called out after him. Mullins almost stopped and went back but with no drink in his system, he was able to remain in control, and he continued on.

He was annoyed enough, however, to stop into the cabin on his way home. As he stepped inside, he was greeted by an atmosphere of abandon and cheerfulness.

"What's going on?" he asked the first man he made contact with.

"The wolf is caught," the man said to him.

"By who?"

"Lord Muc," the man was pointing at the far side of the room. Mullins looked over, and he could see Lord Muc sitting down with a circle around him. As Mullins came closer, he was then able to see the huge animal on the table. In this setting, it looked twice the size it had when he faced it in the alley. There were some heavy wounds inflicted on the animal and Muc was the worse for wear himself. Blood oozed from various cuts, and he was dazed with possible whacks to the head. He was telling his tale of conquest and didn't notice Mullins come in. The blacksmith smiled and backed away, he'd been right about who was going to bring it in.

He left the cabin to its celebrations and walked the short distance home. As he walked, he thought about Scally, and he wondered what he was doing now. He really hoped that he had not become a victim of the killer and his body had not shown up yet. He missed the lad at the shop, and he felt like the world had abandoned him these last few years. It was in a fine melancholy that he found his chair in front of the fire a short time later.

## Chapter 66

When Kate came to she was in a place, she had never seen before. It was a room not too unlike those at Madam Melanie's, but this was not her place, nor did it seem to be any other whorehouse. It was a comfortable room with a fire going against the far wall from the couch she lay on. The attack! It came back to her in a shocking pain in her ribs, and she sat up,

"Don't worry, you're safe here," a voice said calmly. She knew it was Edwards without having to look and she recalled then that he had come to her rescue. She lay back down.

"Did you see who it was?" she asked him.

"No, did you?"

"No."

They were silent for a while. Kate was relieved that she had not been killed, but she resented being in his debt.

"Are you in pain?" he asked.

"Not really," she answered as pain shot up her side. "Why were you following me?"

"In case just such an event were to take place." She thought about thanking him, felt that it would have been appropriate under the circumstances, but she couldn't bring herself to utter those words.

"Why did you tell Tim what I did?" There was a long silence, and finally, she looked over at him for an answer. He was looking at the floor.

"I'm sorry for doing that," he said and then looked up at her. She was taken aback by the look on his face and in particular in his eyes; they were moist, and she had never seen him like this before. It put her on her guard as she felt something akin to her natural pity rise up inside.

"You can see what's happened as a result of it?" she wanted this to hurt him, feeling as she did that he was vulnerable just then. He nodded but didn't say anything. "I've been made homeless by it too," she said.

"You can stay here in this place, it will cost you nothing," Edwards said.

"This is yours?"

"Yes, it looks out over the river," he said indicating the window.

"I'll never forgive you for what you've done," she said, "I want you to know that. I will stay here happily as I have no other place to go, but you have had me in bed for the last time, and I will never hold you in anything other than contempt for the rest of my life!"

"I understand," Edwards replied.

Kate was confused; this was not the Edwards that she knew. She had seen him in dark moods and even cruel ones, but this, this was something entirely different. She wondered what was going through his head. For a moment she felt senses of the night they had been together when Tim was in gaol, and she was surprised the electric jolt it gave her, and she compared it to other times they had been to bed. She was in too agitated a state to notice it at the time, but there was a hunger in him that night that had been more than lust. Now that she was able to look over it with more objective eyes she realised that it had been so different to any time before and then she knew what it was. He was in love with her, it wasn't all just words and games- these were just the only way he knew to go about things- he actually loved her, and he was relishing her that night as he had never relished anything in his life up to that moment. Kate suddenly felt embarrassed in his company, and she looked away from him.

Edwards seemed to get some sense of how she was feeling, and he sat upright and cleared his throat, putting on a more normal and confident air, though one that in this instance she could see through easily.

"You'll need something to eat perhaps before you retire?" he stood up. She went to resist this but she was hungry, and she nodded absently. He left the room, and she looked into the flicker of the fire and wondered what time it was. It was still and quiet outside, but there was no hint of daylight through the windows.

Edwards came back with some bread and cheese. He had a pot of water in his other hand and this he brought to the fireplace and began to heat it.

"This will do fine," Kate said.

"It would be better to get something warm inside you before you go to sleep," Edwards said as he stood up from the fireplace. He stood for a moment as though contemplating something and then he said, "I'll leave you alone, here is the key, I do not have a copy. I will come see that you are able to settle in sometime tomorrow." He moved quickly for the door,

"Wait!" she said, and he stopped, half in the room and half out. She had called out to him in a moment of pity, which was in her nature, but she couldn't tell him anything she thought he might want to hear. "Thank you for saving me," she said.

"I was there, and there was no other course of action I would have been capable of taking," he said, and then he bowed and left the room. She heard a door close down a short hallway, and she was alone.

She moved closer to the fire so as to keep an eye on the water as it heated. The bread was fresh, and the cheese was cut thickly, and she enjoyed the weight of it in her hand. She was reminded of the day she herself was let out of the 'Black Dog, ' and she had slept in a big bed in Edwards' house and the opulence she had seen that she had never been privy to before that day. It was an odd feeling for her to know for sure now that Edwards was in love with her. She wondered why he had thrown her out after only two days at his home, but she knew the answer despite not seeing it for a time. The whole period she was there, from the moment of arrival, straight after they went to bed and all the next day she had asked incessantly about the fate of Tim. This must have heavily jarred on the ideas of a man in love. She had seen men do very odd things over the years and the odder the thing, the more likely it was that love was at the root of it. She had wounded his pride, hurt his love by all but saying that she did not and would not return it, could not return it. He was an impetuous man, she'd always know that about him, but that he was capable of love, this was the first time she had ever thought that.

# Chapter 67

When someone knocked on the door to the apartment on Skinners Row, Mary wasn't too surprised. Neighbours would often drop by looking for something or offering something left over, and Sarah was forever going out without her key. This time, however, the visitor was an entirely unexpected one. Colonel Spencer stood at her door, and he looked to be in an extreme state of agitation. His hair was matted to his forehead, and he started when she opened the door as though he'd not expected it. He rushed into the room and closed the door, and then went to the window and looked down onto the street.

"What's the matter?" Mary asked when she was over her initial surprise.

"Are you alone here?" he asked, and he looked around the room.

"Yes, yes," she said and then she grabbed him by the arm, so he looked at her, "What is it?" she asked again, her voice calm and soft. He stilled and then seemed to be following the lines of the scar on her face.

"I think I've done something terrible," he said, and he rushed to the window and looked out again.

"Is someone following you?" Mary asked, coming over to look outside too.

"Not someone," Spencer answered.

"What then?"

"I've displeased him somehow," he was getting agitated again, so Mary grabbed him once more to make him look at her face.

"Who?"

"I painted him," Spencer said, his voice trembling, "and

since then he has come after me, everywhere I go!" he wept pitifully. Mary recalled the image of the Devil she was sure she'd seen that day in his attic.

"The painting of the Devil?" she asked, and he nodded. "You think the Devil has been following you?" She wondered now if he was not drunk or drugged, she could smell none of these things off him, but that didn't prove anything.

"He's been taunting me, and he's made me do some things, I can't even remember them!" he wailed.

"What things?" Mary was uneasy asking this question, she was not sure that she wanted to hear the answer.

"He sent the wolf after me!"

"The wolf?" Mary said, "The wolf is dead."

"Yes, but before that, he came for me at my home,"

"What have you done?" she asked him and her feeling of dread grew worse as the answer became more and more apparent to her.

"It's me," he said, tears streaming down his face. He dropped to his knees and grabbed hold of her skirts in a bundle. She backed away, and he fell to all fours.

"What are you talking about?" Her voice was sterner now, and she was getting angry at his display of remorse. "Did you do something to John?" she asked, and now it was her turn to weep. He nodded though he was still facing the ground. Mary's heart sank, and she hit out at him, "What did you do, what did you do?" she shouted.

"I'm the one who killed all those people," he said, and he looked up at her. His eyes were wild now, and he looked terrified. "I didn't know I was doing it, he made me do it all!"

"Did you kill John?" Mary asked, dropping to her knees

to be of a height with him.

"I don't know who any of them were," Spence said, "I don't remember anything, but I know I did it all."

"Why?" Mary cried harder now and clumped down on her side. This was the confirmation she had been dreading for weeks now, that John was dead. She could feel the truth of it in her soul.

"He's unhappy with me, I don't know why!" Spencer went on, and then a look came over his face as though he had suddenly realised something. "I have to destroy it," he said. Mary wasn't listening to him now though she heard these words.

He stood up and seemed to have collected himself. Mary sidled up against a chair and looked at him warily. He seemed to have calmed considerably now that he had made his confession. She wondered was he going to kill her now too. She hadn't been this scared since she had witnessed the murder of her aunt by Thomas Olocher.

Spencer looked down on her, and she could see pity in his eyes.

"I'm sorry to have troubled you with this," he said in a calm and gentlemanly voice, "But you are the only purely good person I have ever met." Mary didn't know what to say to this. He ran a hand through his hair and straightened his clothes out, and looked out the window once more. This time he didn't seem at all frightened or worried about what he might see. "I have to go to the hill and destroy it; to hell with what Edwards has to say about it!" Mary started at the mention of the name and wondered if it was the same Edwards who had done so much harm to Kate.

"Did you kill John?" Mary asked feebly once again. He

looked down at her, and she could see he was mostly if not all the way back in control of his faculties.

"Has his body been found?" he asked. She shook her head. "Then I haven't killed him, all of them have been found," he said. She felt relief flood her body.

"Thank you!" she said as though he had done her some great service.

"Don't thank me, Mary, it was luck alone that saved your man, I had no control over this, it was all his doing." Was he still talking about the Devil? "Again, I'm very sorry to have burdened you with this, you must go to the Alderman with what I have told you." He made for the door and opened it and looked back at her one more time, "It was a great honour to paint you, Mary, I hope you find your man soon." She thanked him again, and he slipped out the door. Mary got up, went to the window and looked outside and saw him come out of the building and walk in the direction of Hell. Her hands were shaking as she pulled on her cloak. She had to get to a soldier at once.

## Chapter 68

The light of the day was just about to disappear when Edwards and Lord Muc rode up the pathway to the hunting lodge on Montpelier Hill. They were coming here as payment of Muc's price for following Mullins around. Edwards looked at Muc to see his reaction upon seeing the house.

"I thought it would be much bigger," Muc said.

"It's quite big enough for its use," Edwards said. They rode up to the stables and tied up the horses and then walked the perimeter to stretch out their legs after the long ride out.

"What do you do up here anyway?" Muc asked when they had done a full circuit and were back at the entrance ramp.

"Nothing really, we eat and drink and listen to music," Edwards replied.

"And women?"

"And women, yes of course," Edward smiled as though this was a given that had no need of verbalisation.

"If you get up to nothing, why have this place so remote?" There was suspicion in Muc's voice and look, but it was good natured, as though he knew full well what went on here and he knew he was not going to hear it from Edwards' mouth.

"We like the quiet life," Edwards replied grinning. "Shall we go inside?" he put his hand out to indicate the guest should go first. Muc walked up the ramp and opened the door, Edwards saw him notice that it was not locked. They went in and Muc looked about the room, taking in the stone walls and the paintings and animal heads that adorned the walls. Then his eyes settled on something, and Edwards followed his gaze with pride to the large painting of the Devil that Spencer had done for the club. Muc walked towards it as though he were drawn to it; Edwards certainly also thought it had this quality and he could see why it had driven Spencer so mad. To look into those life-like eyes day after day and week after week would be enough to send any man potty.

"What the hell is this?" Muc said his voice incredulous.

"You've said it!" Edwards laughed. Muc looked at him, and then realising what he meant, looked back at the painting.

"I'd heard rumours about this, but I never thought it would be anything like this." It seemed to Edwards that this might be the first thing to impress Lord Muc in many, many years.

"It really is amazing, isn't it? And a perfect likeness." Edwards couldn't help but smile at this joke of his.

Muc was about to say something else when there was a crash, and both men looked in the direction of the sound.

"Who's there?" Edwards called out. There was no reply, and Muc pulled a long knife from inside his tunic and gripped it tightly. Edwards couldn't be sure, but he thought that for the first time he may have seen a moment of fear in Muc. Could it be that he was a God fearing man underneath all that mayhem and that he was unnerved by the devil?

A loud whoosh sound went up, and flames suddenly streaked across one of the tapestries on the wall and began to spread across some of the paintings.

"The place has been doused in something!" Muc shouted, and the flames went up and took hold of the roof.

There was movement in the back room, and a shape ran past the doorway, and Muc and Edwards set off in pursuit.

As they ran in through the archway, the fire seemed to run on ahead of them, rushing up walls and across the roof with great and terrific speed. The man who ran was pulling things down behind him and spreading the flames still further across the rugs and carpets and up the legs of tables and chairs. Just as it looked as though he were about to escape through a rear door a beam of the roof cracked and he paused long enough for the section of the roof just in front of him to collapse and miss him by mere inches, flecking burning pieces of wood onto his clothes which must have been soaked in the accelerant also as they went up quickly.

Muc and Edwards stopped in their pursuit at the shocking sight of this and looked on dumbfounded. The heat was becoming unbearable, and the man cried out in pain as he rushed about trying to remove his clothes. Through the shimmering heat haze, Edwards saw the man's eyes, and he knew at once that it was Spencer. At that same moment, Muc grabbed Edwards' arm,

"We need to get out of here," and he indicated a door that hadn't been blocked by flames.

"I have to get him out," Edwards said pulling away.

"Suit yourself," Muc shouted, and he strode to the door, uninterested in being of any assistance to Edwards in his folly.

Edwards held his cloak up to the heat and moved through the archway and came to where Spencer was,

"Spencer, it's me, Edwards, we need to get you out of here!" he shouted and he rushed forward and threw his cloak around the spiralling Colonel. As he was wrapped in this Spencer lost his balance and fell over sideways but Edwards managed to take his weight, and he saw the fear in Spencer's eyes. Did he even know what was going on around him, Edwards wondered as he pulled him away towards the door Muc had left by. Edwards' lungs were filling with smoke, and he was feeling weak, but he was near enough to the door now that he could hear the oxygen burn as it whooshed in and he stumbled out into the light, and both of them fell to the ground. There was a blur in the light, and suddenly Edwards was cold and soaking wet, and the shock sent both men to their feet. Edwards looked to see the smiling face of Muc with a long trough, formerly filled with water for the horses, held in the air where he had doused the two men and put out the flames.

"Was that entirely necessary?" Edwards said wiping the run off from his face.

"I could have let you both burn," Muc said with a shrug. He looked at Spencer who was coughing and still looked wild eyes with fright.

"Spencer, it's fine now, you're safe," Edwards said to him.

"You know him?"

"He's one of the members here. A colonel in the army."

Loud cracks came from all over the house, and they manoeuvred Spencer to a safe distance from the building and looked on as it began to crumble to the ground. At this Spencer began to come out his trance and he looked on with seeming hope for something. Edwards was amazed by the spectacle himself, he had never seen a structure burn so fast and begins to fall down like this. Of course, it was only the wooden sections and the ramps of the entrance that were collapsing, the stone structure stayed put, but it was soon a hollow shell, smouldering and reeking of scorched wood and charred fabrics.

"Is it gone?" Spencer said after a time. His voice was filled with a dreaded hope.

"Is what gone?" Edwards asked.

"The painting," Spencer looked at him as if entreating him to go and look as he could not bear to do so himself. So that's what this little escapade as about, thought Edwards. This painting had surely done a number on Spencer's sanity, there was no question about it.

"I'll go look," Edwards said, and he walked over towards the former lodge. He could feel the heat trapped in the stones as he got closer and he knew it would be unwise to try to clamber up into the shell of the building so he walked around until he could see into the room that held the painting. Very much to his surprise he saw those two ferocious eyes looking out at him and the painting completely undamaged, not so much as a scorch mark or peeling of paint that he could see from this distance. A chill went up his spine, and for the first time in life, he felt unnerved by something as inanimate as this painting. He walked back to the two men.

"Nothing left at all in there by the looks of it," he said cheerily. They said little else as they gathered the scared horses and started to ride down the hill away from the former Hellfire Club.

# Chapter 69

The mortuary was dark and quiet when Edwards approached, but he could see the candles lit in Adams' office. He walked across the courtyard, and his steps made loud noises on the gravel underfoot. The candle flickered, and Edwards saw the shape of man come to the window. The man opened it and peered out into the night.

"It's only me Dr. Adams!" Edwards called out.

"Mr. Edwards?" Adams asked, "What has you here at this hour, has there been another murder?"

"How would I know?" Edwards said smiling.

"Go to the door over there, and I'll let you in," the doctor said. Edwards did as he was asked and soon the bolt from inside lifted, and the door opened. "Come to the office, it's the only place with a bit of warmth left tonight," Adams said beckoning him to follow.

They walked along the short corridor and into a small office where Adams had been working. He closed the door and gestured with both arms out for Edwards to take a seat. Edwards did so, and Adams sat down too.

"Will you have a drink?" Adams asked, but Edwards shook his head no.

"I have not come on a social visit," he said curtly. Adams seemed surprised by his tone.

"No?" Adams said, raising a thick eyebrow.

"You went too far in attacking Kate," Edwards said, and there was no hiding the anger in his voice.

"What?" Adams was incredulous, he looked lost for words.

"Don't toy with me Adams, I know what you've been up to."

"I don't know what you're talking about."

"Don't worry, the Alderman isn't close to catching you, he has another man pegged for these murders."

"I don't know..."

"You have been killing these people, starting with the man in the tower," Edwards interrupted him.

"That man died in locked gaol! No one killed him, no one could have!" Adams protested.

"Someone with the skill you have with a bow could have done it," Edwards said, he was very satisfied at having figured this out, and he watched as Adams' face dropped. "How did you do it, climb one of the buildings nearby and shoot with the arrow attached to a string so that you could reel it back in?" Adams nodded slowly with an air of dejection. "That was risky, what if you missed or if the arrow became ensnared in the bars when you tried to pull it back?" Adams shrugged,

"Neither would have mattered. The man in there was of no importance; it was the location of the death that was key. If it had got caught in the bars, I just would have left it there. All that would have been different would be that it would have been obvious as a murder from the off."

"It was some shot," Edwards said appreciatively.

"Sweeter than I had hoped," Adams said with a grin of satisfaction. "He never suspected a thing until it slit his throat."

"The Alderman had that room turned upside down and inside out and then burned looking for something he could have cut himself with,"

"That's why you invited me to go hunting that day, isn't it? To see what kind of shot I had?" Adams smiled at Edwards's cunning.

"And you did not disappoint," Edwards also smiled at his own cunning.

"You've known since then?" Adams was surprised by this. "Why did you not turn me in?"

"What you are doing is of no concern to me so long as certain people don't get hurt," Edwards said coldly.

"This 'Kate' you're talking about?"

"Yes,"

"Was this recently?"

"Very, I was on hand to run you off."

"So you saw me?"

"Not well enough to recognise you if I had not already known," Edwards admitted.

"I didn't know who she was, I still don't know who she is?"

"She is someone who is off limits to you now."

"Fine," Adams agreed, and it struck Edwards all of a sudden how odd this meeting was, it was like a formal business meeting, and they were agreeing on an agenda. It was true that this was not the first time Edwards had dealt with a murderer, but it had never been like this before.

"The Alderman has Spencer, who was with us hunting that day, for the murders. He'll pick him up soon and arrest him," Edwards said.

"Why does he think Spencer has been doing it all?"

"Spencer has become unhinged of late, he thinks that the Devil is following him around,"

"Perhaps he is?" Adams said, and he looked at Edwards with a malevolent scowl.

"You are the man with the red face?" Edwards asked. Adams nodded. "I thought that was all part of Spencer's madness."

"Serves him right," Adam's said bitterly.

"What is it between you and Spencer?" Edwards asked, "You seemed fine in one another's company that day we hunted?"

"He doesn't know who I am, never did, I trained under one of his surgeons in India, and I saw the callous disregard he had for all the troops under his command. He thought nothing of letting his men die for small victories or anything to make a name for himself. I had almost forgotten about him until I came here. So I decided to try to kill two birds with one stone, as it were," Adams smiled evilly. Edwards shook his head in gentle disbelief,

"Well, an axe to grind is a powerful thing," he said wistfully. "Still, I will miss him."

"I had no axe to grind, it was only an afterthought once I saw he was here," Adams scowled.

"You need to finish up soon, go out with a bang," Edwards said changing the subject.

"Is that so?"

"It is so. You will have to kill Mullins, the blacksmith and perhaps Mary Sommers to tie it all in with the Dolocher and then you will have to leave the country,"

"Leave the country!"

"Yes, I can arrange it easily for you, and you can go on with your desires somewhere else, London maybe?"

"What makes you think you can tell me what to do?" Adams sat forward in his chair and Edwards could see that he had clenched his fists.

"You are only a free man right now because I have decided it, I could have told the Alderman at any time."

"If you don't leave here tonight you won't be able to tell anyone what you know." This was as clear a threat as

Edwards could have imagined, but he laughed and shook his head in disappointment with Adams.

"Adams, Adams," he said, "You should know that I would never have come in here with you without some sort of insurance?" Adams looked at him but remained silent. "There is a boy with a letter containing all that I know of this affair, it also says that I am coming here to see you tonight. That letter will be delivered to the Alderman if I do not come to personally reclaim it tonight."

"So you've thought this through," Adams said. He looked like a chess player who could see he was soon to be checkmated but who looked around wildly for some amazing unseen move that would turn the tables completely in his favour. They were silent, and each regarded the other.

"How did you first suspect me, before you knew about the arrow?" Adams asked.

"When I came here with the Alderman, and we waited for you to arrive I was looking under things, and I saw some of your surgical sketches, they bore a keen likeness to the ones on the letters the Alderman had received." Adams nodded.

"What is it to you that I finish this if I don't hurt anyone you care about?"

"It is not so much for my sake than for your own."

"What do you mean?"

"Something is coming soon, something big that will eclipse everything you have done here. It is best for you to finish and revel in your glory before this thing comes to be," Edwards said, his eyes lighting in anticipation of this event that only he had the ability to see at present.

"What do you speak of?"

"I will not say, but you will no doubt hear about it no matter where you go," Edwards smiled. Adams looked rueful and tired and much older than his years suddenly.

"There are more people connected to the Dolocher than the two you mentioned," he said presently.

"I know, but I have told you who should go. I will need the Alderman to see what is coming."

"Don't you want to know why I'm doing all this?" Adams asked, his face betrayed his eagerness to tell, and it put Edwards right off. Edwards had no need to know of the midnight cravings or lure of the moon that no doubt Adams would call on to describe his murderous instinct. Edwards knew this feeling only too well, he knew what it was like to seek out violence, to see it and feel it, to know its power. No, Edwards did not need any of this explained to him by Adams.

"Not in the least," Edwards replied and seeing the disappointment in Adams he went on, "I would like to know what you did with Cleaves' body though when you dug it up."

"It's in the ground on this very site," Adams said, and his eyes drifted out into the night to the area of the barracks it must be in. Edwards nodded.

"I have another question for you," he said as though suddenly remembering something. "The amulet?" Adams smiled at this.

"That was completely by chance!" he laughed. "I snuck into Spencer's attic many months ago to look at his paintings and see how he was coming along with the one for your club so I could model myself on it. I saw the painting of a woman with an amulet on that I knew I recognised. It took a while to come to me but then I recalled it was a woman who had recently passed away in a carriage accident. I took a sketch of Spencer's painting and then dug up the woman and saw that they matched." Adams was still laughing at this turn of luck. Edwards didn't find it funny, luck was a very serious business to him -a necessity for all that he had planned to come to fruition.

"London would be a good place for you to go, I'm not sure how much they might have heard about the Dolocher over there but it would nice to sow that type of fear in the heart of the Empire too wouldn't it?" Edwards said with a wicked grin. Adams regarded him for a long time, his eyes scrutinising Edwards as if summing him up completely. He smiled to himself, and Edwards wondered what he was thinking.

"I find it very odd that to the eyes of the outside world, I would be the evil one of our pair here tonight," he said.

# Chapter 70

Spencer was at home when James and Edwards called. They were shown to his dining room where the Colonel sat at the table listless, wan and tired looking. He looked completely drained of life and energy, and James for his part was shocked at how much weight the man seemed to have lost in so short a time since he had last seen him.

"You've come to take me," Spencer said as though confirming to the men themselves what they were there for.

"Have we reason to leave you be?" James asked.

"I've done terrible things Alderman James, terrible things," he said looking intently at James, "Bur, I was not under my own command."

"I assume you are speaking of the Devil?" James said, and he could see in the corner of his eye that Edwards smiled at this. James was not joking, however, and he looked sharply at Edwards.

"He's everywhere I go," Spencer said.

"Still?" Edwards asked. Spencer shook his head.

"What do you mean 'still?'" James asked.

"Spencer here paid a visit to the clubhouse at Montpelier Hill yesterday and burned the place down, didn't you?" Edwards said, addressing this last part to Spencer.

"I had to get rid of the painting," Spencer replied.

"What painting?" James asked. It didn't concern him in the least that the Hellfire Club had been burned to the ground.

"The one of the Devil," Edwards said. "It was destroyed in the fire."

"I'm sorry for all the bad things that I've done," Spencer

said, "I have no memory of them at all."

"None?" James didn't believe this.

"None," Spencer said.

"You killed all those people, and you claim that you remember not one bit of it?"

"The Devil was controlling me,"

"Rubbish!" James said, angry at this cowardice and unwillingness to admit in full what he had done

"I know how it sounds," Spencer said, his voice reasonable, letting James know that he would not believe this same tale from another man.

"I suppose this means you can't tell me the significance of the amulet?" James asked, his tone exasperated.

"The amulet?" Spencer looked genuinely confused at this. This had not been something that had made it to the public arena, and it looked for all the world as though this was the first time he had ever heard about it.

"The one in your painting of the woman in the attic," Edwards said. Still, Spencer looked confused.

"Can we go and see the painting in question?" James asked, "Perhaps it will jog your memory."

Spencer said nothing but beckoned them to follow him and then made his way up the few flights of stairs to the attic. It was dark up there and very cold, and it took some time for Spencer to light enough candles so that they could see comfortably by.

"Which painting are you referring to?" Spencer said. James looked to Edwards for him to point out where he had seen it. Spencer looked now at Edwards too, his face suspicious.

"It's over here, in this pile," Edwards said making his way over to a dark corner. He moved a couple of paintings and pulled the one out that he was looking for. "Here we are," Edwards said as he held it up to the dim light.

They all three looked upon the painting, and James looked to Spencer for him to say something.

"I did this one a couple of years ago," he said. This is a lady who has since left this country to live with her new husband in England."

"What is her name?" James asked.

"Lady Partridge," he seemed convincing in this.

"And what about the amulet?" Edwards said.

"What about it? She was wearing it, so I included it in the painting."

"Is she still alive?" James asked.

"As far as I know, I've not had contact since the painting was done."

"Why is the painting still in your possession?"

"She didn't like the likeness, she wouldn't pay for it."

"This amulet turned up inside one of the people who was killed," James said.

"I've told you, I don't remember anything about them. I certainly don't ever remember Lady Partridge leaving her amulet behind." Spencer's voice was almost bored now as though he just wanted to be taken away and be done with the whole affair.

"I'm going to have to arrest you, Colonel Spencer," James said. Spencer's face flushed with relief. It was as though he thought he was going to be let away with his crimes and that this was the worst possible outcome for him.

"You don't seem to be too worried about the prospect of the gallows," Edwards remarked.

"The gallows will be a relief to me, Mr. Edwards," Spencer said.

"It's time to go, Colonel Spencer," James said taking him gently by the arm.  James felt sorry for him, his mind had completely twisted, and an insane asylum was more likely to be his new abode than the gallows.  The Alderman couldn't make up his mind which was worse.

# Chapter 71

The water of the Liffey lapped softly against the hull of the ship as it disembarked from Templebar. Doctor Adams stood on the deck and looked back at the city of Dublin as he was leaving. He had enjoyed his time here and thought perhaps he would return one day. For now, however, it had lost all its charm to him. His game was over, and he had no intention of finishing it on Edward's terms. Mullins and Mary Sommers would live- what did he care about those two now?

London would be fine though, he thought, there is always something going on, and there was the opportunity to make an even bigger impression over there once he was established. Still, it would have been nice to finish what he started here and now have to leave in this ignominious way. The part of Dublin he knew best was leaving his sight now, and a hollow feeling of loss came into his breast. As careful as he thought he had been, he had been found out, and a lot earlier than he would have ever suspected.

Edwards' sneering face came to mind, and he couldn't help but smile. What was that man made of? What did he have planned that was so outrageous it would put his own work to shame? Edwards had promised Adam's would know about it no matter where he ended up. Time would tell on that score.

## Chapter 72

"It's time for you to come and stay with me Olocher," Edwards said. He was sitting in Lord Muc's kitchen at a large wooden table with Scally, whom Edwards had started to call by his father's surname.

"Where?" the boy asked.

"Across the city, you will be in luxury from now on, but it was important for you to see life at this level before you came to me."

"Am I done with Lord Muc?"

"I'm still undecided on that, he is a delightfully unpredictable and violent man, and I'm sure he would be very much missed in this part of the city," Edwards said. Olocher looked at him with eyes widened slightly.

"I didn't mean killing him, I meant with the training."

"His death will be the last act of your training and the first of your new mission," Edwards said to him.

"He's been good to me."

"He's been paid handsomely to be good to you." Olocher thought on this for a moment.

"Can we not use him for this mission?"

"No, this will be done by you alone," Edwards looked at him with a big smile. "I'll tell you what, Muc has to go as part of the mission, but he doesn't have to go first." He looked at Olocher and saw his agreement with this in a low bow of his head. "Come along, I want you to see the decoration in the place you are going to stay." Edwards thought of the huge painting of the Devil that hung on the wall opposite the bed Olocher would call his own for the next year. Every night, Olocher and the Devil would look upon one another and get deeper and deeper inside one another until it was time to unleash his creation on the city. It was going to be hell being patient for that long, but Edwards felt that he could do it. Who knows, perhaps there will be another killer in the meantime.

The carriage rattled over the cobblestones and into the fog of the evening, drifting towards the river and away into the mist so that soon all that could be heard was the clopping of the horseshoes on the even rough surface. It was chilly, but the spring was coming soon. A dog scuttled across the road and into Muc's yard. There was a phantom moon through the air as Dublin went to sleep that night.

## The End

Sign up for news of new releases at
http://eepurl.com/bWwroj

If you liked this book please leave a review from where you got it. Thanks for reading.

For more information on European P. Douglas, please visit www.europeanpdouglas.com

**'The Light within the Cauldron'** the next Alderman James Novel is currently in the works and you can keep up news of this at either link above.

I am happy to take any questions or queries at
info@ghostcreativeservices.com

Made in the USA
Middletown, DE
21 April 2017